DISTANT HORIZONS

*The continuing story of Alice Chase
and her family*

It is the early days of the phoney war and
Alice Chase is awaiting the birth of a fifth
child. Alice's eldest daughter, Rose, is
head over heels in love and about to join
up as a nursing assistant, following her
doctor sweetheart. But as the war clouds
gather ever more ominously, new friends
and a new man enter Rose's life, making
her uncertain which way her life should
go...

*Rowena Summers titles available from
Severn House Large Print*

Long Shadows
Blackthorne Cottage
Monday's Child
Shelter from the Storm

DISTANT HORIZONS

Rowena Summers

Severn House Large Print
London & New York

This first large print edition published 2010
in Great Britain and the USA by
SEVERN HOUSE PUBLISHERS LTD of
9-15 High Street, Sutton, Surrey, SM1 1DF.
First world regular print edition published 2009 by
Severn House Publishers Ltd., London and New York.

British Library Cataloguing in Publication Data

Summers, Rowena, 1932-
  Distant horizons.
  1. Pregnant women--Fiction. 2. World War, 1939-1945--
  Evacuation of civilians--Fiction. 3. Great Britain--
  Social life and customs--1918-1945--Fiction. 4. Domestic
  fiction. 5. Large type books.
  I. Title
  823.9'14-dc22

  ISBN-13: 978-0-7278-7827-4

Printed and bound in Great Britain by
MPG Books Ltd, Bodmin, Cornwall.

One

The village of Bramwell was in glorious summer bloom as Alice Chase took her small son on their regular visit with her sister-in-law. It was the kind of day when strangers smiled at one another, and neighbours stopped for a chat and asked after the family, and those who knew that Alice was expecting her fifth child made a special enquiry after her health. Half an hour later, settling down for a gossip, she tried not to let her anxiety show as Helen made her announcement. It wasn't what she had expected to hear, and she just hoped the other woman knew what she was letting herself in for.

'Are you sure about this decision, Helen? And does Mick agree?'

She could see at once that Helen was on the defensive and ready to bristle. 'Well, of course I'm sure, and you don't think Mick and I would have considered it if we hadn't thought about it properly, do you? I don't know why you should be so critical, Alice. Even a bit smug, if you don't mind me saying so.'

'What does that mean? I've only said a couple of words, and I'm only thinking of you, Helen. Two young children are a lot to take on when your one and only has already left the nest.'

She immediately wished she hadn't mentioned Jack. Helen's feelings were still raw, when, a few months ago, her son had left so ignominiously to join the Territorials, just leaving a note for his parents to say he was joining up, long before there was any need to do so. With war so imminent – and even a fool knew it could be only weeks or even days away now – Helen and Mick had come to terms with his decision, and were justifiably proud of him. But this was a different decision.

Helen went on doggedly. 'You've seen the newspapers and listened to the wireless the same as the rest of us, Alice. The government is urging families to send their children away from the cities to the country for their own safety, and I'd have thought that you, of all people, would have appreciated us offering a temporary home to a couple of small evacuees from London, seeing that it's sure to be the first place that will get bombed.'

She paused for breath, her eyes flashing, and Alice wished she'd never questioned it at all. The fact that she herself was a Londoner, had nothing to do with how different life was going to be for Helen if she opened up her house to young city children with no knowledge of country life. She had been an adult when she first came to Somerset, charmed by the country and by Walter Chase, and the whirlwind romance and marriage had followed. After more than twenty years now this village was

6

home to her – even if she was occasionally not-so-subtly reminded that she was still an outsider...

She felt a small flicker under her petticoat, reminding her more forcefully that this fifth child, this precious late baby, even later in her life than Bobby, was alive and kicking. It reminded her too, how much Helen had always yearned for more children, so of course she could understand this desire to take in some small evacuees in the rambling house that she and Mick shared. It must seem even more empty now that Jack was gone. All the same, it was still a big undertaking for a woman with no knowledge of dealing with small children for so many years.

'If you must know, I think it's admirable, Helen,' she said sincerely. 'And you know I'll give you every help that I can.'

Helen gave her a warmer smile. 'I knew you'd come round to the idea, and for good-ness' sake, if I can't cope with a couple of young kids far from home, I'm not much of a woman, am I? We've got plenty of room here, and it's our duty to do what we can.'

'They'll be homesick, you know. They prob-ably won't even have seen farm animals before. I haven't ever forgotten how strange it was for me, with all the country noises – and the smells!' she added with a laugh, remembering.

'Well, they'll soon get used to that, with all the farms around here, and with Mick being a vet. Anyway, it's all settled, and the billeting officer's bringing the children here on Friday. I was rather hoping you'd be here to greet them with me, Alice. You and Bobby, of course. It will help if they see another small child.'

Her voice wavered for the first time, and Alice realized again what a big decision this was for her. It would make a huge change in her life, and in Mick's too. It made Alice feel doubly appreciative of her own large family, even if there was no way they could take in any evacuees in their modest home. Rose still lived at home, although how long that might be once the war began, Alice wouldn't like to guess. Working as a children's nanny for the local doctor's family and with more than a passing interest in his younger brother, she guessed shrewdly that if the young Doctor Matt joined up, Rose would probably think about it too. Lucy was working in the big house, The Grange, although her interest in her job seemed to have palled lately. In any case she came home as often as she could at weekends to be with her family and share a week's gossip with her sister. While their boy, Tom, was doing his furniture-making apprenticeship near Bristol.

She and Walter had assumed that Bobby, now three years old, was to be their last child, born when Alice was forty. But then the unease and queasiness she had felt after her best friend Tilly had died, had turned out not to be nerves, or the horrible thought that close as they had once been, it was nature's way of telling her she might be going the same way as her friend.

8

They were foolish thoughts, of course, but the miracle of another baby had never entered her head until Doctor Stacey had confirmed it. At the news, she and Walter had almost danced for joy and awe – despite his gouty toe – and even though Lucy and Tom in particular had been startled and a bit embarrassed to hear the news, the rest of the family had welcomed it. And so they should. Creating a baby was a miracle, no matter how old you were, and Alice knew she was still young enough and strong enough to carry it and enjoy the prospect.

Oh yes, she could well understand Helen's yearning for another child through the years, and her bitter disappointment when it had never happened. Especially when Alice and Walter seemingly had only had to look at one another and another babe was on the way. She only hoped the evacuees wouldn't eventually have too strong a hold on Helen's heart, though, because in due course she would have to give them back. She couldn't keep them for ever. But this wasn't the time to mention it when Helen's feelings were obviously so fragile.

Aware of Alice's regular visit with Bobby, her brother-in-law came through from the adjoining vet's surgery, drying his hands on a towel. The inevitable smell of animals and disinfectant wafted in with him, and Alice wondered fleetingly if it lingered in the bedroom too. She turned away at the thought, feeling the warm flush on her cheeks. On and off over the years, she had wondered uneasily if she had married

9

the wrong man, and she knew Mick had always harboured fond feelings for her. But all that was over now, and she didn't ever want to think about it again. Besides, in some strange way, the fact that she and Walter were now expecting this fifth baby had seemed to embarrass Mick too. It was an absurd thought, but one that Alice couldn't quite dismiss.

'How's my favourite three-year-old today?' Mick said breezily to Bobby, picking him up in his strong arms, whirling him around and making him shriek with delight. He smiled at the two women. 'Does he know he'll be having some new playmates living with us soon?'

Helen spoke tartly. 'Well, if he didn't before, he knows it now.'

'What will they be called? Will they be boys? I want them to be boys like me,' Bobby shouted at once. He never spoke quietly when he was excited.

'We don't know if they'll be boys or girls yet,' Helen told him kindly.

'I want boys,' Bobby said firmly again, pulling a face.

Alice smiled at Helen over the top of his head. He wanted a baby brother too, but they would have to have what came. He made enough fuss of the Stacey baby Mollie, anyway, and she was sure that he would love it when it arrived, whether it was a boy or girl. Providing it was healthy, Alice thought. She mentally crossed her fingers. That was all that mattered.

* * *

Walking home again with Bobby, she tried to explain what being an evacuee meant. She couldn't imagine it herself, but being thrown into a strange environment away from their families was bound to be distressing for young children at first.

'Won't their mummies and daddies come with them?' Bobby asked.

'No, love. They'll stay at home.'

Bobby's face became puckered. 'Why do they have to go away then? Don't their mummies and daddies love them any more?'

Alice knew this was going to be trickier than she thought. How did you explain to a three-year-old about wars and bombings and the need for families to send their children away to safety, however hard it was for them?

'I'm sure they love the children very much, but this will be like a long holiday for them. They'll have new aunties and uncles, and make new friends. We've all got to make them welcome, haven't we?'

'Will I have to share my toys with them?' Bobby asked next.

'Only if you want to,' Alice replied with a smile.

He broke away from her and began running on towards home.

'I don't want to,' he shouted back. 'They're mine, and I'm not letting anybody touch them. I'm not letting the new babby touch them, either.'

'I think we may have a little problem with Bobby,' Alice said uneasily to Walter, when he came home from the sawmill that evening.

The boy had gone to bed by then, surrounding himself with teddy bears and wooden toys as if in protest about what he thought might happen when the evacuees arrived. Rose had come home and gone out again, and Alice had time to talk with her husband – if he would only listen.

'What sort of a problem? He's not jealous about the new babby, is he? I thought we'd got all that sorted out by now,' Walter said, too busy twiddling the knobs on the wireless to pay complete attention to what his wife was saying.

She looked at him in exasperation. Like every man nowadays, his head was too full of the impending war news to give too much heed to domestic troubles. They were the wife's department, not his. He finally found the station he wanted on the wireless, and listened to the sombre words of the announcer, finally grunting that if you took notice of everything they said, you'd believe the Germans were about to bomb them all out of existence.

'So why don't you listen to what I'm saying instead?' Alice said. 'I said I'm a bit anxious about Bobby, Walter.'

'Why? What's he done?' Walter said with an impatient sigh as he turned off the wireless to save the precious battery. 'You should be able to keep him under control.'

'Is your toe playing you up tonight?' she said intuitively, counting to ten and wishing she'd never bothered him with another problem.

He grunted. 'No more than usual, I daresay. So out with it, Mother. What's the little runt done now?'

'Don't call him that, just because he's small for his age! And don't call me Mother,' she added out of habit. 'No, my dear, it's not the new baby our Bobby's jealous about. He's excited enough about that.' She overlooked Bobby's last remark. 'It's these evacuees Helen and Mick are going to get. You know what a pet they make of Bobby, and I'm sure he thinks his nose will be put out of joint when these other children arrive.'

'He'll have to get used to it then, won't he? He can't be a pet all his life, and he's nearly four years old now and going to school soon. He'll have to put up with the rough and tumble of other kids and you can't mollycoddle him for ever.'

Alice knew he was right, but she could hardly be blamed for wanting her ewe lamb to be protected as much as possible. Bobby had always been the least robust of her children, and it was her mother's instinct to want the best for him.

'I wonder how difficult it will be for them adjust to such a different life from all that they're used to as well,' she began, and then she felt Walter put his arm around her shoulders and ruffle her hair.

'Don't fret, old girl. One step at a time, eh? You just look after yourself, and let the rest of them get on with it. You never know, these

London kids might take a real shine to the country and to Bobby too. You didn't have any trouble, did you?'

She gave him a swift smile. 'I was older – and besides, I had you, charming the life out of me, didn't I?'

Walter laughed, the gleam in his eyes reminding her that he was still the same old charmer he had always been. The proof of that was in the baby she carried beneath her heart. They were so lucky to have their large family, and even though Tom had moved away from them now, he was happy and fulfilled in his apprenticeship, and kept in touch regularly. They had never considered this coming baby as a replacement for Tom in any way, but it would fill a large gap in their lives all the same.

Walter slid down beside her on the sofa as she put down her knitting, and her head rested on his shoulder for a moment. His hand moved lightly over her belly, where the baby was just beginning to make its presence felt.

'I wonder if it'll be a boy or a girl,' he said, as he frequently did.

'It's one of the mysteries of life that we're not meant to know until it's born,' she reminded him. She wouldn't want to know in advance. If God had wanted women to know beforehand he'd have given them eyes to see into their bellies, and that was a prospect Alice couldn't even imagine. Whether it was a boy or a girl, she knew the whole family would love it.

* * *

Walking home from the cinema with Matt Stacey later that evening, Rose tucked her arm in his. They were also discussing her family's new baby, and how much her parents were looking forward to it.

'I think Dad would have a football team if he could,' she remarked. 'It's weird to think you know more about these things than I do, Matt. I mean, as a doctor, of course, not personally.'

'I should think not,' he said with a grin. 'It doesn't bother you that I have to examine patients, does it?'

'Of course not. It's what doctors have to do, isn't it? I'm not sure I'd enjoy it, though. Doctors have to have strong stomachs, don't they?'

'Sometimes, but even if you were a nurse, you'd have to attend to plenty of unpleasant jobs, Rose. I know we've talked about that, or are you having second thoughts about volunteering if necessary?'

'No, but I suppose if I'm honest, I'm putting it to the back of my mind unless – well, unless, you know!'

'You mean until war breaks out, not unless,' he said deliberately. 'There's no sense in shunning from saying the words, Rose, and it's not unless. It's *until*. You know it as well as I do. The only doubt is when it will happen. But happen it will, and pretty damn soon now.'

Rose shivered, not wanting this lovely evening to turn into something gloomy.

'You're starting to sound like my father now. I swear I think all men are eager for it to begin.'

He hugged her arm to his. 'I may sound like him in one respect, but I'm not thinking like him in the least. Every sane person knows the war is imminent, but there's no need to let it spoil our evening, is there?'

'That's what I've been telling you.'

He was suddenly serious. 'No. I think you've been telling me you won't want me to join up, which I have every intention of doing, of course. And that your fine ideas about being a nurse are flying out of the window. Isn't that it?'

She looked up into his handsome young face, and had a quick vision of every other young man of his age, rushing into war for king and country, because that was what young men did. Brave, reckless young men, who wouldn't hesitate to do what they thought was right, and she was briefly ashamed because what he had said was so true.

'If you go, then so will I,' she said huskily. 'Though how I'd tell my mother, I don't know. She'd probably think I was mad.'

Matt glanced around, and seeing there was no one else in the vicinity, he kissed her quickly on the cheek.

'She'd think you were wonderful, just as I do,' he said.

If Rose thought her parents were unaware of her vague plans, she was wrong. Lying in bed that night, Alice listened to Walter's heavy breathing as he settled down to sleep, and knew very well that her oldest girl would follow whatever that young man of hers did. It was inevitable that doctors and nurses were going to be needed in time of war. Rose wasn't a fully-fledged nurse, but she had looked after the Stacey baby for months now, and she was a natural at caring for people.

Oh yes, another of their children would leave home soon, and it was the way of things. It was right for fledglings to leave the nest and spread their own wings. As for following her man, wasn't that what Alice herself had done, all those years ago when she came to live in Somerset? She had known no one except Walter and his brother when she left her London home and all her friends, but together she and Walter had made a home and a life for themselves, and she wouldn't have had it any other way.

She felt him stir in his sleep and she wrapped her arms around him. The swelling of the baby nestled between them, and as always, she felt a little glow of excitement inside, imagining what this unexpected new child would be like. One of the pleasures about this greatest of mysteries was wondering if it would be a boy or a girl, and who it would resemble. Alice wasn't the kind of woman to indulge in too much dreaming, but this was an exception. In her opinion, any woman who didn't dream about the child she was carrying wasn't a normal woman.

'Go to sleep, Mother,' she heard Walter slur quietly, and she smiled again, no longer as affronted at being called Mother by him as she had once been. She wasn't his mother, but she was mother to four of their children, and soon to be five. There was no sweeter word in all the world, and Alice was perfectly content.

An hour later, she was feeling far less than content after Bobby came whimpering into their bedroom saying he felt sick, and promptly threw up the contents of his stomach over the bedroom floor.

Alice staggered out of bed to pick up his wan little body in her arms and take him back to his own room to clean him up, sitting him on his bed for a few moments while she gathered up the rag rug in her bedroom to put straight in the washtub in the morning.

'There now, love, you'll be as right as rain in a minute or two,' she soothed the boy. 'Let's wash your mouth and make you feel better. Something didn't agree with you, did it?'

'I was dreaming about the baby,' he snuffled. 'It was bigger than me and it wanted all my toys.'

She gave a small laugh. 'Well, that shows you it was just a dream, you silly. The baby will be very small when it arrives, and it will be a long time before it's able to play with toys at all. It will need a big brother to look after it. I told you all that, didn't I?'

She saw Bobby scowl. He had been charmed at the thought of being a big brother, but now it seemed it wasn't such a thrill.

'When I go to school it will be here all alone with you, won't it?'

18

Alice could almost sense the jealousy oozing out of him. She cuddled him close to her.

'Yes, it will, and it will be sleeping for most of the day, so I'll have nobody to talk to until you come home again.'

Bobby obviously hadn't worked that out.

'I might draw a picture of it tomorrow,' he offered, and Alice knew he was settling down again.

'Good. And then we'll start thinking of a name for it. You can help us choose, Bobby, so get your thinking cap on in the morning.'

Before he could open his mouth and ask her what his thinking cap was, she settled him down in his bed again, kissed him firmly and said goodnight, promising to leave his bedroom door open, and hers too, in case he woke up again. Hopefully, thinking about a name for the new baby, which was too superstitious a thing for any of them to do just yet, would keep him happy. Alice had a vague hope it would be born on February the eighteenth, her old friend Tilly's birthday. Then again, she fervently hoped it wouldn't arrive on that day. It would be too weird. It would be as though Tilly was sending her someone to love, replacing her in a sort of ethereal way, especially if it turned out to be a girl.

Alice shivered as she climbed back into her own bed, her side of it grown cold now, and felt Walter grunt in his sleep beside her. He would not be thinking of such things, of course. Walter didn't have a superstitious bone in his body –

and always laughed at his womenfolk if they ever mentioned such things. Alice had never thought she believed in omens and superstitions either, until Tilly died...

She tried to squash the feelings, knowing she would never get to sleep again at this rate. She tried to think ahead to better things, the way she always tried to do when she was troubled. She tried to think of holding this new baby in her arms and smelling the sweet baby smell of him – or her – and knowing that between them, she and Walter had created this perfect miracle. They were the lucky ones.

Her thoughts strayed to the children Helen and Mick were taking into their home. Children who would be strangers, feeling lost and bewildered, and probably hating these new aunties and uncles they had never met before. Helen was a good woman, but she had never really been the motherly sort, and Alice hoped again that she wasn't going to take on more than she bargained for.

On Friday she and Bobby made their second visit to Helen that week. By then Bobby had been instructed to make friends with these new cousins. She and Helen decided that if the kids were to call them all aunties and uncles, it was easier on Bobby for him to think of them as cousins.

There was an unfamiliar black car standing outside the vet's house. There weren't that many cars in the village, and any new one always caused a stir of interest among the local children. There were several of them hanging about now, and they catcalled to Bobby as he and his mother arrived.

'There's a couple of crybabies in there to keep you company, Bobby Chase,' they jeered.

'Take no notice of them, Bobby,' Alice said swiftly, praying they weren't going to be met by weeping evacuees, and knowing they should have got here sooner before the billeting officer arrived. Helen would have wanted that too. Alice could see that by Helen's flustered look as they went inside.

The billeting officer was a woman called Mrs Willmott, who was very firm as she explained to Helen that these children were a brother and sister from the East End of London. They lived with their grandmother as their mother had gone off long ago, and their father worked at the docks. The children were seven and five, and were properly house-trained, she added, as if she was referring to a household pet. Alice wondered if she thought she was being funny because these children were allocated to a vet's home, or if she was spectacularly insensitive.

She got a good look at the children for the first time. They still had their outer clothes on, far too warm for this time of the year, and their gas-masks in their cardboard boxes still hung around their necks. They each wore a name label pinned to their coats, and at their feet were their small suitcases. They didn't look ill-cared-for, just frightened. The five-year-old girl was snivelling, and the boy was doing his best not to do the same. They clutched each other's hands, their legs tightly held together, and Alice prayed for all their sakes that they weren't about to disgrace themselves and widdle on Helen's clean floor.

Since nobody seemed to know what to say for a moment, she was the one who broke the awkward silence.

'Well now, Patty and Johnny,' she said brightly, addressing them by the names on their labels, 'come and meet your new cousin, Bobby.'

The children both swivelled their eyes to look at Bobby. For a second Alice had the vain hope that they were about to smile at each other and then Bobby gave a great howl of terror and clung to his mother's skirts.

'I don't like them,' he shrieked.

'Oh, for goodness' sake, Bobby,' Helen said in distress, 'you don't even know them yet. You're all going to be lovely playmates together, so let's get Patty and Johnny's coats off, and we'll all have some milk and biscuits. I'm sure they're hungry after their journey. '

Her eyes were desperate as she struggled to get the children's arms out of their coats, and Mrs Willmott tut-tutted at such a fuss, clearly thinking Alice would have done better to keep her unruly child away.

'I'll leave the paperwork with you, Mrs Chase,' she told Helen, 'and I'll return in two weeks' time to see how you're all settling down.'

The next minute she was gone, and the women could hear the sounds of the local children cheering as they ran after her car.

'Do you know my gran?' the small girl said nervously to Alice in a pronounced cockney accent.

'I don't think so, but I might have done once,' Alice said, realizing at once that the girl recognized the accent Alice had never lost among these strange country ones, and that she probably considered Alice a small link to home. 'London's a big place, love, but we might have met sometime. What do you think, Helen?'

She willed Helen to agree to the impossible idea. This wasn't such a good start. She didn't want these children to cling to her, and neither would Bobby, who still had his face buried in her skirts. Helen shrugged slightly.

'I daresay you might have known their gran,' she agreed, just to keep the peace, but her eyes were burning with resentment.

Alice could see that her wonderful plan was falling apart. She had gone into this with the best of intentions, meaning to care for these lost children so far from home, but it wasn't turning out at all as she had imagined. But for pity's sake, they'd only been here five minutes! What did she think was going to happen? That they would fall into her arms and call her auntie the minute they arrived?

'Why don't Bobby and me get the milk and biscuits?' she suggested. 'I'm sure the children would love to see their bedroom, Helen.'

She knew she was taking charge, but since Helen seemed to be at sixes and sevens, it was the only thing to do, and at least it would separate them all for a little while. Helen picked up both suitcases and told them to follow her, and they trailed after her as if they were going to their doom.

'Now then, Bobby, you're to stop acting so silly, and behave yourself,' she told her son severely. 'Patty and Johnny don't know anybody here but us, so we have to be nice to them.'

'I still don't like them,' he groused. 'The girl talks funny.'

Alice smiled. 'Not to me, darling. I used to talk a bit like that when I lived in London, so that's why they feel at home with me – just a bit. So try to be nice to them. And don't worry, you're still my best boy.'

He gave a weak grin, but she knew she had won. Ten minutes later the trio came downstairs again and tackled the milk and biscuits Alice had prepared for them. They looked fractionally brighter.

'We ain't never slept in a room of our own before,' Johnny muttered, his eyes still wary. 'I slept with me dad and our Patty slept with me gran.'

'I slept with our Tom until he went away to make tables and chairs,' Bobby burst out. 'Now I sleep on my own, until the babby comes.'

The other two looked at him as if he was crazy, not understanding any of what he said.

24

Helen gave a small smile, finally starting to relax.

'I'll explain it all to you later,' she told her charges.

On the way home, Bobby looked at Alice curiously.

'Why did that lady say their mum had gone off? Where did she go off to?' he said, and Alice knew there were yet more delicate explanations to be made.

Two

Tom Chase was definitely enjoying life. He knew he had found his niche in the furniture-making business. He'd been happy enough working with his father at the sawmill, but it was nothing like the satisfaction he felt at shaping and planing a piece of wood until it shone, and feeling the smooth perfection of it come to life between his hands. Or the extraordinary sense of achievement he felt at turning an ordinary piece of wood into something beautiful. Not that he was very experienced as yet, and he was told it took years to make an apprentice into a craftsman, but he had a natural empathy for the wood, and an inborn ability. This was his destiny, he thought happily, and even if he never achieved fame and fortune, he was doing what he liked best.

Whenever he could, he caught the local bus into Bristol, and spent his time hanging around the docks where the seamen gathered to spin their yarns of faraway places; of grappling with mountainous seas and great sea monsters that rose out of the waves. He didn't believe all their outrageous tales, but he relished being allowed to listen to them. What he didn't do was to get caught up in their drinking bouts. He'd had enough of that on the one time his father had caught him drinking and forced him to drink rough scrumpy cider until he was sick. It had effectively cured him of the need for ale. It had also told him that he simply didn't have the head for it, either.

He knew he didn't have a head for a lot of things he'd once fancied. Such as being an airman. In fact, listening to some of the sailors' saltier tales of faraway places, dusky maidens and all, he was more and more taken with the idea of going to sea one day. He knew better than to mention it to any of his family on his weekend visits home, though. They had always considered him to be a scatterbrain, flitting from one thing to the next, and although he considered himself very grown up now that he'd left home, and fast approaching his fifteenth birthday, he knew they'd scoff at his new ideas and tell him he had a lot to learn yet.

Well, so he did, and for the time being, this apprentice job he'd landed was the best in the world. There'd be time enough for travelling the seven seas and seeing new places, when he'd made his fortune, maybe. He grinned to himself, just for the hell of it, and for all the opportunities open to a lad with ambition. Tom Chase was nothing if not an optimist.

On his next visit home to Bramwell, he decided to call in on his Aunt Helen to find out where his cousin Jack was now. By then, he'd heard about the two London evacuees his aunt and uncle had taken in, but with any luck they'd be out when he turned up. He didn't mind small kids, but Bobby had been all over him that day, and he'd had enough of them for a while, thanks very much. Besides, it was good to get out of the house once he'd said hello to his parents and sisters, told them how he was getting on, and found out what everyone was doing. There was only so much repetition you could cope with every couple of weeks when nothing much ever changed in the country.

He heard the rumpus before he reached the vet's house, although it didn't seem to be coming from the house at all, but from the surgery alongside it. Tom grimaced. Some poor pooch was probably getting his uncle's treatment and didn't like it one bit. He couldn't blame him. The next second he saw two small children come hurtling out of the surgery to go running along the road in Tom's direction with his uncle hollering after them.

'Stop the little devils, Tom,' Mick yelled. 'Don't let them get away!'

It was an automatic reaction. One minute it

27

seemed as if two small bodies were screeching and hurtling along the road, and the next, Tom's arms had been flung out to stop them. The small girl didn't have as much momentum as the boy, and was captured by Tom's right arm. The boy cannoned straight into Tom's outstretched other arm, and was floored at once.

'You silly bleeder, now look what you've done to me knee,' the child howled as blood spurted out from the deep graze.

Tom yanked him to his feet, as outraged by the kid's language as by the fact that he'd nearly been winded himself by the impact.

'You'd better wash your mouth out with soap, you little sod,' he snapped, 'and you'd best not let my auntie hear you using that language.'

The boy stuck out his tongue at him while he slapped a grubby hand over his knee. Tom couldn't identify the sweetish whiff coming from him.

'She ain't *my* auntie,' he yelled. 'I never asked to come and live in this dump!'

The girl was snivelling now, lying limp and heavy against Tom's arm as his uncle caught up with them. He looked meaner than Tom had ever seen him. He remembered his Uncle Mick as being the mildest of men, far more than his own dad. But Mick was looking anything but mild now.

'Right, Tom. I'll take over now. It's time these brats learned a thing or two about how to behave in somebody else's home.'

Like everyone else, Tom knew all about the

evacuee situation and why they were being sent to the country, and he also knew very well his auntie wouldn't hold with them being called brats any more than his mum would have done. So something must definitely be up to get his uncle so riled.

'Shall I come with you? I was coming to see Aunt Helen, anyway,' he offered. In any case it didn't seem such a bad idea since the girl was clinging on to him like a leech.

Mick shrugged. His own hand was gripping so tightly to Johnny Gregg's hand that the boy was squealing anew and trying to pull away from him. But there was no way Mick was letting go, not when the kid had caused such havoc in his surgery, and put both himself and his sister into danger into the bargain. Snotty-nosed brats, he found himself thinking savage-ly, and then found himself looking into the frightened, wide-eyed stare of the girl, brim-ming with tears, and his heart softened.

'Yes, come with us, Tom,' he said, more normally. 'Perhaps you can help explain to these two just why a vet's surgery is out of bounds, and full of things that children should not touch. You and Jack were never allowed in there when you were children, and these two must learn to respect the sense of it.'

Tom found the girl's hand clutching his now, and although he felt a bit of a fool holding on to a five-year-old's hand, at least it wasn't far to go back to the house, and he could see his Aunt Helen hurrying along the road towards them.

'What's happened?' she exclaimed at once. 'I could hear all the shouting from Kelsey's shop. Have you had a hand in it, Tom?'

He gave a snort. This wasn't the visit he had intended by a long chalk, and he wasn't about to get the blame for something he hadn't done.

'It wasn't him, missus,' the girl suddenly piped up in defence of Tom. 'It was our Johnny taking the stuff off the shelf and sniffing it. And then the dog barked and Johnny dropped the bottle and it broke, and the man came and shouted at us.'

'It was only a bottle of ether, that's all!' Mick said, furious again. 'They could have knocked themselves out for hours – or worse,' he added meaningly. 'As it is, Mrs Potter's dog is out for the count for a bit longer than he should have been.'

Tom felt a wild urge to laugh at the thought of the dog passing out with the effects of the ether, until one look at Helen's face stopped it dead. But she was glaring at Mick now, not the children.

'I asked you to keep an eye on them for half an hour. Was that too much for you? How do you expect them to understand what's out of bounds if you don't tell them?' Without waiting for a reply, she turned to Tom. 'I'm sorry, Tom, this was an unfortunate thing for you to see on your one day home.'

'It's all right,' he said, the urge to laugh still simmering. 'I really wanted to know how Jack was faring, but I can wait until you've got these two sorted out.'

'Well, let's all go inside the house before we start a peep show,' she said quickly. 'The smell of that stuff is sickly, and these two will have to change all their clothes before we do anything else.'

Tom had always thought his Aunt Helen the most unruffled person he knew. There was nothing unruffled about her now, though. She was flushed and flustered as she hustled the two children into the house ahead of her, with himself following. His uncle was nowhere to be seen now.

'So how's Jack doing?' he finally got around to asking, in what seemed a long while later. By then, the evacuees had been cleaned up and had been sent upstairs to tidy their bedroom before they came down for some lemonade with this new cousin. And he was twiddling his thumbs, and wishing he hadn't bothered taking time out from his brief visit home to come here at all.

Helen sniffed. 'He's doing very well, thank you, though I doubt the Territorials will be enough for him once Mr Chamberlain sends us all to war. It'll be the real army then and no mistake.'

Tom looked at her uneasily. 'I'd like to drop him a line sometime if you can give me his address.'

Helen spoke more sharply. 'I'll do that, Tom, providing you promise me you won't get any wild ideas of your own about following him. What Jack did, going away like that without a word, wasn't very kind to his family, and I wouldn't want your mother to go through the same worry that I did.'

''Course I wouldn't. I'm not fifteen yet, so nobody would want me, anyway!'

He kept his fingers crossed as he said it, knowing that he'd jump at the chance. At least, he thought he would. Six months ago, he wouldn't have given a second thought to what he'd be leaving behind if he did as Jack had done and gone away to join up before there was any need. But six months ago he didn't have the wonderful job he did now. Six months ago he hadn't seen what it did to his aunt and uncle when Jack left without a word. He wouldn't want his mum and dad to feel like that on his account. He might be only on the verge of being fifteen, but six months ago he wasn't as grown-up about things as he was now.

Before anything else was said between him and Helen, the evacuee children came stumping down the stairs to join them. Johnny glared at him, but Patty managed a feeble smile. He suddenly felt expansive and a bit sorry for them.

'So you two live in London, do you? My mum used to live there a long time ago. Did she tell you that?'

Johnny's brows darkened still more. 'We ain't got no mum no more. She's gone off. We live with our gran and our dad when he comes home from the pub.'

Tom didn't know what to say to that. Then

Patty spoke up.

'Our gran smells of cabbages.'

'Patty, that's not a very nice thing to say,' Helen said at once. 'I'm sure your gran looks after you very well, and it's probably just the smells in the house when she cooks your dinner.'

Patty shook her head vigorously. She had fair curly hair that bounced on her shoulders, and she sucked a strand of it when she was nervous. She was doing it now, and her lips wobbled with remembering.

'No, it's me gran,' she whispered. 'She farts a lot.'

Trying hard to conceal his laughter now, Tom heard his aunt's outraged gasp. He didn't fancy being here if the kid was going to get a telling-off and start blubbering, and nor was he prepared to act as a sort of nursemaid-cum-big-cousin to these two. He knew he'd been here long enough. His boss would be calling to collect him and take him back to Bristol in a couple of hours, and he needed to spend time with his own family before then.

'If you'll just give me Jack's address, Auntie Helen, I'll be getting home.'

Outside again, he heard his name being called. He gave a groan. It wasn't that he didn't like his sister Rose, because he did, but she had two kids in tow now, his brother Bobby, and the doctor's baby. And he'd had enough of kids for one day.

'Tom, will you take Bobby home with you?'

Rose said. 'Mollie's being a bit fretful and she needs a feed. By the time I get home and back again she'll be bawling her eyes out.'

She grinned at him, and then noted his less than cheerful expression.

'What's up?'

He jerked his head backwards. 'Those two staying with Helen and Mick. I don't know how you cope with somebody else's kid, Rose. They're enough to give anybody the willies.'

'What are the willies?' Bobby said at once.

'Nothing,' the other two said together. Rose looked sympathetic. 'I'm sorry for them, and for the others who have been landed down here so far from home. They must wonder if they'll ever see their own families again.'

Tom snorted. 'The girl says her gran smells and I won't tell you why, though it's probably no worse than the smells in Uncle Mick's surgery.'

Rose tightened her grip on the pram handle as Mollie began grizzling. 'You're being a pig, Tom, and I'm not listening to any more of it. Take Bobby home with you and I'll be there later.'

She turned and strode away, leaving her two brothers to get on with it. She had enough to think about without listening to his whining about the two kids her aunt and uncle had taken in. She had Matt to think about, and his plans for the future that were becoming ever more likely. As well as that, she had to think about whether she was brave enough to share them,

34

and what her mother's reaction would be if she did.

Alice told herself not to hover near the window. Tom was only home for a few precious hours, and it was foolish of her to be jealous because he'd gone out to find news of his cousin. Jack had always been something of a hero to Tom, but she thought those feelings had faded slightly in recent months. Of course, Jack wasn't around any more, and nor was Tom. They had gone their separate ways, when at one time they had seemed to be as close as Siamese twins, despite the four year difference in their ages. They were as close as Alice and her friend Tilly had once been.

As her friend's name came into her mind, Alice felt the familiar stab of pain, knowing she would never see Tilly again. To die horribly in one room of a lodging-house as Tilly had, with no-one to comfort her, must have only added to her agony, and Alice thanked her lucky stars every day, for her large and loving family.

As if to remind her that there was another part of it still to come, she felt the small ripple of the unborn baby's movements inside her. There were still six months to go until the birth, so she'd thought it was too soon to feel anything, and that it was probably just her imagination, until Doctor Stacey said that once a woman had experienced childbirth it was quite usual for her to know the signs very early. And Alice had experienced childbirth four times already.

She saw Tom push Bobby ahead of him through the door, and sighed. Tom was growing away from them, and who could blame him for that? He was finding his feet in the world, and no mother could begrudge her son his independence. All the same, the feeling that the family with whom he lived now were becoming more important to Tom than his own, was something she couldn't quite dismiss. Nor the eagerness with which the boy looked forward to being collected in Mr James Conway's fine motor car to take him back to Bristol.

'Our Tom don't like the vaccies,' Bobby shouted in his usual excitable way as soon as he got inside. 'He was laughing 'cos they made a mess in Uncle Mick's surgery and spilt some stuff and made a bad smell. Uncle Mick called them brats, and our Tom called the boy a little sod, and he said Auntie Helen made them go upstairs and tidy their room before they could have any lemonade.'

'I didn't say all that,' Tom snapped, knowing damn well that he had, just to spin a tale on the way home. 'It's time you learned how to keep your mouth shut, you little liar.'

'That's enough, Tom,' Alice said at once. 'I don't like that kind of talk, and if you can't be nice to your brother, perhaps you shouldn't come back at all.'

She drew in her breath, hardly able to believe she had said it. But it was certainly true that life was more harmonious since Tom had gone, and she was only just realizing it. She caught sight of his face then, red and furious, and was immediately upset at her words. Walter would be furious too, if he heard about them. And Bobby the blabbermouth would be sure to tell him...

'Look, Tom, I didn't mean that the way it sounded,' she began, but he brushed her aside angrily.

'I don't know how else you could have meant it. It sounded plain enough to me. You don't want me here any longer, and that suits me. I'd rather be where I'm appreciated, anyway.'

Bobby began howling, and a sudden lurch from the baby made Alice feel momentarily dizzy. Today had started out so well, and now it was all going wrong. Right on cue, having heard his boys return home, Walter came stumping in from his shed in the garden where he spent so much of his time.

'What's going on in here?' he said.

'Ask *her*,' Tom said rudely while Alice was still catching her breath and her equilibrium.

'That's no way to refer to your mother, boy,' Walter snapped. 'Is somebody going to tell me why the child's bawling, and why you two sinners are glaring at one another?'

Alice could have laughed if it hadn't been so serious. For years Walter had referred to her as *Mother*, and now she was a *sinner*, for pity's sake. Tom was still his precious *boy*, though, she noted, and she sobered at once.

'I told Tom if he couldn't treat Bobby more kindly, perhaps he shouldn't come home at all,' she said, her voice tight and strained. 'I didn't mean it, of course. It was one of those things people say on the spur of the moment. Of course I want to see him here where he belongs.'

Walter sat down on his chair, his arms folded, his face black, every inch the judge and jury of his domain. He heeded the first part of her explanation, and ignored the rest.

'Well, this was a nice welcome for the boy, I must say. It's no wonder he felt the need to leave home if this is your attitude towards him.'

It was too much. Alice found herself screaming at her husband, while Bobby was subdued now, cowering behind her skirts.

'*My* attitude towards him! You seem to have forgotten it was you who put the idea of leaving home into his head, not mine. It was you who brought Mr James Conway and his wife here, and between you all you persuaded him that there was a better life for him away from his family.'

Tom's temper had disappeared, and he looked from one to the other of them in genuine alarm.

'Mum ... Dad ... I never meant for any of this to happen. Please don't argue over me. I'll have to leave soon, and I don't want all this bad feeling between us.'

Whatever else might have been said between them was disturbed by the honking of a car horn outside the house. The silence between them all was brittle, and only Bobby's snivelling could be heard. And then Walter shrugged.

'Your chauffeur's waiting,' he said. 'I'd prefer it if you didn't wait for him to come inside today, boy.'

Alice could see that Tom looked close to tears now, and she hated Walter for making him feel so inadequate. Tom was no longer a child but a young man, and she went straight to him and put her arms around him.

'It will all blow over, Tom,' she said quietly in his ear.

She couldn't say any more, for fear the words would choke her. He gave a brief nod and moved out of her arms.

'Right. I'll see you all next time, then,' was all he managed to say, and then he was gone. They heard the car door open and close and then the purr of the engine as the car glided away and out of the village.

Alice caught hold of Bobby's hand and told him they were going to make some cakes. It was the last thing she felt like doing, but she had to keep her hands occupied somehow. The thought flashed through her mind that she actually felt more like throttling Walter instead.

He sat where he was for a few minutes longer and then she heard the door slam and knew he was going out to his shed again. Best place for him, she thought savagely. She could beat the living daylights out of the cake dough, and he could hammer some sense into a piece of wood. And perhaps by the end of it they would both have calmed down.

'Is Tom coming home again?' Bobby said in a

small voice.

'Of course he is, love,' Alice told him at once. 'He just made a bit of fuss over nothing, that's all.'

'Dad's not going away too, is he?'

She looked down at his worried little face, and felt her heart contract.

'No, love! Whatever made you say such a thing?'

'Those vaccies said their mum's gone off, and their dad's at the pub, and you went away to London after Auntie Tilly died. I don't want you and my dad to go away,' he said, his face crumpling.

'We're not going anywhere, you silly boy,' she said, holding him close.

She felt suddenly stricken. She hadn't thought how all of these arguments would affect him, nor that he still remembered so vividly the sad week she had spent in London just a few months ago, arranging her friend Tilly's funeral. Bobby was barely four years old, but the loss of his mother for those days had obviously stuck in his mind, and the arrival of the evacuees had evidently stirred it all up again.

Walter came back indoors, saying shortly that he'd been in his shed for long enough, and there were more important matters to think about. He switched on the wireless, and listened intently to the sombre voice of the announcer as he heard the latest news. As if aware of the silence inside the house now, he turned the wireless off just as quickly, and cleared his throat noisily.

'It seems we've all got hot under the collar over trifles, Mother, and the best thing to do is to forget it. If you've a mind to it, we'll take this young 'un out for a spell tomorrow. The blackberries are ready for picking in the hedgerows, and a nice apple and blackberry pie will go down nicely for Sunday tea.'

It was rare that Walter wanted to do anything so mundane, and Alice knew this was his way of saying sorry. She didn't need to comment, since Bobby was already jumping up and down and begging his mother to say that they could. Over the top of his head she gave Walter a half-smile, and all was forgiven.

A long while later when Bobby was in bed, Walter stretched out his legs in front of the fireplace, adorned with Alice's tapestry fire screen in front of it in the summer months when fires weren't needed to warm the cottage.

'I suppose Helen will be getting the new kids churchified,' he said. 'From what I heard today, she'll have her hands full trying to tame those little heathens.'

Alice resisted the temptation to be sharp about his uncharitable words. Instead, she nodded ruefully.

'You could be right. It's not easy for little folk to be taken from their homes and have to learn a whole new way of living. Especially coming from the city to the country where everything's so strange for them.'

41

'You managed it, didn't you?'

'I was hardly a little person at the time, Walter.'

'That you weren't,' he said, with a reminiscent smile. 'You were all woman then, and you're all woman now.'

He didn't often say such things and she felt herself blush.

'A woman and a half now, you might say,' she said a little ruefully, patting the soft swell of her belly.

'Ah well, a woman blooms when she's expecting a babby, and there's none who'd dare to say otherwise.'

Her eyes widened over the small garment she was knitting. That was two compliments in one evening! He must really be regretting all the fuss between them that afternoon – especially with Tom in the middle of it. Her hands shook for a second and she tutted as she almost dropped a stitch. Walter noticed, and as if knowing exactly the reason for it, he spoke more gently.

'You don't need to fret about our Tom, Alice. It's a sure bet he won't be bothering about it by now, and you'll see him as usual in two weeks' time. Good God, it'll be September then, and didn't Tilly always say you should never carry a grudge from one month into the next?'

'So she did!' Alice said in astonishment. 'Fancy you remembering that, Walter. I'd forgotten it myself.'

'Ah well, I mind her saying it when she came down here when you were girls, and there's certain things about that time I'll never forget, if you get my meaning.'

He was definitely doing his best, she thought now, and it cheered her. He could be a stubborn old cuss, but there were still times when she knew exactly why she had married him. He knew how hard it had been for her at first, living in a new environment, but she had succeeded, and so would those kids living with Helen and Mick now. Like her, they were Londoners, and Londoners knew how to survive.

She put down her knitting. It was time to forget them all, and time for bed, and with it the reminder that just as he said, she was all woman now. And through all the years they had been together there had been nothing like the stimulus of a good old argument to make the making-up even sweeter.

Three

September the third dawned bright and sunny, almost as balmy as an Indian Summer in the country, and hot and stuffy in the towns. But this was a day like no other, because it seemed as though the entire country was holding its breath for the broadcast by the prime minister at eleven o'clock that morning. Since it was a Sunday, many people were at church, but for those who weren't, every family who owned a wireless set was crowded over it, in order not to miss a single word of Mr Chamberlain's announcement. The Chases were one of those families.

'He couldn't have a more monotonous voice if he tried,' Alice commented, never one to care for politicians.

'Shush, woman,' Walter said. 'What the devil does his voice matter? It's what he says that's important, and this is no time for him to be sounding cheerful.'

Bobby had been sent out in the garden to play, too young to know the significance of this day. They could hear him now, shouting and laughing as he chased butterflies. Alice wished so hard that such moments could be captured for ever. She could see Rose's hands clasped together in her lap, her eyes downcast, and thought she could guess so well how her elder daughter must be feeling. She would be wondering if or when Doctor Matt would be enlisting, and how she was going to feel about it. In those intense moments before the fateful words were spoken to the nation, Alice's thoughts flew to her other two children. No longer children, of course, but both still vulnerable.

Lucy had already said that she wasn't putting on any old uniform other than the one she wore at The Grange where she worked. It was bad enough to feel like a servant. But Tom ... Alice drew in her breath. Lord knew where Tom's thoughts would go if the worst happened – as it was surely about to do. The baby inside her lurched, and she put her hand protectively over her belly. At least this one was safe, the thought whispered inside her head, not daring to think for a moment what all that implied for the rest of them. Even though – her heart lurched again. This baby would be born in wartime, and that was a reminder that nobody would have wanted for their child.

'Here it comes, Mother,' Walter said, still twiddling with the knobs on the wireless in order to hear the crackling words more clearly.

It took such a small amount of time. Before the broadcast began they had still been in the glow of an Indian Summer, the very best of times in the English countryside, and in moments all that was about to change for ever, as the threatening war bickering became a reality. Even if the weather didn't really change, it was as though a dark cloud had gone over the sun as Mr Chamberlain's sombre voice announced that the German Chancellor had been given an ultimatum for them to suspend their attack on Poland and that the time for receiving the reply had passed.

'...I have to tell you now, that no such note has been received – and that consequently – this country is now at war with Germany.'

Walter's breath exploded in his usual bellow at the man's exquisite pauses. 'God Almighty! A bloody *note*. Is that all the bugger can call it?'

'Walter, language!' Alice chided him, seeing Bobby glance their way through the open window. Her heart thudded all the same, because now it was speculation no longer. It was real.

Walter snorted again. 'A bunch of warmongers, that's what they are, the lot of them. God knows whether it could have been prevented, any more than we know how hard they tried.'

Rose intervened as she saw her mother's face redden. 'I'm sure they tried as hard as they could, Dad. No sane person wants to go to war, do they?'

'Is that your young doctor friend's opinion?' he said rounding on her. 'How soon before he pushes off from the village to join up and get blown to bits in some Godforsaken battlefield? None of his fine medical learning will be a ha'porth of good to him then, will it?'

'That's a rotten thing to say,' Rose said. 'And if he goes, so will I.'

She jumped up from the sofa and rushed outside to swing Bobby up in her arms, making him squeal with fright and excitement.

'Shall we go and visit baby Mollie?' she asked him, sure of his response, and knowing full well there was an ulterior motive behind the innocent words. She meant what she said. If Matt joined up, then so would she, and she had always known it would come to that.

Holding Bobby's hand tightly, she called out to her parents through the open window. 'We're going for a walk. Back later.'

Bramwell was a sleepy country village where nothing much happened on a Sunday. On a normal Sunday the churchgoers were out and about for the hour of the morning service and then went home to prepare the Sunday dinner, having done their pious duty. Others stayed indoors with their families, enjoying the proverbial day of rest. By then, Bramwell was a proverbial ghost town, and that was the way they liked it. But today was no normal Sunday.

The Chase cottage was a little way out of the village, but as soon as Rose and Bobby neared it they could see the crowds gathering on the village green and outside cottages and shops. The Pig and Whistle had its usual quota of old men outside on the benches, and it was obvious that everyone was aware of the prime minister's announcement, and the consequences. It was as though no one could stay indoors any more. People needed to be outside, sharing in what had just happened. Faces were drawn on those who had seen it all before. Younger ones couldn't quite disguise the excitement and anticipation of something they had never experienced, and were uncertain what to expect.

Crazy imaginings ran through them like wildfire. Would bombs come raining down on them in minutes? Were they all going to be killed in their beds by the enemy? Or would they have to learn to speak German if they were invaded? It was as though there was a ground-swell of different emotions washing through the whole village, and even before Rose and Bobby reached the doctor's house, she could see her aunt and uncle with their two young charges coming their way. She gave a sigh, knowing she would have to put off seeing Matt for now. Families were more important, and at times like these families needed to be together.

'You've heard the news then,' Helen said, as soon as they got near enough. 'We were just coming to see you all. These two have been hopping up and down for the last ten minutes, wanting to know if their house is going to be bombed and if their gran can come down to stay with us.'

Rose saw the desperation in her aunt's eyes. It was one thing to take in the evacuees. It was quite another for a homely woman like her, with no knowledge of handling boisterous young children since her own son was grown up, to know how to deal with this situation. But none of them knew how to deal with it. None of them had been faced with it before.

The evacuees were looking warily at Rose now. They didn't really know her, but they did know Bobby. When nobody quite knew what to say, Bobby spoke up.

'If your gran comes here to stay, can we share her?'

Patty giggled and Johnny the spokesman sniffed, as aggressive as ever.

'Don't be potty. You can't share a gran. You've either got one or you ain't, and you ain't having ours.'

Helen could see Bobby's frown and spoke quickly.

'Nobody's house is getting bombed, Johnny, and I'm sure your gran wouldn't want to come here to stay. She'll want to stay home where she belongs, and keep the house nice for when you go back.'

At any minute now, they all knew Johnny was going to ask why *they* couldn't be at home with their gran where they belonged, and Mick took his hand firmly and strode on ahead of the others.

'Come on, the lot of you. I want to see the rest of the family, and we're wasting time standing here arguing.'

Rose had no option but to turn around with Bobby and go with them, ignoring his wailing that he wanted to see baby Mollie.

'We'll see her tomorrow,' she told him, knowing that she would be seeing Matt long before that. At the first opportunity that day she was going to rush back to the doctor's house and ask Matt what he intended to do and how soon he was going to do it.

Tom Chase had listened just as avidly to the news that morning. The Conway house had a far more impressive wireless set than his own family in Bramwell, but the news was the same, wherever you heard it. Like his own family, the Conways, with their disabled son Graham, were gathered around the wireless to listen to the prime minister's words. James Conway switched it off as soon as it was over.

'So now we finally know. It's been a long time coming but there's no turning back now. I hope your parents won't want to review your situation here, Tom.'

His words were a complete shock to Tom. 'Why would they do that?'

James Conway spoke very evenly. 'We're very close to Bristol and the docks, as you know, Tom, and if this war is fought in the air as well as on the ground, as all the signs point towards, Bristol docks will be a prime target for the enemy. Your father may well decide you'd be far better off working back at the sawmill with him, than in an area that's likely to be attacked.'

'Well, I won't go!' Tom said, his heart jumping about in his chest at the thought. 'He can't make me!'

'I'm afraid he can, Tom,' James said calmly. 'You're still a minor, and you'll have to abide by what he says.'

His wife broke in. 'I'm sure it won't come to that, Tom. In any case, there's no point in worrying about things before they happen. But you know as well as I do, that Mr Conway makes a study of these things, and if he and your father do decide that you'd be better at home, just temporarily, of course, you'll realize that they're only thinking of your own good. I'm sure your apprenticeship can always be continued at a later date.'

'Temporarily until the war's over, you mean,' Tom said heatedly, ignoring all the rest. 'And how long will that be!'

He had never spoken so freely with his employers before, and he knew he was being impolite to speak to Mrs Conway in that way. He wished to God he was a couple of years older, and then he'd damn well go and enlist tomorrow, regardless of his apprenticeship, and to hell with the lot of them. Nor could he help thinking, and God help him for doing so, that at least they could be complacent about their own son. Graham would never be called up...

'I think we all need a little time to cool off,' he heard James Conway say next. 'I'm going into the city for an hour or so and I'll be back later.'

'And the boys and I will take a walk before dinner,' his wife said firmly, and that was the end of it. 'I'm sure we can all do with some

fresh air while we think about what's happened.'

That was typical of them, thought Tom,
fuming. He liked them enormously, but they
didn't ever have a rip-roaring argument like his
own family did when they needed to thrash
something out. They each went their separate
ways to think and consider problems, and in the
end nothing was ever sorted out convincingly.
Problems were just pushed under the table and
life went on in its own sweet way.

At that moment, he realized guiltily how
much he had always relished the family rows in
which everyone could get involved and have
their say. He didn't blame Graham for never
saying anything much. It was the way he had
been brought up, and a peaceful life suited him
fine. With more of an adult insight than usual,
Tom found himself wondering how much of a
peaceful life anyone was going to get in the
future.

The children were sent out into the garden,
where Bobby was trying to persuade Johnny
that chasing butterflies with a net was fun. Patty
was happy to do so, her blonde curls bouncing
up and down in the sunlight, but Johnny clearly
thought it was beneath him to join in such a
piddling little game. He was only seven years
old, but he thought the countryside was tame,
and wasted no time in telling this little squirt
how he spent his time in London.

'Me and Patty used to go and sit outside the

pub of a Saturday night-time, waiting for our gran to bring us pork scratchings while she was drinking her beer,' he told Bobby importantly.

Bobby retaliated at once. 'You can't go in pubs.'

'I didn't say we went in them. I said we sat outside, dummy. Ain't you got ears?'

'I don't like you,' Bobby said flatly.

'Well, I don't like you neither, so there,' Johnny said.

Patty put her hand in Bobby's, glaring at her brother.

'I like you, Bobby, and our Johnny's a rat-arse.'

Bobby's mouth dropped open. He had no idea what it meant. He only knew he didn't like the sound of it, and he shook the girl away from him as he screeched at her.

'I'm telling on you for being so wicked.'

Indoors, all his relatives were talking solemnly about the imminent effect on the community now that they were officially at war with Germany, but they all stopped talking abruptly as the little whirlwind rushed inside.

'That girl said something awful!' he shouted. 'She said Johnny's a rat-arse. What's a rat-arse, Dad?'

After a startled second when all the women gasped, Walter looked thunderous. 'Don't you ever let me hear you using words like that again, do you hear? And Helen,' he turned on his sister-in-law furiously, 'I suggest you set some rules in your house for those two brats and teach them some manners before you bring them anywhere near my family again.'

Helen's face was scarlet with embarrassment and fury.

'If that's the way you're going to speak to me, Walter, I promise you it'll be a long time before any of my family comes near yours again!' she snapped.

'Helen, for God's sake,' Mick remonstrated as she headed for the door with her chin held high. She didn't heed him, and as she flung open the door, they were all met by the sight of the evacuees scrapping and bawling as loud as they could.

'I want to go home,' Patty yelled, her eyes streaming now. 'I want my gran and my dad. I hate everybody here and I hate the country. It smells like a lav all the time, and it's scary.'

'Well, you can't go home,' Johnny yelled back. 'There's going to be bombs falling soon and killing people, and we've got to stay here until they stop doing it, so you've got to put up with it, same as me.'

Neither Alice nor Helen could stand this sight any longer. They both rushed outside to catch one of the children in their arms. Johnny's arms flailed furiously against Helen's embrace, but Patty seemed to melt against Alice's rounded shape. The women looked at one another, and then Helen gave a tight smile.

'Maybe the damn governments can't sort out their problems, but we should be able to sort out ours.'

Alice looked directly at Johnny, who still looked ready to kick Helen at the least provocation.

'Why don't we all go for a walk in the woods?' Alice said. 'Bobby can come too, and we'll leave the men to themselves for a while. Have you ever seen a squirrel or a field mouse, Johnny?'

'*No,*' he said belligerently.

'Have you and Patty ever picked wild flowers, or collected fir cones and leaves and twigs to stick them on to paper to make a picture?'

She had caught his attention now, and Patty had stopped crying and was looking curious. At their age, it took so little to divert their attention, Alice thought – if you knew how to do it. But she knew too, that she had better involve Helen in the plan before her sister-in-law felt completely useless.

'Auntie Helen will tell you what else we can see in the woods, while I go and fetch Bobby and see if Rose wants to come with us. Auntie Helen knows a lot about small friendly animals and birds, and about trees and plants as well,' she went on, crossing her fingers that this was the right way to go about things. She had never thought of herself as a mediator, but she knew a thing or two about bringing up children, and she saw the grateful look that Helen flashed her.

And sometime soon, she thought grimly, those two also needed to be educated in what words were unacceptable to a decent family, but today it was more urgent to calm them down and make the rest of the day as pleasant as possible. Her heart suddenly jolted. It was appalling, and somehow terrible, to think that in the midst of this small domestic upset, the wider implications of the recent wireless announcement had slipped from her mind. But it wasn't going to go away for long. The dreaded news, and all that it meant, was here to stay.

Rose declined to join them on the walk, saying she would stay behind and prepare dinner for them all, while Walter and his brother went outside to Walter's shed, the male sanctuary where so many decisions had been made over the years.

'This is a bad business,' Walter said at last.

'The war, or my wife's outburst?' Mick countered.

Walter laughed gruffly. 'For God's sake, man, we've weathered more than a tiff with a female over the years. I mean the bloody war, of course. Aren't you worried about your boy now?'

Mick looked at him thoughtfully. He'd always been the thoughtful one, the one who thought things through, while Walter was more inclined to hit out and apologize later. Perhaps if he hadn't kept his counsel to himself years ago, and worn his heart on his sleeve instead of hiding his feelings, he might have been the one sharing years of married happiness with Alice ... but those youthful days, like old yearnings, were long gone, and best forgotten.

'Of course I'm worried for Jack, but you can't live your kids' lives for them, can you? He's doing what he wanted to do, and I wouldn't wish for anything else for him.'

'Even if it kills him?'

Walter groaned, even as he said it. The words should have been kept inside his head where they belonged, not brought out into the open like that. Only a fool believed that there would be no killing in a war. Countries declared war to fight one another, but it was the people who suffered, the people who were wounded and killed, the young men ... Walter shuddered, and accepted the lit Woodbine that Mick shoved into his hand. He didn't smoke to excess like some of his pub cronies, but there were times when it was the only companionable thing to calm the nerves.

'We've got to be realistic, Walter, and we've also got to keep the worst thoughts to ourselves for the sake of the women, and the kids too. I never wanted these evacuees, but Helen wanted to do her bit, and if the worst should come to our house, they'd be a kind of comfort.'

He was floundering, because he knew there would be no amount of comfort for Helen if anything happened to Jack. But he was damned if he was going to let such dark thoughts colour his days and nights for God knew how long this war was going to last. By the time the wood-shed was so thick with smoke that they could barely see across it, the two men stumbled outside, leaving the door open to air it, and since Rose was still busy in the kitchen they told her they were going down to the village to see what was what, and they'd be back in an hour.

She didn't mind. After the earlier furore, she rather liked the thought of being in the cottage alone for a while. Everyone had to sort out in their own minds what to make of what had happened, and she already knew without telling what she and Matt were going to do. Discussing it would be no more than a formality, since they had spoken about it so many times already. Telling the family would almost certainly cause another upset, but she knew without saying that if Alice had been her age, she would do exactly the same as Rose intended to do.

She knew that Matt, being the conscientious doctor that he was, had already discussed it with his own brother, the senior doctor in the village. He had found out all the details of what to do if a person wanted to enlist. He knew the procedure and he had his brother's full approval – and Rose's as well.

By the time everyone was together again, the men had discussed the reality of war to their satisfaction, Rose had some soup simmering on the stove, and the walk in the woods had certainly done enough to put smiles on the children's faces when they returned with her mother and aunt. They were all chattering over the things they had seen, and Patty clutched a bunch of wilting wild flowers in her hand. They had glimpsed several squirrels and a nest of baby birds. They had seen a field mouse nibbling at some straw, and had picked a small basketful of blackberries. The country was obviously a mite more attractive to the visitors now, but Johnny was still determined to be contrary.

'Animals are all right, I suppose, but they all smell,' he said.

'Cats don't smell, Johnny, and you and Patty both loved the baby animals, didn't you?' Helen said quickly, seeing Mick's raised eyebrows. 'We might be able to get a kitten when Mrs Dobson's cat has hers.'

'Can I have a kitten as well?' Bobby shouted at once.

'I don't know about that,' Walter began, but Alice told him they would think about it, knowing there was no sense in sending him off into a tantrum when it was reasonably amicable there.

Mick took control. 'Before you decide all animals smell, Johnny, you can come out with me on my rounds tomorrow and see a few larger animals than the ones you saw in the woods today. You'll see what happens when farm animals need treatment, too, and it might keep you out of my surgery in future, unless you're invited inside,' he added, reminding the boy that he hadn't forgotten what had happened when he had rampaged through there before.

'All right,' Johnny said sullenly.

'So now let's all have some soup before it gets cold,' Rose said, before the mood descended again. 'I have to go out this afternoon, Mum.'

Bobby immediately asked if he could come, but since all the adults knew exactly where Rose would be going and why, Helen said at once that Bobby could go home with her and spend the afternoon with Johnny and Patty if he wanted to. For a moment it was a gamble which child was going to object first, but in the end none of them did, and it was agreed.

There were fewer people about in Bramwell during the afternoon, as families remained indoors to discuss the personal implications of Mr Chamberlain's broadcast. But Rose Chase had other business away from her family, and as she walked through the village to the doctor's surgery she saw her old employer and his son measuring up their shop windows. Henry Kelsey nudged his son as he saw the girl approach, and Peter scowled.

'I'm not interested,' he told his father coolly.

'You should have hung on to her, boy, a good-looker like her.'

Rose caught the end of the sentence and her face burned. She had never liked Peter's father, and it was obvious to her now, that it was his crudity that had rubbed off on her one-time young man.

''Afternoon, Rose. What about the news then? I daresay you'll be putting on a fancy uniform soon,' Henry called out, never one to let her pass without some snide remark.

'I might,' she replied, and then curiosity got

the better of her. 'What are you doing?'

Peter snorted. 'Dad thinks we're about to get bombed any minute, so we're measuring up for blackout curtains so the enemy planes can't pick out our little shop in the middle of nowhere,' he said, heavy with sarcasm.

'Why would they bomb a little place like this? There's nothing here for them,' Rose said uneasily.

'Once they start, the buggers will drop bombs everywhere,' Henry said, annoyed with the pair of them for belittling his efforts. 'You might scoff, but everybody will be following my lead soon, and then we'll see who's laughing.'

'Nobody's laughing today, Mr Kelsey,' Rose said stiffly.

She walked on, annoyed for letting herself take any notice of the man. He was an oaf, and Peter wasn't much better. Not that she had thought that way once. Not so long ago she had thought he was the man of her dreams. But that was before she fell out of love with him, and before she met Matt Stacey.

Her heart jolted. It had been such a wonderful day when Matt first came to Bramwell to join his brother in the local doctor's practice. Even in those first dreamy days of knowing him, Rose's imagination had foreseen a future for them, settling down in this idyllic village and eventually raising a family of their own.

All that was changed now. Because of that one earth-shattering announcement on the wireless that morning, there was no secure future for any of them, and she knew that she and Matt would fulfil the plans they had spoken about in the event of war. The only people who knew of it were Matt's brother and his wife, since Rose would have to give up her job of caring for the Stacey baby. It gave her a pang to think of it, knowing how fond she had grown of baby Mollie.

But she wouldn't think of that too deeply. The important thing was for Rose and Matt to make their final plans, and the next step would be to tell her parents together. She knew how her father would react. They had already lost Tom in effect, even though he was within easy reach of home, and now they would be losing Rose to who knew where? But in time of war families were always split apart. They had to make sacrifices, and if this was the extent of her own, then it was little enough. So many people would make so many more, Rose thought with a shiver of premonition.

Four

Alice saw her elder daughter and the young doctor walking down the lane towards home, their heads close together as if in earnest conversation. He was a fine-looking young man, Alice thought, and with far nicer manners than the Kelsey boy, whom Alice had never thought good enough for her daughter.

Lucy had come furiously pedalling home on her bicycle earlier that afternoon, missing all the fuss with the evacuee children, but agitated and excited at the same time over what the war was going to mean to everyone. Seeing her sister and Matt together though, Lucy's thoughts were momentarily diverted.

'He's like a film star, isn't he, Mum? Rose was always the lucky one. First Peter Kelsey, and now him. It's not fair. Why couldn't I have been born first?'

Alice sighed, wishing she could hold the image of two attractive young people walking down a country lane in her heart for ever, instead of wondering what the future really held for them. If Rose had thought Alice didn't know what she had in mind, then she didn't know her mother very well.

'You do ask some daft questions sometimes, Lucy,' she told her younger daughter, finding her remarks completely irksome.

'No, I don't! Mrs Frankley at The Grange thinks I'm very sensible, but you and Dad have never taken much notice of me. You only care about Rose and Tom and Bobby – and now the new one, of course.'

Surprised by the sudden air of rejection in her voice, Alice looked at her sharply. 'That's another silly remark to make, Lucy. We care about all of you, although sometimes it seems as if you'd rather be at The Grange than here with us.'

'Well, I wouldn't if you must know. They've been talking about the war for ages and what's going to happen, and today they're going on and on about it, of course, and who's going to be a hero and who isn't. I hate it. I'd much rather be home with you. I don't even feel like going back there today. Can I say I've got a cold and you had to keep me home?'

Her eyes were large and pleading, but she sounded almost comical at the same time, and if she hadn't been so obviously clutching at straws, Alice would have laughed and told her she was being foolish and dramatic as usual. A real watery-eyed music-hall turn ... and so like Tilly when she wanted something. Alice caught her breath as her old friend's name came into her mind as it often did so unexpectedly. As if trying to offer an answer ... but before she knew quite what to say, Rose and Matt had arrived, and the moment had gone.

'Where's Dad, Mum? We've got something to tell you, but we want you to hear it together,' Rose said at once.

'He's in the shed with Bobby. I'll go and get him,' Lucy said. Her face was red and blotchy by now, and Alice guessed the girl thought she had revealed too much, and was glad to get out of the cottage for the moment.

But within minutes they knew there were other things to think about than a young girl's dissatisfaction with her lot. Doctor Matt was probably going to be called up soon, but he wasn't waiting for his official calling-up papers to arrive, and Rose was going to enlist with him. Doctors and nurses were going to be needed now, and what Rose didn't know, she intended to learn.

'I had an idea something like this was brewing, and I suppose you've thought it out properly, have you?' Walter said, his voice harsh with suppressed emotion. He'd always feared that Tom was going to put his age up and enlist in a burst of patriotism, but in his opinion girls should stay at home. It may be an old-fashioned view, but that was the way it had always been, with man the hunter, and woman the homemaker. Girls weren't meant to go to war in any shape or form. Even so, he had to concede that in such perilous times everything changed. War did that to people. As far back as the Crimean conflict Florence Nightingale had shown that women were just as valuable as men when it came to saving lives. Much as it pained Walter to think of Rose being anywhere near danger, or having to deal with unspeakable wounds alongside army doctors, and witnessing sights no young girl should ever have to see, he couldn't be anything but proud of her.

Rose was somewhat taken aback by his reaction. She had steeled herself for a huge row. She had expected him to put his foot down immediately and say that he wouldn't allow it, but it seemed he had gone some way to accepting the inevitable already. Or else her mother had begun oiling the works even before Rose had said it. Her mother, the peace-maker, Rose thought with a rush of intuition.

'We've been thinking about it for a long time,' she said. 'It's something we both feel strongly about, and now that there's no turning back we're going to a recruiting centre to enlist as soon as possible – with your blessing, of course.'

'Oh, so you are waiting for my blessing then?'

'I've always needed that, Dad,' she said simply.

'What about your job?' Lucy interrupted the charged atmosphere in the room. 'I thought you liked looking after the Staceys' baby.'

Rose turned to her. 'Well, of course I do. I like it very much, but this is more important, and we all have to do our bit when we can. Matt will be leaving the practice as well, but Doctor Stacey managed on his own before, and he'll do so again, I'm sure.'

Bobby had partly caught on to what was happening, realizing that if Rose went away he wouldn't be able to see baby Mollie with her. He began to wail.

'I don't want Rose to go away. I want to see baby Mollie, and I don't want to have to play with the vaccies all the time. I hate them!'

Alice caught him as he rushed into her arms. Nothing in this family was ever simple, she thought wryly.

'I'm sure you'll be able to see baby Mollie sometimes,' she said soothingly. 'The other children will be going to school soon, so you wouldn't be seeing much of them, anyway.'

'Won't Mrs Stacey want someone else to look after her baby?' Lucy said.

In the fractional silence, it seemed as if everyone looked at her in the same instant, as if noticing her flushed face and moist eyes for the first time. Matt was the one who answered, his voice casual, the professional doctor putting the anxious patient at her ease.

'I don't know. Are you thinking of applying for the job?'

'Do you think she'd consider me?' Lucy said, suddenly breathless.

'You're surely not serious, are you, Lucy?' Rose said.

They had decamped to the old bedroom they had once shared, while Matt discussed their plans in more detail, leaving their parents and

Bobby downstairs.

'Why not? Don't you think I'm capable of looking after a baby?'

'Of course you're capable. I just thought you were happy at The Grange, that's all. Has something happened that you're not telling us?'

Lucy's face crumpled. 'Not really. Oh well, if you must know, there was this boy who I liked, and I thought he liked me. It's just like before, when that other boy I fancied got caught for stealing and was dismissed. And now there's this gardener, a bit older than me, who's playing me and Sophie off one against the other, and I don't like it, Rose. It makes me feel cheap, and I'd rather get away from there, only for goodness' sake don't tell Mum my reasons, will you?'

Rose realized how twitchy her sister was becoming saying all this.

'If you're really unhappy, then you're better off out of there, but I'm not sure it's a good enough reason for wanting to be a nanny, Lucy. You can't take on a responsibility like that on the spur of the moment. Besides, you have to like babies to look after them properly.'

'I do like babies! I looked after Bobby as much as you did when he was born, if not more! I'm looking forward to the new one as well, now I've got used to the idea of Mum having another one. But this seems like the perfect opportunity for me, Rose, so please put in a good word with Mrs Stacey for me. *Please*.'

Rose's heart softened. 'Why don't you see

what Mum and Dad think about it, and if they don't object, then come back with Matt and me this afternoon and we'll talk to Mrs Stacey about it. I can't guarantee anything, mind.'

She was rewarded by her sister flinging her arms around her neck. At that moment Rose felt so much older than the two years between them. Lucy was past seventeen, but she was still a child in many ways, and Rose could understand her fury if this gardener was playing fast and loose with two of the young girls at The Grange. Knowing how she herself had felt when Peter Kelsey had wanted more from her than she was willing to give, she couldn't blame Lucy for wanting to put plenty of distance between herself and temptation. Nor could she be sorry for that.

She found herself thinking it was strange how everything changed so rapidly, as they went downstairs to face the music, as Lucy called it. She and Matt had known for a while that they would enlist when the time came, but for Lucy to come back to the fold, which in effect it would mean, was something none of them had anticipated. Rose also knew her mother would be glad to have Lucy living at home again. The family would be almost back to normal again – as normal as any of them could be in wartime.

It felt strange to be even saying the word in her head. When they had woken that morning they had still been at peace, yet in a moment, everything had changed. Was it really wartime now? It still seemed so unreal. Nothing had happened. No bombs had fallen. No sirens had sounded. No marching feet were invading the beautiful English countryside, defiling it with their weapons and their guttural foreign voices. She shuddered, knowing she was letting her imagination take her to places she didn't want to go. In any case, it may well be that she and Matt would be sent to foreign places themselves, to offer what help they could to the wounded and dying. It never occurred to her that they may not be together.

Violet Stacey looked up in surprise at the small deputation entering her sitting room. As her young brother-in-law, Matt was free and easy in the doctor's house, where he had his own room. Violet was well aware of the attachment between him and Rose. She approved of it, and she always welcomed the girl after working hours. But today, on this momentous day of days, there was someone else with them, and she quickly recognized the other girl.

'Why, it's Lucy, isn't it?' she said. 'I haven't seen you in a while, and you're quite the young lady now. Are you still working for the Frankleys at The Grange?'

Unwittingly, it was just about the worst opening remark she could have made. Now that the moment was here, Rose could see that Lucy was going to be tongue-tied after her impulsive suggestion. She broke in quickly before her sister appeared completely dull-witted.

'She is, Mrs Stacey, but she's hoping to find

70

something more suitable where she can live at home again. My mother will be glad of her company now that she's expecting, especially when I'm not there to give a hand with the new baby and with Bobby too, and that's what we've come to see you about.'

She knew she sounded a bit more garbled than usual, and she mentally crossed her fingers, having put the onus on her mother's needs, but it didn't take Violet more than a moment for her to guess where this was leading. She gave a small smile.

'I see. You know where the kettle is, Rose, so why don't you make us all some tea? I was just about to wake Mollie up, so do you want to come with me, Lucy? You haven't seen her lately, and I swear she grows bigger every day.'

'All right,' said Lucy.

Once they had left the sitting room, Rose and Matt went into the kitchen to make the tea, and Rose raised her eyebrows at him.

'So what do you think?'

He laughed, putting his arms around her waist and nuzzling his face into her neck. 'I think if she's got as much charm and is as devious as her big sister for getting what she wants, then the job's as good as hers.'

It was much later when Lucy returned home to tell her parents it was all settled. Lucy had fallen in love with Mollie just as quickly as Rose had done, and Violet Stacey told her she was pleased with the way her baby took to her.

So now that it was all agreed, bar the fact of Lucy giving in a week's notice at The Grange. Alice welcomed the idea of Lucy living at home again. Alice had always had all the protective instincts of a mother hen, wanting her brood around her as much as possible, even though it was inevitable they would eventually go their separate ways and make lives of their own. It was the natural way of things. You couldn't keep your children – or your friends – with you for ever.

She could see that Walter too was oddly elated. If Rose had to go and do her patriotic thing, as he was now resigned to, then it would be good to have the house filled with female chatter again. He realized anew how proud he was of Rose, especially a week or so later when his cronies at the Pig and Whistle congratulated him on having such a fine daughter and stood him a round of drinks when he told them she was planning on joining the nursing profession.

He was proud of Tom and Lucy too, of course. A man shouldn't put one child's accomplishments above another. The most important thing every parent wanted for their children was for them to be happy. He was a lucky man, Walter thought expansively. The little nipper wasn't doing so badly either, and they had a new babby to look forward to. Boy or girl, it didn't really matter a jot to him, just as long as it was healthy.

He soon learned that it wasn't only Rose and Matt Stacey who were excited about getting their calling-up papers. In the thick, smoky fug of the pub, when he had been there for a while, comparing notes with some of the older men, he heard Henry Kelsey's raffish tones. Once the shopkeeper caught sight of him, he raised his glass to Walter in greeting.

'We're just giving a send-off to the boys here, Walter,' he called out. 'Do you want to come and join us for a jar?'

Walter saw that his son and several village lads were there with him. He was about ready to go home, and he didn't particularly want to join them, but he knew it would look churlish to refuse, so he nodded, and the group of young men made room for him on the wooden bench.

'What's the occasion?' he asked without thinking, though it was obvious what any send-off of young men was all about. He and Alice had been so wrapped up in their own family and the send-off that they were shortly going to give to Rose and Matt once their orders came through that he hadn't considered anything else.

'Our Peter and his mates are joining the Navy,' Henry said expansively. 'They'll be sinking a few Jerry U-boats between them, I've no doubt.'

'Winning the war all on their own, eh?' Walter said.

He hadn't meant to sound sarcastic, but he didn't miss the way Peter's eyes narrowed at his words. He was an arrogant young man, full of self-importance like his father, and Walter knew how much he had resented it when Rose had finished with him at the beginning of the year.

'We'll do our best, won't we, boys?' Peter said coolly. 'Pity your Tom's not old enough to sign on, Mr Chase, but I daresay it means he can be mollycoddled a while longer.'

The others laughed at his daring, and Henry smothered a grin while he reprimanded him.

'Now then, Peter, I'm sure Tom would be the first to go if he could. He and that cousin of his always had some fancy ideas between them, but old Walter will have to be content with a household of women.'

Walter's eyes flashed. 'That's just where you're wrong. Rose has already signed on, and there's nothing lacking about my family wanting to do their bit for the war effort, same as my father did in the last.'

'Ah well, good luck to her then,' Henry said grudgingly. 'She was always a sparky sort of a girl, I'll give her that.'

'She used to be your girl, didn't she, Pete?' one of his mates said, nudging him and giving him a sly wink.

'Until I got tired of hanging around with her,' Peter Kelsey drawled. 'There's more sport to be had with your mates than with some of the local girls. Wait until we get our uniforms though. Then we'll show them, won't we?'

The raucous laughter started again, and when it was coupled with whispered innuendoes that brought on even more sniggering, Walter had had enough of it. He slapped his empty glass on the table, wiped the foam from his lips and turned away from the lot of them. He hardly noticed Henry following him outside into the fresh evening air. Walter was too busy drawing deep breaths and trying to control his temper. He was thankful to be out of the smoky atmosphere and glad to be away from young Peter Kelsey before he told him exactly what he thought of him for slighting his daughter like that. Truth to tell, for one minute when he felt his blood pressure rise, he'd almost lost his rag and belted him one.

'Hold on there, Walter,' Henry called out, as the other man strode off. 'Peter didn't mean to offend you, but now that they've signed on and there's no going back, I reckon they're all feeling more nervous than they let on. These are worrying times for all of us, and they have to let off steam any way they can. You and I both know that, don't we?'

Walter's footsteps slowed, and he turned around to face the man. He couldn't miss the fact that Henry appeared less than his usual bumptious self now. He recognized the other's anxiety, because it was something he shared.

'I daresay we do,' he said at last, 'and there's enough worry with countries fighting one another without neighbours doing the same, so I reckon we'll say no more about it.'

He gave a nod and went on his way, hardly knowing why he was being so bloody magnanimous towards the man when he still felt more like lashing out at him, and anybody else who came near him right then. But common sense was taking hold of him too. While the young uns did their patriotic duty and signed up, and probably thought it a bit of a lark to do so, the older folk knew they were all in for some hard times ahead. What he'd said was true. There was no sense in neighbours squabbling when they should all be pulling together. He knew damn well Alice would be saying the same thing, and wouldn't think too much of him if he'd lost his temper and went home with a bloody nose after exchanging a few punches with Henry Kelsey – or the lusty young lads who'd have made mincemeat of him.

He found himself thinking of the terrible day when he and his brother Mick had heard the news that their father had been killed in the last war. The war to end all wars, they had called it, and now they were starting another one. They had all known it was coming for a long time, but when a day like that Sunday actually arrived, the shock of it was still real. It changed everything. It changed the way people thought and the way people behaved – even in his own family.

Like most women in the village, Alice had been busy making blackout curtains to be put up at the windows every evening as soon as darkness fell, so that enemy bombers would be unable to see the slightest chink of light from the houses far below. If some folk thought it a waste of time in a small village buried deep in the Somerset countryside, there were regulations that everyone had to follow, and heaven help those who didn't. Already the villagers were organizing themselves into air-raid wardens and firewatchers. It was still a game to some, and deadly serious to others.

Walter gave a deep sigh. It wasn't time for the blackouts to be put up on this mild autumn evening. The sun was still setting in a beautiful blaze of red and gold, and creating an idyllic setting of the village and the surrounding countryside, worthy of an artist's hand. He was a practical working man who scoffed at omens or the intuition of women, but with a rare and unwelcome touch of insight he fancied he could see blood in the sky, and he swore savagely at himself for seeing things that weren't there. He wanted more than anything to be back inside his own four walls where a man felt safe. It was a disturbing feeling for someone like himself.

'So you're back at last,' Alice admonished him when he went indoors. 'I'm having trouble fastening these curtains tonight, and I need you to do it for me. If I sit here knitting when it gets dark I'll drop half my stitches and the baby will end up wearing a rag-tag of a matinee coat.'

Her voice was so blessedly normal, the grumbling so endearingly *Alice* that all the tension Walter had been feeling for the last hour or so was suddenly released. He put his arms around her and hugged her close, breathing in the scent of her hair and feeling the comfort of her body, alive and warm and so very loved. Any weird fantasies he'd been experiencing were soon put to rest by the living, breathing woman in his arms, just as they would always be.

'What's come over you, Walter?' she said with a laugh. 'You'll be crushing the babby if you're not careful.'

'I'd never do that,' he said huskily, 'but we've proved we could always make another one, haven't we, girl?'

He didn't know why he said it. He didn't mean such a daft thing, and he didn't mean to be cruel. He wanted this baby as much as Alice did, even if it had come as a complete surprise to both of them. But he might have known she'd take it seriously. He knew it as soon as she wriggled out of his arms.

'I'm not sure that's a very nice thing to say, Walter, and I don't know that the baby will care to think he can be so easily replaced either,' she said, her hand going protectively over her belly.

'For God's sake, woman, I didn't mean it like that, any more than I think that what's in there can know anything that's being said until it's born.'

'You do want this baby, don't you, Walter?' Alice said, aware of the irritation in his voice about something so irrational.

'About as much as I want you. Does that answer your question?' He gave a heavy sigh. 'Oh, take no notice of my babbling tonight, Alice. I've had a bugger of an evening, and I'm not thinking straight.'

She forgave him instantly, thinking that men were strange creatures sometimes. All this endless talk of war, and now the reality of it, was bound to make a mush of their brains. But if all it took was a woman's softness to change a man back into the loving husband she wanted again, what did a little soft soap matter? She moved back into his arms and looked deep into his troubled eyes.

'Well, think straight about this, then. Bobby's fast asleep so we'll have a nice bit of supper together and go to bed early while we've still got the house to ourselves. Rose is out with Matt this evening and won't be home until much later and once Lucy comes home to live it'll all be mayhem again. I think we should make the most of it while we can, Walter.'

It was an invitation that he couldn't mistake, and nor did he want to. Feeling safe in familiar surroundings was going to be a luxury for many folk from now on, and he found himself thanking God for the perceptive woman he had married all those years ago.

As September merged into October the whole mood of the Chase family had changed. Bobby had a chest infection that caused Alice sleepless nights in attending to him. Lucy had come home to live, exuberant about her new job looking after the Stacey baby and wearying Walter with her constant tales of how sweet baby Mollie was and how she loved being part of a doctor's household, and that they weren't nearly as stuffy as the people at The Grange. And Rose had had her orders and had to report to a hospital on the south coast near Brighton the following week.

'I thought Matt and I would be sent somewhere together, but he hasn't even heard anything yet,' she almost wept to her mother. 'We made it plain that it was what we wanted. Would it have been so difficult for the army to allocate us to the same hospital?'

Alice knew she had to tread delicately, but she was so tired from being up with Bobby for the last four nights, and with her unborn baby beginning to make its presence felt, that it was hard to be sympathetic.

'The army doesn't cater for couples, my dear, but I'm sure if you made your wishes clear, they will have noted it.'

It was a feeble sort of response, but it was the best she could do, and she knew it didn't satisfy Rose. All along, Alice had had her doubts over this romantic plan of theirs, to be serving side by side, saving souls, being unsung heroes ... but Rose was unqualified, and would probably be given menial jobs until she proved herself, while Matt was a qualified doctor and would assuredly be sent wherever skilled men were needed. Rose wasn't stupid, and she must have known it all along. She had just refused to see it.

All the same, it was a tearful goodbye on the day she had to leave. By now she had been sent her railway pass, and knew she would be met at her destination, and Matt was borrowing his brother's car to take her to Bristol Temple Meads station. They all hugged one another, and Alice knew how guiltily grateful she was that at least Rose wasn't being sent to an overseas military hospital. Everyone knew by now that there were already troop movements to France, however cagey and ambiguous the reports were. It was easy enough to read between the lines in the newspapers, and to decipher the flowery words of the wireless announcers, no matter how much they tried to disguise what was really happening.

And yet, what *was* really happening? Nothing much, as far as anybody could see. There were no bombing raids, no invasion, only a country seemingly bolstering itself up for something on the distant horizon that hadn't made itself felt yet.

Oh yes, they all knew that sirens had been heard in London, even on the first day of the war – just for practice, of course. Enemy planes had been heard over the south coast cities and the sound of gunfire was apparently a familiar one in some areas. That was probably just for practice too, Walter said scathingly – and still railed at the fact that everyone now had an identity card, just as if they didn't already know who they were.

Walter was constantly angry, made worse by his frustration over being able to do little himself other than join the local fire-watching group, and suffer the recurring gout in his toe that, lately never seemed to let up. He didn't hold with the new-fangled idea that such pains were made worse by stress. What the devil did stress have to do with a bloody pain in the toe?

The only thing that made the war seem real in their rural community was when young men got their calling-up papers and reported to their various units. And when young women who didn't need to do so, volunteered for jobs they were totally unsuited to. Regardless of whether it was unpatriotic or not, and regardless of the fact that Alice was proud of her daughter, by now she couldn't help feeling resentful that Rose had done this when there was no real need for it.

She hadn't slept at all well the night before Rose left. She could hear the murmur of her two girls talking long into the night in the room they would be sharing for the last time for a while. For the life of her Alice couldn't stop thinking of her best friend Tilly, and the times long ago when they too had whispered and told each other their innermost secrets long into the night.

Would Tilly have done exactly the same as Rose was doing now, if she had been the same age? Alice knew that she would, recklessly and without question. Tilly had always had that kind of bravado. In an odd sort of way the thought of Tilly going into battle like some fearless Boadicea and facing the enemy single-handed, made her smile, just as thoughts of Tilly always did.

Five

After Rose's initial disappointment that she and Matt weren't going to be together immediately, she settled into the hospital routine with amazing ease. As Alice had warned her, the job of an orderly was a menial one compared to real nursing duties, but the letters Rose wrote home were full of the names of the other girls she worked with, the new friends she had made, and the larks they had in their off-duty hours. They heard frequent sounds of planes over the coast, and the gunfire sometimes seemed a bit too near for comfort, but apart from that all was well.

'She hardly sounds as if she's away because of the war at all, does she?' Lucy said one evening in November, reading the latest letter over her mother's shoulder.

'She certainly doesn't sound as though she's missing home,' Alice said slowly.

Why did she feel so unsettled by the ease with which Rose seemed to have cut off ties of home? It was as though moving away from the cosily insular environment of Bramwell had released something inside her daughter that Alice had never suspected was there. She daren't say as much to Walter, who would certainly scoff at such high-falutin' ideas.

'That's a good thing, isn't it, Mum?' Lucy said, in answer to her mother's comment. 'You wouldn't want her feeling homesick all the time like those blessed vaccies at Auntie Helen's, would you?'

'Well, it's a bit different. Rose is hardly an infant! I'm just surprised, that's all. She only mentions Matt once, to say he's now at some big training hospital in London, and he hopes to get to Brighton to see her one day soon.'

'I know. Mrs Stacey told me,' Lucy said importantly, secure in her new job now, and loving the freedom of caring for the infant Mollie.

Alice was hardly listening. She was feeling increasingly large and uncomfortable since the baby was lying awkwardly in her belly now, despite still having three months to go until her time. Her ankles swelled up by evening, and if she didn't think it highly unlikely that she would be having twins, as there were none in either hers or Walter's family, she would have wondered about it.

But that one mention of London had brought about other thoughts. She really did seem unduly scatter-brained these days, she thought anxiously, in a way she had never been before. It only took that one mention of London, in her imagination she was instantly back in her old home when she and Tilly were girls, full of life and expectation about the future.

It was a very different London from the one of

today, she thought more soberly. Today's London was a place where people were prepared with their air-raid shelters even though there had been no air raids yet, and so many of the children in the capital had been sent away to live with strangers for their safety. And how long would it go on? The last war had gone on for four terrible years, despite those who said it would all be over by Christmas.

Alice shivered with a premonition she could not shake off, as if she was already seeing the city she loved burning and in ruins.

'Are you all right, Mum?' she heard Lucy say. 'That's the second time I've asked you if you want a cup of tea.'

'I'm fine,' Alice told her with an effort. 'But what did you mean about the evacuees at Auntie Helen's feeling homesick? I thought they had settled into the village school by now and were making new friends.'

'That's not what I heard, but I'm sure Auntie Helen will tell you herself the next time you see her.'

Alice went to see her the very next day. Now that he was four, Bobby would also be starting at the village school in the new year, and she had had vague thoughts of Patty and Johnny Gregg taking him under their wing. He was sent out to play while she and Helen discussed things, and she quickly learned that what Lucy had said was true.

'You've heard that some of the children are going back to their homes, I suppose, Alice?

Not just to London, but to the other cities as well. We didn't have a great number of evacuees here, but some of those at the village school have been sent for by their parents, and it's unsettling all the others.'

'Going back? What on earth for, after all the disruption of sending them away?' Alice said.

Helen looked at her thoughtfully. 'I know you've got a large family of your own to look after, Alice, but sometimes I think you've got your head buried in the sand as far as the outside world is concerned.'

Well, that was rich, coming from a woman whose only outside activities until the arrival of the evacuees was doing the church flowers and involving herself in a few Good Works! But Alice could see the real worry in Helen's face and bit back the retort she had been tempted to make.

'So why don't you tell me what's happening?' she said instead.

Helen shrugged. 'The grandmother's not an educated woman, but she writes to the children and tells them about their dad and so on, just to keep in contact. It has the opposite effect of what she expected, and now that the few friends they've made at school are going back to London, they want to go as well.'

'But you can't let them go, Helen! It would be stupid and dangerous!'

'Why would it? This war has all been a farce so far. Men have been called up with nowhere to go, and women are working in munitions factories, according to the newspapers, but what's really happening? Nothing! And besides all that, you don't have to listen to Patty crying in her bed every night, and Johnny having a job not to do the same. She's even wet the bed a few times and although I don't think she misses her dad much, she keeps calling for her gran. It's sometimes more than I can bear, Alice. It's worse now that the teachers at the school have been showing them how to make Christmas decorations. For heaven's sake, it's still weeks away, but it takes time for little fingers to make trimmings, I suppose. But now it's started the kids thinking about Christmas and wanting to be at home.'

After this tirade, her hands were shaking so much as she fumbled for her hanky to mop her eyes that Alice felt alarmed. She had no idea things had got this bad, and she realized that Helen was right about herself. She *was* far too wrapped up in her own family affairs to see what was going on right under her nose.

'So what are you going to do?' she said at last.

'I don't know! Me and Mick have talked about it until we're blue in the face. He's all for sending them home, rather than seeing them so unhappy, but it makes me feel such a failure. God knows we've done everything we can for them since they've been here, but nothing seems to be enough.'

'You knew you were taking on a lot, Helen, and we all admired you for it. But nobody would blame you or call you a failure if they went home. You have to think about them more than yourself. Does their gran know how they feel?'

'I know they've told her in their little letters to her. Neither of them are capable of writing very well, of course, but the woman must know how they feel. I'm almost waiting for the day when she turns up here to take them back. It's making me quite ill with worry.'

Alice could see that it was a situation that couldn't go on. Helen was looking decidedly unbalanced, and for a woman who had always seemed so much in control of her life, she seemed to have lost all sense of direction. This wasn't the time for 'I-told-you-so', either. She needed somebody to advise her, and she needed it now.

'Why don't you or Mick contact the billeting woman who brought the children to you and explain the situation, then?' Alice said. 'If it's true that some of the children have already gone home, she'll be aware of it. She'll know what to do, especially if it's taking a toll on your health as well as making the children so unhappy.'

The look of relief on her sister-in-law's face almost transformed her.

'Now why didn't I think of that? You always have the answer, Alice, and it's such a godsend to have you to lean on at times like these. I'll get Mick to contact her right away. He's always been better with words than me.'

Alice nodded. Oh yes, Mick was always good with words. For a time, she'd strongly suspected that he'd dictated the letters Walter had written to her all those years ago, using words that had charmed her into wanting to marry this lovely man and live with him in the country for the rest their lives. For a time, she had even wondered if she had married the right brother after all. Older and wiser now, and with her fifth child growing inside her, there was no longer the slightest doubt.

Walking home through the village with Bobby a while later, she realized how the talk with Helen had somehow cleared her brain. So Rose was not only making the best of her new life at a hospital in Brighton, but enjoying the freedom of meeting girls from different backgrounds. Wasn't that what she would have wanted for her daughter, after hearing about the unhappiness of two small children far from home? Mick and Helen had given them a comfortable life, with nourishing food and a clean bed every night, but it wasn't home, and Alice could totally understand that.

'I sometimes think I was born to be fickle,' Rose Chase said, lying flat on the narrow bed in the room in the Nurses' Home that she shared with three other girls.

Elsie Venn laughed. 'You're not fickle, mate, you've just discovered that you like having a bleedin' good time, and what's wrong with that?'

The other two agreed. The elegant Daphne Poole leaned up on one elbow, while the third girl, the quieter and newer one of the group, merely giggled at Elsie's strong cockney accent, and her rich choice of words.

'But that's what I mean,' Rose said. 'I'm crazy about Matt, and I can't wait to see him again, but I thought I was crazy about another boy less than a year ago, so what does that make me if I'm happy to go to the occasional dance and the pictures and enjoy the company of other chaps?'

'It makes you normal, you dope,' Daphne drawled, in the fake American accent she was adopting whenever she remembered it from the Hollywood films they saw. 'Do you think your medical bloke's whiling away his spare time in London reading about operations and suchlike? Of course he's not. He's making the most of his free time, same as we are.'

'That doesn't make me feel any better,' Rose said, throwing a pillow at her.

'Well, it should, Rose,' the third girl piped up. 'We all have to make the most of things these days, and who knows how much longer this phoney war is going to last before things start hotting up? That's what they're calling it now, in case you hadn't heard, so it is.'

'Blimey, it speaks,' Elsie grinned at her. 'So what did you get up to back in the Irish bogs, kid? They always say the quiet ones are the worst.'

Orla Flynn coloured up as usual. 'I didn't get up to anything! I lived in a tiny village in the west of Ireland with my mammy and daddy, and there was never any shenanigans going on there.'

'That's why she's taking advantage of them over here, isn't it, Orla, sweetie?' Daphne said.

'No, I'm not!' she began heatedly.

'Oh, take no notice of their teasing, Orla,' Rose said easily. 'I lived in a small village as well, but it doesn't mean we're all dumbbells, does it? Anyway, I reckon you caught the attention of that nice Canadian airman at the dance the other night. I bet he'll be looking out for you at the next one.'

'She wasn't the only one to catch a Canadian's eye, was she?' Elsie said. 'What did you say his name was? Elliott, or something?'

'Eldon,' Rose corrected, realizing too late that she'd fallen into the other girl's trap as the others all started laughing. 'Anyway, you can't *catch* somebody's eye. He wasn't throwing it around the room.'

'Oh Jeez, now she's going all correct on us,' Elsie groaned.

Daphne sat up straight, glancing at the smart watch on her wrist, a gift from her parents last Christmas.

'Well, I say we all stop chattering and get changed if we're going out this evening. We might as well make the most of our free time while we can, girls. Let's take a stroll along the sea front while it still belongs to us and not the Jerries.'

'Well, that's a bleedin' cheerful remark to make and no mistake,' Elsie grumbled, but following suit all the same.

If Rose was the pretty one with the soft West Country way of talking, Daphne was the undoubted leader. It came with breeding, Elsie had confided to Orla when she was explaining who they all were when the little mouse first appeared in their midst at the Nurses' Home. Orla needed taking out of herself, Elsie had decided then, and if meeting a good-looking Canadian was the way to do it, then good for her. She just hoped the kid knew the facts of life – and if she didn't, then Elsie was just the one to make sure she knew them before anything bad happened.

Blimey, she thought, changing out of her uniform into a blouse and skirt, topped by a woolly jacket with fancy wooden buttons down the front, I'm acting like the mother here. It was a thought to make her smile, because she wasn't ready for any of that malarkey yet, no siree. Like she said, she just wanted to have a good time, while she could. And it was sheer good luck that there was a small Canadian airbase not far from the town, whose members were partial to a bit of female company now and then.

Rose brushed aside her uneasy thoughts that she might be fickle. Of course she wasn't, and Matt knew very well he could trust her. In any case, they weren't engaged, or even courting, well, not properly. And certainly not now, when they hadn't seen one another for several months. It made her wonder how people managed when they were separated for months or even years, as was possible if ever a war lasted beyond the hoped-for quick ending. How did they cope then?

'Which one are you daydreaming about now, Rosie?' Daphne asked, as they got ready for the evening.

'None of them,' Rose said, 'but if we don't go out soon it will be too cold and dark to bother. I don't fancy finding my way back in the blackout.'

'So that'll be the perfect excuse to go into that new canteen where the boys hang out, and get them to walk us back,' Elsie added with a glint in her eyes. 'Come on, all of you, for Gawd's sake.'

Rose wasn't the only one of the Chase siblings to be finding her feet in ways she hadn't expected. The unexpected freedom of living and working away from home, and meeting new friends, was a heady feeling. Tom knew that feeling too, but in his case good luck had fallen right into his lap. At least, that was what he called it in his enthusiastic letters to his cousin Jack, now that they had finally got in touch again. It didn't bother him that Jack didn't write as often as he did. It was probably not so easy to find time for ordinary pursuits when you were a proper soldier now. As soon as war had been declared, he had transferred from the Territorials, just as everyone had predicted, but Tom made it his mission to give Jack a bit of spice with news of his own doings. He wrote, full of excitement:

I've met this girl, Jack. She's the daughter of one of the Conways' old friends, and she's come to live with the family for a while. Her home's in Brighton, and I suppose they think that's a risk area from the Jerries. You know our Rose is working in a hospital there now, don't you? Anyway, this girl is called Mary, and she's just like a film star, with long blonde hair and a shape that goes in and out in all the right places, if you know what I mean, ha ha. She's a couple of years older than me and she's a hairdresser, so she always smells nice. Who's the lucky one now then, eh Jack? Not that she looks twice at me yet, except in an older sister way, but I'm sure I can change that! I'm not such a kid any more!

Even writing the words in his bedroom that night, Tom knew he wasn't a kid any more as he felt the usual uncomfortably exquisite feelings in his groin. Just thinking about the luscious Mary whose shape went in and out in all the right places, could do that to him, and he cursed himself for not being a few years older. If only he was ... he'd be courting Mary by now – if he wasn't away fighting the Germans and turning himself into a hero ... the rush of sensation died down a little as he thought instead of the temptation to put his age up and sign on anyway. Plenty did so, and it was still fifty-fifty whether or not the attraction of girls and being a war hero was more important to him. And if the truth was told, he was still young enough to do nothing about it but dream, he thought with a grin.

A few weeks later when the weather had turned cold enough to freeze a brass monkey, and the shops were starting to display their Christmas cards and 1940 calendars, he was still debating on whether he dared to buy Mary a small Christmas present and hope for a kiss in return. Such sweet and daring hopes were completely and horribly dashed when a police constable arrived at the house late one night, with the worst of news.

'How did it happen?' Mrs Conway asked, as white as parchment and finding it hard to hold back the tears.

James Conway held on tightly to his wife's hand, while Tom and their son Graham were mute with shock, hardly able to take in what was being said.

The constable cleared his throat and consulted his notebook. It was almost like watching a bad play on the stage, Tom thought incoherently, with the village bobby flexing his knees and revealing what had happened in that well-practised voice for all occasions.

'It seems the young lady was walking away from the city centre when she stepped out into the road without looking. The driver of the car is in a terrible state, but he didn't stand a chance of avoiding her, what with the blackout and the car's headlights almost covered, according to current regulations. A couple of witnesses said it all happened very quickly, and she couldn't have suffered very much. Your address was in her handbag, Sir, and I'm to take you to the hospital if you wish, and of course her next of kin will need to be informed. I'm very sorry.'

He closed his notebook. Closing Mary's life, Tom thought wildly, feeling the bile rise in his stomach as the hideous images the constable had outlined seared into his brain. Almost as an antidote to throwing up all over the Conways' expensive Axminster carpet and disgracing himself, he found himself shouting, using words he wouldn't normally use in his employer's house.

'She'd come here to be safe, not to be killed. It's not bloody well fair, is it? And it's all the fault of the Germans and that bloody Hitler.'

Graham began to snivel beside him, and as if the sound of Tom's anguished young voice had galvanized her into action, Mrs Conway swiftly took charge.

'I think it's best if I stay here with the boys, James. We have a telephone number where I can reach Mary's parents, and I'll busy myself doing that while you go with the constable. I'll go to the hospital tomorrow. I'm sure her parents will be here as soon as possible. They'll want to ... make arrangements.'

Her voice cracked then, and her husband squeezed her hand as he prepared to leave the house, saying that they all had to be strong now.

Tom felt numb from head to toe. You had to be strong when you were a serviceman, doing your duty. You didn't expect to have to be strong when you heard that a beautiful young girl with the looks of a film star, had been knocked down and killed in a blackout. The stupidity and folly of that thought surged into his head like lightning. Because of course that was what any of them could expect from now on. You would have to be strong for all kinds of different and terrible reasons that had never arisen before.

Mrs Conway's voice somehow penetrated his senses. 'We've all had a shock, my dears, and you boys can have a drop of brandy for once if you feel you need it.'

Tom realized she was opening the decanter on the sideboard. Such an ordinary task in a middle-class household, on a night that would never feel ordinary again. Maybe the world would never feel ordinary again...

'It would probably choke me, and I'd rather go to bed,' he said in a strangled voice, and Graham, ever his shadow, echoed his words.

Once in his own room, lying in the darkness and curled up as tightly as he could be, the unmanly tears streamed down Tom's face, and there was only one place he wanted to be. He wanted to be home. It was the only safe place in the world. Every noble thought he'd ever had in his head vanished like the morning mist. He wasn't ready to be away from home and learn-ing a fine career and pretending he was almost a craftsman. He wasn't ready to be a soldier, either. He was just fifteen years old and he wanted to be home safe with his mother. The shame of it overpowered him and he buried his face in his pillow and wept.

He didn't know how to explain, and nor did he want to, since it would only expound his feeling of shame. But in the end there was no need for him to say anything. The following day was Saturday and although it wasn't Tom's weekend for going home, the Conways had already discussed things thoroughly.

'I'm going to the hospital this morning, Tom,' Mrs Conway told him, in a disjointed voice, 'and Mary's parents will arrive this afternoon to stay for a while. They're obviously distraught, especially as it's so near to Christmas when they had planned to be here for a few happy days. You would have been going home for Christmas too, and we think it best if you went today, Tom. We have a great deal to do, so Mr Conway has arranged for a taxi to take you back to Bramwell in an hour's time. As their oldest friends, we must give Mary's parents as much support as possible in their grief. You do understand, don't you?'

'Of course,' he said, almost stammering in his relief. It might be cowardly, but he couldn't wait to get away from here now, and he couldn't bear the thought of meeting Mary's weeping parents.

'Stay home until the new year, Tom,' James

added. 'I'll be in touch then, and I'll see that your wages are sent on to you, so you won't lose by it.'

Amid his guilty relief, the unworthy thoughts whirled around in Tom's head that this was how moneyed people could behave. They could dispense with an apprentice for a few weeks, so that he didn't intrude into a family's grief while they comforted close friends. They could afford to send him all the way home in a taxi and think nothing of it, and still pay his wages even though he wasn't doing his work. It was a far better way to live than grubbing for a living in some miserable job. It was a far better way to live than dying in the road in the dark...

'Thank you both,' he said hoarsely. 'I'd rather be with my family now, so I'll go and pack my things.'

Mrs Conway pressed his hand. 'We know you thought highly of Mary, my dear. We just have to believe that she's gone to a better place now.'

He almost laughed. He almost bloody-well *laughed*, and how awful would that have been, when Mrs Conway was looking so white and puffy-eyed as if she hadn't slept all night? But for anybody to think that dying was going to a better place than living, was about as daft as you could get. It was also about the first positive thought he'd had since the constable broke the news last night.

In her steamy kitchen, Alice brushed a flowery hand across her forehead as she diligently continued with her baking. She refused to let bad thoughts cloud her mind, but realistically, who knew whether or not this would be the last Christmas when they would all be together? Rose had written joyfully to say she was sure she would be able to have a few days off for Christmas and should be there on Christmas Eve, and they knew Tom and Lucy would be here too. Helen and Mick had heard from Jack that he was due for a week's leave at Christmas, so the family would be complete. Therefore Christmas puddings had to be steamed and cakes baked, and the plans for a big family celebration were under way.

Alice had no thoughts of anything else that Saturday afternoon. Walter had taken Bobby off her hands and she hummed as she worked, while she had the house to herself. If you ignored the newspapers and the wireless reports, you could almost imagine that they weren't a country at war, she thought cheerily, and that this was going to be just a normal, traditional Christmas, with everyone's stocking containing an apple and an orange and a nut, and whatever little gifts they could all manage for one another. They didn't go in for fancy treats. The money didn't stretch to it, but being together was all that mattered.

The unusual sound of a motor car in the lane outside didn't disturb her very much, and she assumed it would be passing by. She thought no more about it until she heard the car door slam, followed by the sound of footsteps crunching on the gravel outside. She gave a small sigh, wondering what this was going to be about, and expecting a knock on the door at any minute. It wouldn't be anything important, and maybe she could ignore it, she thought...

The next minute the front door had been flung open, giving her the fright of her life. Tom burst in, hurling his bag of clothes on to the sofa. It took less than a heartbeat for Alice's initial alarm to recede, and without fully registering her son's tormented eyes, she looked at him angrily.

'For heaven's sake, Tom, what's happened?' she exclaimed. 'Have you been up to something? Your father will have something to say if you've disgraced yourself with Mr Conway!'

For a moment, he simply couldn't bring himself to answer, and then to her horror he burst into tears, and she knew at once that something was seriously wrong. Alice went to him at once, and put her arms around him. Whatever the trouble was, she was still his mother, and he had come to the right place.

'Why don't we sit down, and you can tell me all about it?' she said gently.

Six

In the midst of Tom's sobbing and incoherent explanations, the smell of baking from the kitchen told Alice she would have to attend to it very soon or they would be having burned offerings for Christmas Day. But which was more important? Listening to a young boy's first real experience of death, or checking on the progress of the Christmas cake? Tom had known of his mother's own anguish when Tilly died, of course, but she had shielded all her children from the trauma of it as much as possible. Tom had never been personally involved in such an event, as he seemed to be now. Alice couldn't remember hearing about a girl called Mary, but this wasn't the time to ask the kind of pertinent questions a mother would like to ask. This was a time for compassion and understanding.

'I really liked her, Mum,' Tom managed to say at last, his voice wobbling. 'She was only seventeen and she'd never done any harm to anyone, so why did such a terrible thing have to happen to her? And don't start telling me it was because God wanted her for a blooming sunbeam or any of that Sunday School rot, because

I don't want to hear it.'

'I wasn't going to, my dear,' Alice murmured.

That may have been something Helen might have said, but not her. Everyone questioned their faith at times like these, and God knew Alice herself had done it, after Tilly. Everyone also needed time to come to terms with it in their own way, as Tom would, eventually.

'Coming home was the best thing you could have done, Tom,' Alice said, when she had finally heard the whole story. 'It wouldn't have been right for you to stay at the house with Mary's parents there.'

'Mr Conway sent me home in a taxi. That'll make the village look up, won't it?' he said, attempting to lighten the mood. 'So I'm home for Christmas, not that I feel much like celebrating, but I'll try not to put a damper on everything for the rest of you. I'm glad we're all together, anyway.'

His voice wobbled again, and Alice took a determined breath.

'Now listen to me, Tom. You've had a shock, and it will take a little time to come to terms with it. Go upstairs and have a lie down in your old room before your father and Bobby come back, then you can leave it to me to do all the explaining. Try to get some sleep, because I daresay you didn't get much of it last night.'

Gratefully, he did as his mother said, knowing he could always rely on her to say the right thing. The last thing he wanted was to have to tell the same sad story over and over again, and it was true that he felt more weary than he had in his life before. It was bad enough having the nightmares about the car accident, without listening to Graham in the next bedroom wailing and muttering in his sleep all night. He lay down thankfully on his old bed, willing himself not to think any more, and almost instantly he had fallen asleep from sheer exhaustion.

It seemed only minutes before he felt something bouncing up and down on his chest and a voice screeching with delight that he was home again. Something was trying to prise one of his eyes open and when he jerked them open himself, it was to see his small brother's face peering down at him, inches above his own.

'Mum told me you were here,' Bobby shouted. 'Are you sleeping in my room with me tonight, Tom?'

He groaned. 'Looks like it,' he grunted. 'Get off me, you twerp.'

'Our Lucy's home now as well.' Bobby continued shouting. 'Me and Lucy are going to help Mum look after the new babby when the doctor brings it.'

'Is that right?' Tom said, feeling his mouth twitch, despite himself.

How could he have forgotten, so soon, what it was like to be in the middle of a big family like his, with everything that went on, day by day? Normal things, big and small things, his own family things.

The Conways were good people, but they were so well organized in everything they did, to the point of obsession at times. While here, in Bramwell, his own family life could sometimes be one big, glorious muddle, and that was the way he liked it – the way families were meant to be.

He was bright enough to know it was the reaction to all that had happened in the last twelve hours that made him feel this way, and that he would be glad of the order that ruled the Conway household, but not yet. Not blessedly yet.

He leaped off the bed and grabbed his squealing brother in his arms, tickling him ruthlessly until Bobby begged for mercy, and his father was roaring up the stairs for him to stop tormenting the child or he'd be peeing himself. Oh yes, he was home all right, he thought, with a surge of relief.

Lucy was surprisingly sympathetic towards him. With only two years between them, there had always been a certain rivalry. But now they had both grown up in their different ways, and they were no longer children – at least not the wide-eyed children they had once been.

'It must have been horrible for you, Tom,' she said, as they walked to the village together to buy provisions for Alice. 'You don't have to talk about it if you don't want to, mind. I know all about wanting to keep personal stuff to yourself.'

'Do you?' he said. He'd never thought of her as a kind of ally, and he'd never questioned why she'd wanted to leave that cushy job of hers at The Grange to look after the Stacey kid. Maybe there was more to it that she let on. He glanced at her sideways. She was quite a looker now, as the Yankee film stars said. You didn't usually think such things about your sister, but he could see that other blokes might think the same, and that she might have had a fling with some boy.

Lucy was the same age as Mary, and remembering his feelings for Mary that had come to nothing, he felt an overwhelming need to protect Lucy.

'Don't think you're getting anything out of me,' she said crisply, totally unaware of his thoughts, and reverting to the old Lucy. 'Nor that this sudden affection will last for long. I know you too well.'

He laughed. He knew her too. Or he thought he did – as much as you knew anybody. He squeezed her arm.

'At least we're getting on better than we used to, and that will make the parents happy over Christmas, won't it?'

She agreed. 'Rose will be home on Christmas Eve too. It wouldn't have been the same if she hadn't been here. I think Auntie Helen said Jack's due for some leave, but I can't really remember.'

Tom didn't answer. He seemed to have gone so far away from the young boy who had hung on his cousin Jack's coat-tails, believing every word he said, and admiring him as a hero. It hadn't changed until the day he'd found his cousin drinking with other lads, and persuaded Tom to do the same, making him sick and ill and disillusioned.

That was also the day his father had found him in his inebriated state and marched him to the Pig and Whistle and forced him to drink even more cider until the very smell of it made him retch. Walter Chase might not have such a clever brain as James Conway, but he knew human nature, and how to deal with his son.

Jack was still his hero in a different way. Even a hero had feet of clay, and it didn't change the person he was inside, and Tom had long forgiven him for his part in that awful day. The fact that Jack had gone and joined the Territorials so soon afterwards, had told Tom his own story of his cousin's guilt and remorse.

'I'm going to see Auntie Helen to see if she's got any more news,' he said now. 'You can get the groceries, can't you? You've got more muscles than I have.'

Lucy gave him a gentle swipe and told him to get on with it then. She watched him walk away from her for a moment more, seeing the swagger that hid all the insecurities he couldn't quite hide.

Tom heard the noise coming from his aunt's house before he reached it. There was a black car outside that he didn't recognize, and if they had visitors he wondered if this was such a good idea after all. But he was quickly recognizing that he felt like a fish out of water in his village now, and he needed the familiarity eople he knew. Resolutely, he knocked on door and opened it, knowing he had no need to stand on ceremony.

Five faces turned to look at him. They were all sitting around the table, and he registered them all in an instant. There were his aunt and uncle, and a strange woman that he'd never seen before. She wore dark clothes and a serious expression on her face. And there were the two evacuees his aunt had taken in, the little blonde girl looking red-faced and tearful, and the boy looking angry as usual. Alongside the grown-ups, they looked small and fearful.

'Tom, this is a surprise,' Helen said, flustered, and he realized at once that they had no idea why he was here. It was odd to think that something that was so momentous in his life, had no meaning for them. They didn't know that a girl he'd been fond of had been killed so horribly, nor that he'd been sent home in a taxi while he came to terms with it – and how pathetic his pride in that seemed now – or that he'd wept uncontrollably in his mother's arms as he told her what had happened. Nobody here knew, and it was clear that there was trouble in this house that he didn't know about either.

'I'm home for a few weeks,' he said in a cracked voice. 'I wanted to know if Jack was likely to get leave for Christmas, but I can see that you're busy, so I'll come back some other time.'

He could feel himself mentally backing away,

even if his feet weren't actually moving. He vaguely remembered learning about the home situation of these London kids at the time. So if something bad had happened – if the kids' father had had an accident, or something had happened to their gran – he didn't want to hear it. He had his own misery to cope with, and he couldn't deal with any more.

'No, Tom, don't go,' his uncle said at once. 'We're always glad to see you and hear how you're getting on in Bristol. We just have a few things to sort out here.'

He felt trapped. He didn't want to stay, and it seemed rude to have to listen to what was going on, but just as rude to leave now. He slunk across to a chair near the window and tried to make himself as invisible as possible as he heard the woman in the dark clothes give a loud sniff and consult the papers in her hand.

'So these are my conclusions, Mr and Mrs Chase,' she said in an officious voice. 'Naturally, we don't want any of the children to be unhappy, but is the idea of sending them back to the East End of London where bombs may be falling at any minute, the best alternative? You have a good home here and the children have been well cared for, so we have to ask ourselves what the problem really is?'

Tom sensed the situation in an instant. As the kids began to realize that they might have to stay here after all, Patty Gregg began snivelling, and Johnny kicked her under the table, which made her sob even louder. The stranger in their midst tut-tutted, and for the second time in a period of his life that seemed increasingly bizarre, Tom felt like laughing.

Was the woman totally insensitive? He guessed she was the billeting officer who had either been summoned here to sort out the problems, or was making a regular visit to see how the kids were getting on. But couldn't she see that no matter how dangerous it might be that these kids needed to be with their family? No bombs had fallen anywhere near London yet, and according to Mr Conway, who read every inch of the newspapers, Hitler was trying to make the Allies accept peace even now. It was their own prime minister, Neville Chamberlain, who was holding out and refusing to allow it after the Nazis had marched into Poland and Czechoslovakia so ruthlessly. You couldn't live in a middle-class and well-read household like the Conways, and not be aware of the political situation.

Before he had time to think, Tom found himself clearing his throat, and the adults in the room glanced his way for a moment. It was long enough.

'I think they should go home if that's what they want. Has anybody listened to them properly?' he blundered on. 'Home is the best place to be when you're miserable and unhappy. You need to be with your own family, not sent to live among strangers.'

He was talking as much about himself as the evacuees, but he didn't miss the hurt look in his aunt's eyes, and he knew he'd have to put things right with her later. He wasn't slighting her, for God's sake ... but to his horror, the woman now directed her words to him.

'And what do you know about being miserable and unhappy and being sent to live among strangers, young man?' she snapped.

'I know a good friend of mine has just been killed in a blackout in Bristol, and that the only place I wanted to be was here at home,' he blurted out in a strangled voice. 'It didn't need any of Hitler's bombs to kill Mary, either.'

His aunt had crossed the room and was putting her arms around him before he had time to think what he had just said.

'Tom dear, I'm so sorry,' Helen whispered in his ear. 'We'll talk about this later once Mrs Willmott has gone. If you want to wait in Jack's room, that's fine.'

He practically fled, knowing he had done this all wrong. He'd just come here wanting news of his cousin, and he hadn't intended to say anything about Mary. He felt ashamed of his outburst – yet a little relieved too. At least he'd said it, and he wouldn't have to say it here again. Telling people was one of the worst things, he was discovering, but perhaps the more times you said it, the less painful it became. Perhaps.

By the time he heard the slam of the car door outside, and then heard it drive away, he sat up on Jack's bed where he'd been lying for the past half hour, and prepared to face the music. Helen came into the room, her face flushed, and closed the door to shut out the excited chatter of the children downstairs.

'I know you realized what was going on earlier, Tom,' Helen said quietly. 'But first let me say how very sorry I am about your friend. It must have been a terrible shock for you.'

'It was. But I made a fool of myself downstairs, and I didn't mean to be rude to you, Auntie Helen. I'm sure you've done all your could for those kids.'

'But you were quite right. They have been miserable and unhappy, and quite unable to settle here, so once Mrs Willmott has contacted their family and made the arrangements, they'll be going home before Christmas.'

'Well, I'm glad for them, but sorry for you, Auntie Helen. Mum always said you looked forward to having kids in the house,' he finished lamely, since it seemed such an odd conversation for a fifteen-year-old boy to be having with an adult.

Helen gave a brief sigh and leaned forward and kissed him. She smelled of lavender, he thought briefly.

'So I was, but I can't deny that it hasn't all been easy,' she finally admitted. 'There have been times when I'd have dearly liked to pack them off back to London on the next train – but don't you dare tell your mother that, Tom, or she'll be saying I told you so. It's our little secret, all right?'

It was doubtful whose eyes were the most watery at that moment. His aunt was treating him as an adult for the first time, as far as he could remember, and it was time he behaved like one.

'Your secret is safe with me,' he said steadily, quite sure that eventually Helen would be pouring it all out to his mother over the afternoon tea-cups, anyway. But it had to be in her own good time, and they had wallowed up here for long enough. 'So is Jack getting leave for Christmas?'

In between her shifts, Rose read the latest letter from her mother, telling her what had happened to Tom's friend. Alice warned her that he was still feeling wretched about it, and was very down at times, despite the news that Jack was definitely getting a week's leave for Christmas.

'You know what that means, don't you?' her friend Elsie said, when Rose mentioned the contents of the letter that left her subdued.

'Yes. It means my little brother has had his first bad experience of what war means,' Rose said tersely.

'No, not that bit. I'm sorry about that, o' course, but I mean the other bit. Jack's your cousin, ain't he? Nice looking, is he?'

Rose shrugged. 'Well yes, in a cousinly sort of way, I suppose. They'll all be pleased he's getting a week's leave, and it'll be good to see him again, providing there's no sinister reason for it.'

'Blimey Rose, cheer up. These rumours about sending troops to France soon are a waste of time. There ain't that much going on for old Neville to send our troops over there for yet, and Jerry's just biding his time.'

Rose shivered. Elsie didn't bother her head with politics much, but Rose was pretty sure that once the war really did get going, and they stopped referring to it as the phoney war, it wouldn't be long before Jack, and young men like him, including Matt Stacey, got their embarkation orders. She knew both of them would relish being in the front line of wherever they were sent. It was the reason they had enlisted. Men always wanted to be heroes. While she would be stuck here, doing dull, ordinary jobs ... she felt briefly ashamed of the thought. She had to admit, though, that apart from the regular sounds of aircraft and gunfire that didn't seem to be too troublesome, the war seemed to be going nowhere, leaving everybody frustrated and wondering what it was all about.

But they all knew that when things really did begin to happen the hospitals at home would be stretched to their limits, and it would be a heartless dimwit who didn't know that the jobs of changing bed sheets with their precise hospital corners, rolling bandages and sluicing bedpans, even writing home for some of the patients, was every bit as essential as the work of doctors and nurses sent overseas.

When it happened, she and Matt would be even farther apart than they were now. They

114

had met just a few times since leaving home, and each time it had left Rose more frustrated than the time before. She was no recluse, and she went to the dances and social evenings with the other girls, and she enjoyed joking with the Canadians, but none of them was Matt. None of them was the man she loved.

'Have you gone off into a trance now?' she heard Elsie say crossly. 'My old mum always said that country girls had their heads full of bleedin' hayseeds, and now I'm sure of it.'

Rose forced a laugh. 'And if my mum wasn't a Londoner, I'd have said all Londoners thought far too much of themselves! So are we going to do a bit of Christmas shopping or not? We've only got an hour or so and if we don't go soon, it won't be worth the bother.'

They were always on different shifts than the other girls. Rose wished this one could have coincided with Daphne instead of Elsie. She wasn't a snob, and Lord knew she had no reason to be, but she sometimes thought Elsie was too damn coarse for comfort. Daphne came from a different background, and heads always turned when she came into a room – even to getting a good table at a crowded café for a cup of tea.

Rose pulled on her jacket and gloves and rammed a woolly hat on her head. There was no use worrying over who was sharing rooms with who any more. They were in this together, for however long it took. For the duration, as people were starting to call it.

'Come on then, let's go. I want to get something for Mum, and a bit of tinsel to brighten up our room wouldn't be a bad thing.'

'Making it more like bleedin' home, you mean?' Elsie grumbled. 'I've seen more space in a rabbit hutch.'

'Oh yes? And when did you ever see a rabbit hutch?'

'Me dad bought me a pet rabbit when I was a kid, if you must know, Miss clever-clogs country girl. We didn't know it was having babies at the time, and eventually there were six of the little squirts. Poor little buggers didn't know what was coming to 'em.'

Rose knew it was best not to ask, but she couldn't resist it.

'What was coming to them then?'

The two girls had left the Nurses' Home now and were walking briskly towards the end of the road where they could catch a bus into the town. December was feeling decidedly wintry, with a keen wind blowing in from the sea.

'Me dad said I shouldn't keep looking in the hutch at the babies until they'd grown a bit. If people did that, the mother rabbit could get shirty and eat 'em.'

Rose began to laugh. 'You're making it up!'

Elsie glared at her. 'Oh, no I ain't! I was only a kid, and I was excited about these cute little bunnies all crawling over their mum, so I kept sneaking a look at 'em whenever I could. Until the day when I seen the six of 'em lying in the bottom of the hutch with their heads bitten off.'

Rose stopped walking abruptly. 'That's a horrible thing to say, Elsie.'

'Well, it's true! That's what bleedin' cannibal mother rabbits do when they don't want people looking at their babies. Me dad heard me screaming and started cussing and blinding at me for not doing as I was told. Then he took the lot of 'em away, mother rabbit, hutch and all, and that's the last pet I ever had, or ever want,' she added fiercely. 'So don't talk to me about the delights of the bleedin' country and how lovely it is to be looking after animals, because it ain't.'

Rose didn't know what to say. Elsie always seemed so superficial, but right now she seemed genuinely upset. You just never knew what went on inside people, Rose thought. You only saw what was on the surface, and what they chose to show you about themselves. For the life of her, she couldn't think why Elsie had confided in her about the rabbits, and she made a shrewd guess that she wouldn't want her weakness passed on to their room-mates.

'Well, it's a sad story,' she said, tucking her arm inside Elsie's as they waited at the bus stop. 'And I might be a country girl, but there's plenty of animals I'm not too keen on. I could not do what my uncle does, that's for sure. He's a vet.'

The bus trundled into sight while Elsie was still digesting this information, and by the time they arrived at their shopping destination Rose was heartily wishing she'd never mentioned

Uncle Mick at all, as Elsie demanded to know what kind of gruesome things a vet had to do.

At least it took her mind off her brother for a while, although what her mother had told her was deeply upsetting to Rose. Far more so than the tale of six baby rabbits, she admitted. Losing a friend was far more personal. It brought back all too sharply the memory of her mother's pain when her old friend Tilly had died all alone in a London boarding-house. Alice had behaved so valiantly in those dark days, making the traumatic journey back to London where they had once lived and worked. Seeing to everything so that Tilly had a decent send-off. Alice had been more than a best friend to her. She was the sister Tilly never had.

'Next Saturday's dance will be the last one before Christmas, mate, so we might as well make the best of it and enjoy ourselves,' Elsie's voice broke into her thoughts. 'Gawd knows where we'll be this time next year!'

Rose dragged herself back to the present. Elsie might be superficial most of the time, but she had the right idea. Only God knew where they would all be this time next year so they might as well make the best of it now.

There were other dark thoughts in Bramwell. Alice repeatedly told Helen she was doing the right thing in letting the evacuees go home, even if she wasn't sure she truly believed it herself. Wasn't it obvious that in due course London would be the target for most of Hitler's bombs? Anyone with half a brain knew it, but the sight of those two kids, so animated now in a way they hadn't been since they had arrived in Bramwell so scared and waif-like, was enough to sway anybody's mind.

'I still hope I'm doing the right thing,' Helen fretted. 'Mrs Willmott's contacted the children's gran, and she says she's willing to have them back. They'll be put on the train in care of the guard, and met at Paddington Station. The dad just sends his regards, which sounds a funny old set-up if you ask me.'

'The main thing is that they're family, Helen, and that's important. It doesn't matter how kind and loving the home is for these children, it's not their own home, is it? We all want our own family around us. It's human nature.'

'It still makes me feel like a failure, though,' Helen muttered.

'You're anything but that! You've been wonderful and patient with them, and they're not the easiest of kids, are they?'

Helen spoke wryly. 'Not exactly.'

'Well then. And you've got Jack's homecoming to look forward to, haven't you? Life's not all bad, Helen!'

She hardly knew what to say next. Everybody had problems, but it didn't seem appropriate to hark on about Tom and his misery. Although she had to admit that he had definitely perked up in the last few days, and had been going back to work with Walter at the sawmill. If you ignored the fact that it was wartime and there was a blackout, so that every walk home in the dark was a hazard now, it was quite like old times. At least her close-knit family seemed reasonably content – but Alice mentally crossed her fingers as she thought it.

As for herself, the baby inside her was constantly giving her twinges now, reminding her that it was impatient to be born. It was becoming uncomfortable to sit on Helen's sofa, or anywhere else, for very long. Two more months and they would all know whether it was a boy or a girl, and Alice longed for the day to arrive when she would hold this unexpected little bundle in her arms. But you couldn't hurry one of God's little miracles, and Helen would be the first to agree with that.

Seven

Jack Chase was looking forward to a week's leave. It would be good to get back to the place he knew best, and to forget all the slog of the boring army training that seemed to have no real meaning. He was impatient to be sent to France, or anywhere else in the world where he could do the job he'd been trained for. You didn't join the army just to go on endless manoeuvres in the flat Norfolk countryside, fighting an imaginary enemy. You needed a real opponent, or what was the point of it all?

He was keen to see his family again, even his cousin Tom. He knew he'd been Tom's hero when they were younger, but he doubted that Tom felt the same way about him now. The kid had once followed him around like his shadow, until the night he'd introduced him into the pleasures of alcohol. He still felt bad about that night. It was the final push Jack had needed to leave home and join the Territorials. And now here he was, Private Chase, a fully-fledged member of the British army, with no one to fight.

He hauled his kitbag off the train at Temple Meads station, and said goodbye to his temporary companions in the compartment. It had been an endless journey back from Norfolk in several packed and steaming trains, full of sweating servicemen like himself, going home for Christmas leave. It was Christmas Eve and bloody cold. He went outside the station and shivered in the frosty air as he looked around for his father's car. There was no sign of it yet. He prepared to wait, and then his attention was caught as he heard someone's voice calling his name.

'Jack! Hey, Jack!'

He turned around and saw a female vision running towards him. His face broke into a delighted smile.

'My God, Rose, what are you doing here?'

'Waiting for a lift home, same as you,' she said with a laugh. 'I phoned your dad a couple of days ago to ask if there was any chance he could meet me here, and he said your train would be arriving around the same time, so he could meet us both. Bit of luck, eh?'

She didn't bother telling him she'd been waiting on the draughty station for over an hour. When Mick had told her the time of Jack's train, she'd simply said that would be fine, and she'd give him a nice surprise. From the look on his face, it seemed she had certainly done that.

'Is your bloke coming home on leave?' Jack asked next.

'I haven't heard, but I hope so, fingers crossed. It was easier for me, being only a lowly ward orderly, but a doctor's far more important, and people don't stop getting ill just because it's Christmas.'

She tried to keep the smile on her face as she said it, but inside her she knew she would be heartbroken if Matt didn't manage to get home to Bramwell.

'Going well, is it?' Jack said with a grin.

'Of course – as well as can be expected,' she said with a grin, trotting out the usual platitude that doctors gave anxious relatives.

It occurred to Rose that they were making the sort of inane conversation that people made when they hadn't seen one another for some time. You couldn't just fall into the easy sort of chatter you once had. It took time to readjust your thoughts. Maybe it would be the same for her and Matt.

To her relief – and Jack's too, she suspected – they saw his father's car coming towards them. Both Mick and Helen were inside, and they leaped out and hugged the two people waiting for them.

'Isn't this lovely!' Helen exclaimed. 'It's like a small family reunion already. Get in the car, both of you, and let's be on our way. It's too cold to be standing around.'

Amen to that, thought Rose, since her feet felt ready to be frozen to the cobbles. She didn't miss her aunt's bright eyes, and wondered if she dared ask about the evacuees. Alice had told her they might be going back to London, and common sense told Rose it must have happened already, or Helen wouldn't have left them at home alone. She wisely decided to say nothing.

'Have you seen Tom?' she asked instead. 'How is he, Auntie Helen?'

'Your brother has grown up a lot recently, Rose. Losing that friend of his hit him very hard, but the shock of it seems to have made him more tolerant of life in general, and he's even mellowed towards young Bobby. He's also been working back at the sawmill while he's back in the village, and you can imagine how that pleases your father.'

'Would somebody tell me what you're both talking about?' Jack said, mystified. 'What's happened to Tom?'

Rose let his mother make the explanation, realizing that such news hadn't been of sufficient importance to tell Jack in a letter. She could tell he was concerned at what had befallen his young cousin, but however close they all were, Jack's family was still one step removed from her own. Jack had a new life away from them all now, the same as Rose did. You met new friends, saw a different kind of life, embraced new horizons. It changed your attitudes. It changed you.

'You're looking very well, Rose,' Mick said, glancing back at her as they headed out of the city for the open roads. 'Nursing obviously suits you.'

'I'd hardly call it nursing, more like being a general dogsbody on the wards, but I'm enjoying it all the same. And I work with a nice group of girls.'

'Are they country girls like yourself?' Helen asked.

'Hardly! Orla's from Ireland, and she's sweet and a bit dippy at times. Elsie's from London, as sharp as a tack, and Daphne's the posh one. But they're all great fun, and we have some good times together.'

Jack laughed. 'Sounds as if you're having a good war, kid.'

She gave a strained smile. She supposed she was. But right now she wished they would all stop talking and asking her the questions she would have to answer all over again once she got home. She felt tired and grubby from travelling, and from being squashed up with all the other people trying to get home for Christmas. Surely Jack must feel the same. To her surprise,

124

she felt him squeeze her hand briefly.

'Bear up, kid,' he said softly. 'They'll soon get used to us again.'

He was more perceptive than she had expected. But it had to be the same for him, of course, and he'd been away far longer than she had.

Helen spoke brightly again. 'Your mother wanted to cook Christmas dinner for all of us as usual, Rose, but this year I insisted that you must all come to us for the day. She's already made the cake and the puddings, and they're safely in my larder now. In her condition, it wouldn't be fair to put any more work on her,' she added delicately.

'You mean she actually agreed to that?' Rose said. 'I can't imagine Mum admitting to not being capable of anything!'

Her dad wouldn't be too keen on moving out of the house on Christmas Day either. Once the meal was over, he liked nothing better than to put his feet up and loosen his belt, belching gently until the effects of the fire and the food overtook him, and they usually heard the rhythm of his snoring for the next couple of hours. It was the same ritual Rose had known since childhood, and Rose too, had been looking forward to relaxing at home for her seventy-two hours' leave, not having to turn out for the day. Blast and double blast, she thought irreverently.

'Your mother wasn't keen on the idea at first,' Helen admitted. 'But I managed to persuade her it was for her own good.'

Well, since Alice was the most capable woman in the world, Rose wondered just how she would have reacted to that! She still felt ruffled. She had imagined Lucy and herself helping their mother as always, everybody getting in the way of everybody else and not minding, allocating tasks, peeling sprouts and parsnips, scraping potatoes, basting the chicken, and taking a hand in stirring the gravy from the meat juices. She could feel her mouth water at the thought ... and now Auntie Helen was taking all that away from them.

'I'll be really glad of some help from you girls, Rose. I'm not used to catering for a large number of people.'

As Helen's voice became less certain it only took a few seconds for Rose to realize what this was really all about. Helen had probably been dreaming of a household much like Rose's own this Christmas, with the excitement of the two small evacuee children making the house a real home. Rose's slight resentment that Helen was denying her own mother the pleasure and chaos of Christmas Day was tempered in a wave of understanding.

'Of course we'll all dig in and help. It will be fun,' she said at once, 'though I doubt if you'll get Mum to put her feet up for long!'

By the time Mick stopped the car at his brother's cottage, Rose was more than ready to get out, and longing to stretch her legs. She hadn't expected them all to come inside with her, but of course there were last-minute arrangements to be made for tomorrow. Her parents would want to see Jack, and Jack would want to see Tom. The cottage was soon full to overflowing, and Alice began to look more harassed than usual.

Her aunt was right, Rose thought. Alice did need a break from all this tomorrow, and she was slightly shocked at how much larger her mother had become since the last time she saw her. She didn't know much about pregnant women, though she had learned a bit more since working at the hospital. In the easy jargon that the young nurses used among themselves, Alice looked about ready to pop.

Maybe the baby would come early, even on Christmas Day. A Christmas baby! How lovely that would be ... and how bloody awful, Rose amended. With Bobby racing around and climbing on to Jack's back and asking him to be a horse now, and Walter bellowing at him to calm down, there was enough mayhem here already without adding to it. Once she got her mum alone in the kitchen she asked her bluntly how she was feeling.

'All the better for having my family all together again,' Alice said. 'Don't worry, I'm sure the babby's not going to embarrass you all by coming early, though it would be good to have my ready-made nurse on hand if it did.'

'You mean me? Good Lord, Mum, don't say such things. I wouldn't know the first thing to do,' Rose said in a mild panic, until she saw that

Alice was teasing.

'No, we'd need Doctor Stacey or Doctor Matt for that. Have you heard if he's getting leave?' Alice went on, unconsciously touching a raw nerve.

'Not as far as I know. He seemed a bit cagey about it the last time I heard from him. I'm not even sure he wants to come home,' she said, finally saying the thought that had been nagging her.

If she had been enjoying the freedom of her new life with the other girls at the hospital, why shouldn't Matt have been doing the same? He would have been mixing with far more important people than a girl from a small country village, and from one or two things he had said, she knew that Matt had ambitions. He didn't intend to end up as a doctor with a small country practice like his brother. His time in Bramwell had only ever been a temporary measure. He hadn't exactly said as much, but the longer they were apart, and the farther away from each other they were, the more Rose knew it.

Alice cleared her throat, seeing more than Rose said. 'If you're going to call on Mrs Stacey while you're home, I'm sure they'll have heard from Matt too,' Alice went on. 'Lucy's doing very well in caring for the Stacey baby, by the way. She's surprised us all with the way she's taken to it.'

So nobody seemed to need Rose at all. Lucy had stepped into her shoes in looking after baby

Mollie, and would be there to help Alice when the new baby arrived. Then her mother put her arms around her and gave her a hug, and with her words the brief sense of gloom vanished.

'I'm so glad to see you, Rose dear, so grown up and independent, and a credit to us all. It's what every mother wants for her children.'

On Christmas morning, Walter was still grumbling that this December was as cold as charity. He'd much prefer not to have to go to his brother's house for their Christmas dinner, but he could see the sense in it. The younger ones had set out early, noisy and excited by what they had found in their stockings, and ready to make the most of the day, but in her condition, Alice shouldn't be walking so far, even though she pooh-poohed his final objections as they prepared to leave.

Alice looked at her husband in exasperation. 'For heaven's sake, Walter, having a baby is perfectly natural. I've had four already, in case you've forgotten.'

'Yes, and you were younger then, woman.'

'Well, thank you for that! I'm not exactly in my dotage now, am I? A woman in her forties is perfectly capable of childbirth, and anything else,' she added tartly.

Walter chuckled as her eyes sparkled at any suggestion that she might be getting past it. 'I'll vouch for that, and once this babby's born we'll have some high old jinks again, won't we?'

She had no ready answer to that and in any

case her thoughts were halted by the sound of a car horn outside.

'Who the devil's that on Christmas morning?' Walter said, frowning.

The next minute Mick came into the house, bundled up in a heavy jacket and rubbing his hands together.

'Helen dragged us off to the church carol service last night, and it was cold enough to freeze the you-know-whats off a brass monkey, and getting colder,' he said by way of greeting. 'But she said I should come and fetch you two in the car to save Alice the walk.'

'That was very thoughtful of her,' Alice said, more grateful than she was willing to admit that she didn't have to walk through the village.

No matter what she said, the baby was lying very heavily now, dragging her down and leaving her frequently short of breath. She felt a brief anxiety, unable to remember feeling quite this way before – not until the very last stages of pregnancy, anyway. And there were still two months to go. Unthinkingly, she passed her hand over her belly, as if to tell the unborn child to be calm and to bide its time, because everyone knew that a seven-month baby carried a risk. It may be an old wives' tale, but it had been ingrained in many an old wife for years, and Alice wasn't about to dispute it.

'Are you all right, Mother?' Walter said, seeing her stand so very still.

'Of course I am,' she snapped. 'And stop calling me Mother.'

He grinned, just as if she was making a joke of it. And because Mick was looking uncertainly from one to the other, she forced a smile back and squeezed her husband's arm.

'I just think we should get started if I'm to help Helen get everything ready. And before you start objecting to that, I'm not an invalid, Walter.'

He didn't normally treat her as if she was walking on eggshells, and she decided that without realizing it, she must have been extra edgy these last few weeks. And why wouldn't she be? What with the coming baby, and the worry over Tom, Bobby still finding his feet at school, and both her daughters changing before her eyes, didn't she have every right to be on edge? In fact, the only constant in her life was Walter, and he was the one who always seemed to bear the brunt of her moods. Without thinking, she reached up and kissed him.

'Bloody hell, now I know it's Christmas,' he blustered.

Helen had long been acknowledged as the family's best organizer, but she had never been faced with the prospect of cooking Christmas dinner for nine people before. She had woken up that morning in a panic, but once she had retrieved her lists of things to do and when to do them, she now had everything under control. And her nieces were two willing helpers. Rose and Lucy began to enjoy being in the middle of a big noisy kitchen while keeping Bobby out from under their feet, and scooting Tom and Jack away to Jack's bedroom while the women got on with it all.

Nobody mentioned the evacuees at all. They had been sent back to London a week ago now, and if Helen missed them, you would never know it. It was something Rose really admired in her, she told Lucy later when they had snatched a few moments out of the steaming kitchen. Helen was the most self-sufficient person they knew, and when circumstances changed, Helen just adapted to them.

'I never realized how alike she and Mum were in that respect,' Rose said suddenly. 'I know it took Mum a while to get over Tilly, and Auntie Helen's never been tested in such a bad way, but they're quite like sisters, aren't they?'

'I can't imagine anyone less like Mum than fussy Auntie Helen. I bet those kids practically had their hankies tied to them like nose-bags to stop the snot getting on her precious furniture,' Lucy said with a snort.

Rose looked at her in astonishment. 'That's a horrible thing to say, and on Christmas Day too.'

Lucy shrugged. 'I don't see why peoples' feelings should change just because it's Christmas Day. It's being a hypocrite to pretend to like everybody, even if you only ever see the good in people. And before you start going on at me about that remark, of course I like Auntie Helen and Uncle Mick. I just think she's too darn fussy, that's all, and I still wish we hadn't had to come here today of all days. It would have been far more comfortable at home.'

A quick vision of the chaos they had left behind in getting ready to come out of the cottage at all today, made both of them smile at that.

'Oh, take no notice of me, Rose,' Lucy went on. 'I get these moods now and then, and they don't mean anything. Mum says it's just growing up, but I should be over all that by now. I'll be eighteen in a month's time in case you've forgotten!'

'If I have, I'm sure you'll keep reminding me. Anyway, if you ask me, I don't think we ever grow up,' Rose said.

Lucy's opinion on that remark was lost as Bobby came hurtling towards them to say they were needed in the kitchen.

Upstairs, the two cousins sprawled uneasily on Jack's bed. It should have been an easy reunion but somehow it wasn't. There had been too much between them in recent months, and now there was the episode with the girl who had been killed in a road accident. Jack didn't know how to broach it, nor if Tom wanted to talk about it. Eventually he cleared his throat and said it, anyway.

'That was a bad business with your girl, Tom.'

For days now, Tom knew that people had been skirting around the subject of Mary. He had become more twitchy by the day, and Jack's words seemed to act like a hair trigger to his nerves.

'She wasn't my girl. She was just a girl I knew. I liked her, but because of her I've been slung out of a good job and a cushy number, and now I'm stuck back here working with my dad again – back where I started.'

He hadn't meant to sound so bloody resentful. He hadn't even put such things into words or even into coherent thoughts before. He saw Jack sit bolt upright as he realized just how awful it had sounded. Because of Mary dying he'd had to come home. Because of Mary dying...

As he saw Jack's outraged face – his brave soldier cousin's face – he found himself snivelling, like the weakling he was. He wrapped his arms around himself, turning his head away sharply from Jack, and cutting himself off from those accusing eyes.

'I didn't mean it like that,' he muttered.

'I'm damn sure you didn't, or you're not the kid I grew up with,' Jack snapped. He gripped Tom's arm, pulling him around, forcing him to look at him. 'You've had a hell of a shock, and it takes time to get over it. How long has it been – a few weeks at most? You can't get over something that fast, Tom, and it's a fool who thinks you can. If you did, it would mean you don't have any compassion in you, and I know that's not true.'

'Your mother seems to have got over losing those evacuee kids pretty fast.'

Jack swore beneath his breath. 'You can't compare that to what happened to you. Besides, everybody's different. She's an adult and you're still young and wet behind the ears. Besides, my mother can be a cold fish when she wants to be. The thing is, you *will* get over it, kid, so remember that. But this is just a taster, and there are going to be plenty more times in this war when we have to come to terms with losing people.'

Tom swallowed. He'd never heard his cousin speak so seriously before, nor sound so much older than himself. You were supposed to grow closer as you got older, when the years between didn't matter so much, but right now he felt eons younger than this sophisticated cousin of his. Four years' difference suddenly seemed to stretch into infinity.

'I know,' he mumbled. 'And I do like working with my dad,' he added, just in case Jack thought he was being totally disloyal.

'So cheer up, for God's sake. It's Christmas, and who the hell knows where we'll be this time next year? Let's go downstairs and tease the life out of the girls and the young 'un.'

They discovered it was as chaotic as Helen's house could ever be. Even in the midst of it all, there was still order and organization, Alice thought admiringly. She had been told to sit down with her feet on a footstool in the centre of operations. Just as if she was the queen, Mick had told her with a grin, his eyes telling her she was just as beautiful. Alice ignored the thought. It wasn't decent to be thinking such things on a family day. And she had to admit she was enjoying being made to feel special for once. Letting everything mull around her as if she had no real part in it. The house was mesmerizingly warm, the chattering voices seeming to fade into a pleasant hum all around her. She was no more than a relaxed observer, and the rest of them seemed to float and swan around her like busy attendant bees.

It was all Mick's fault for calling her the queen, she mused. Even Tilly was there, grinning at the unusual sight of her, so fat and buxom now and teasing her for being the queen bee ... such a young-looking Tilly, so well and happy, just like when they were girls...

'Mum. *Mum*! Are you all right?'

Someone's voice was bellowing right in her ear. Someone's face was close to hers, with frightened eyes and trembling mouth. Not Tilly. It couldn't be Tilly. She wasn't Tilly's mother. She struggled to retrieve her senses.

'Rose, what happened?' she said with a gasp.

'I don't know. I think you fainted.'

She realized that Rose, her capable nursing attendant daughter, was feeling her pulse now, trying to be efficient even while she was shaking, while all around them there was a crowd of people. People she knew and loved. Walter. Family. All of them watching her, expecting – what? She had no idea. Then she registered the wonderful aroma wafting from the kitchen.

Helen's kitchen. Roasting chicken, and parsnips ... Christmas fare. The table was already laid for a special meal, and Alice swallowed hard, forcing herself back from wherever she had gone for those indefinable moments.

'Don't be daft,' she said in a stronger voice. 'I've never fainted in my life. I must have just dropped off for a few minutes, that's all. And me and this babby would be a whole lot better if you didn't crowd around us as if you'd seen a ghost!'

Walter pushed forward then, grabbing her arm, the relief in his eyes worth more than a king's ransom.

'Thank God, girl. You gave us all a bit of a fright, muttering in that strange way and sliding down in your chair like that.'

She smiled into his eyes. 'Well, I'm not a gonner yet, so stop fussing and give me room to breathe.'

They all did as they were told, even if Rose looked at her quizzically all during the meal and for the rest of the day until it was decided that Mick would drive her and Walter and Bobby home while the others stayed behind for a while longer. Alice made her goodbyes and thanks with a sharp feeling of relief.

Once Bobby was in bed, she and Walter sat companionably around the fire with cups of cocoa and a mince pie. Alice felt strangely calm and at ease. She was also very tired, as if she had come a very long way in the space of a few hours.

'Should we wait up for the kids to come home?' she said.

Walter shook his head vehemently. 'They're grown up enough to see to themselves, and you're the one who needs a bit of looking after. I meant what I said, Alice. You gave us all a fright, and me in particular. For a moment I thought I was losing you, girl.'

Hearing how his voice faltered, Alice put her hand over his.

'It would take more than a small feeling of faintness to see me off, my dear. There's nothing to worry about, I promise you, and I did justice to my Christmas dinner, didn't I? I'm eating for two, remember.'

As she felt the baby stir she gave a secret smile, and Walter chuckled.

'Oh ah, there was nothing wrong with your appetite, I'll give you that, even if you did say we were looking at you as if we'd seen a ghost.'

'Did I say that?' Alice said with a shaky laugh. 'There's nothing ghostlike about me, Walter. It's all substance!' she added, patting her swollen belly.

Besides, it wasn't her who was the ghost. And it wasn't the rest of them who had seen it. Far from being the alarming thing some folk thought it might be, it was wonderfully comforting to know that there was a good friend watching over her. The world might be in danger of crashing down all around them, but for one small family in a remote Somerset village, Alice knew it boded well for the future.

Eight

1940 came in with a flourish of bad weather and the coldest January for many a year. The Chase family abandoned any idea of their usual New Year celebrations. Tom was still not back to his usual self and seemed reluctant to go back to Bristol. Rose and Jack had gone back to their respective units, and Alice was too heavy with the coming child to want to put herself out. Since Christmas, the baby had begun to lie heavily and awkwardly, and although Doctor Stacey assured her everything was going well, his very cheerfulness was making her unusually irritable. Her mood had transferred itself to Bobby, who was increasingly fretful and complaining about going to school in the ice and frost when the term began again. His only consolation was that the village pond was already frozen and the ice would soon be strong enough for skating.

'Don't worry, Bobby,' Lucy told him cheerfully. 'With any luck the water pipes at the school will be frozen as well, and you'll have a bit of extra holiday.'

Alice groaned at the idea of having Bobby home all day. The thought of him going back to school would be giving her a bit of a respite. She couldn't remember getting so breathless with any of the others, nor needing to sit down now and then, nor to have her ankles swelling quite so badly. It had alarmed her to see them like that every night, although Rose, with her new-found medical knowledge, assured her it was perfectly normal, and they would soon go back to their usual slim size once the baby was born.

Alice hadn't realized how much she would miss having Rose around. She had always considered herself a capable woman, able to deal with whatever came her way, and the thought that this one tiny baby was causing her more emotional turmoil than she let on to any of her family, was disturbing in itself. She couldn't confide in Lucy in the same way, and Walter ... well, dear as he was, Walter was a man and wouldn't understand. Besides, there were some things about the workings of a woman's body that you didn't tell a man.

But as January wore on, Lucy's predictions about the school were true and all the local children had an added holiday. The frozen village pond became the focal point of their day, and there were plenty of bruises, and cut foreheads, and the occasional sprained ankle to keep Doctor Stacey busy. By the middle of the month Tom's employer had written to say that he would be glad to have Tom back any time he felt able now, and that his job was still open to him despite all the recent upsets.

Alice's feelings were mixed when she saw the big sleek car pull up carefully outside the cottage for Tom to make his goodbyes. She knew she shouldn't be sorry to see any of her offspring leaving home and making their way in the world. It was the proper order of things. On the other hand, it was one less body to cook for. One fewer set of clothes to be washed and ironed, once she could get them dry in the frozen air. One less person to worry about. That was the guilt of it.

'You're looking peakier than usual, Mother,' Walter told her one evening, when she dozed in front of the fire while Lucy washed up the supper dishes.

She felt so weary she couldn't be bothered to tell him not to call her Mother. There were many moments lately, like this one, when she felt as if she was Mother to the whole blooming world. It surely couldn't be right to feel so distressed, together with the thought that had been nagging her lately, that there could be something wrong with the baby. It was uppermost in her mind again now.

'I think I'll go on to bed,' she said. 'I need to get my feet and ankles up on a pillow because right now they feel like cotton wool.'

Walter looked at her cautiously, afraid of saying the wrong thing, since she was more inclined to snap at him than usual.

'I think you need a tonic, old girl,' he said. 'That would soon put you right.'

Once, she might have laughed off his clumsy

attempt to help. Once, she didn't have this awkward great lump where her belly used to be, so large that she couldn't even bend to fasten her shoes without a great effort. Once, she was far more tolerant than she was now.

'Don't tell me I need a tonic,' she snapped. 'What I need is for this baby to be born so that I can be my old self again, but there's no hurrying nature, is there? If there was, women wouldn't have to go through this for nine long months, and men wouldn't say such stupid things. The day a miracle happens, and the first man has to go through having a baby, then you'll know!'

Furious at her lack of self-control, she felt her eyes fill with tears. She so rarely cried, and never in public. Nor over taking offence at a harmless and stupid remark that was just meant to be helpful. She staggered to her feet, and then she felt Walter's arms go around her.

'Don't you know I'd go through it for you if I could, sweetheart?' He spoke roughly into her ear, yet still so tenderly that she felt either like hitting him for being so damned considerate when she was being so hateful, or choking with love for him.

She went limp against him – or as near to him as she could get, considering the bulk of her that was between them. And then, as if in protest at what these annoying parents were ranting about, she felt the baby give an enormous kick. Walter felt it too. It was like an intrusion between them, but a sweet intrusion

142

for all that, and his startled exclamation made her giggle like a young girl.

'Bloody hell, girl. Did you feel that? We've either got a ruddy footballer in there or else it's twins!'

'Language, Walter,' Alice said weakly, through tears laced with laughter.

He squeezed her shoulders. 'Come on, we'll both go to bed. I'll give those feet of yours a rub and we'll leave Lucy to lock up.'

When Rose returned to her room at the hospital after her short leave she didn't know what to make of the letter waiting for her from Matt Stacey. For no real reason that she could think of except intuition, she had a feeling it wasn't going to be good news. But nor did it make her heart jump when she saw his writing on the envelope. This wasn't the way a girl was supposed to react, she thought uneasily, wondering again if she was fickle after all. First Peter Kelsey and now Matt.

Out of sight, out of mind, was one way of putting it, but wasn't absence meant to make the heart grow fonder? She couldn't get the ridiculous sayings out of her head, and she sat on her bed without moving, just holding the unopened envelope in her hand.

Elsie Venn found her still there as she entered their shared room, bundled up to the nines in a thick coat, woolly scarf and hat, and rubbing her hands together in an effort to warm them.

'It's cold enough to freeze the bleedin' thingummies off a brass monkey out there,' she complained. 'We got back earlier, and Daphne's waiting for us in the canteen. I came to see if you were back and wanted to join us. I suppose you've heard the latest about Orla?' she added without pausing.

Rose came to with an effort. 'I haven't had time to hear anything. I've barely been here for half an hour and just found this letter in my cubbyhole. What's happened to Orla?'

'Nothing to her personally. Her mum's had a whopping heart attack and a stroke, and isn't expected to live much longer, so Orla's packed up here and gone back to Ireland to look after her dad and her three small brothers.' Elsie snorted. 'She'll be nothing but a drudge if you ask me. Catch me looking after a parcel of smelly little boys. Anyway, what's with the letter? Aren't you going to open it?'

'Later,' Rose said, stuffing it into her pocket. Whatever it contained she had no intention of sharing it with Elsie and listening to her caustic comments. 'Didn't you say something about the canteen?'

Before Elsie could say she was bleedin' peculiar at not wanting to open a letter straight away, Rose had jumped up from her bed and put on her coat and outdoor things again. Anything to delay the evil moment ... and why she should even think like that, she didn't bother to guess, except that maybe it had been coming for a little while. Maybe a sawmill worker's

144

daughter and an up-and-coming young doctor weren't ever destined to be soulmates. She was angry with herself at the thought, but there was no hiding the fact that the doctors here definitely thought themselves a cut above the rest of them. It was very likely that Matt had found the same kind of treatment where he was, and was thinking he could do better than to be courting Rose Chase from a small Somerset village in the back of beyond.

'What's wrong with you?' Elsie said, tucking her hand through Rose's arm for added warmth. 'Didn't you have a good Christmas? We had a whale of a time at home, with all the aunts and uncles staying the night and sleeping where they could, though it wouldn't have been up to Daphne's standards, of course. They've got dozens of fancy guest bedrooms, I bet, and I don't think rationing has reached the huntin', shootin' and fishin' set, if you know what I mean. They probably pot a couple of rabbits before breakfast. Or their butlers do it for them.'

'You do talk a lot of rot sometimes, Elsie,' Rose said, starting to laugh despite herself. 'For your information I had a very nice Christmas. My cousin Jack was home on leave as well, so we were quite a crowd.'

'Is he a looker? You're not bad yourself, Rose, especially with a bit more make-up than you usually wear, so I daresay good looks run in the family.'

'Shut up, you idiot. Jack's just my cousin,

that's all, and I never really think about what he looks like.'

All the same, she had a quick mental image of him at that moment. And yes, he was good-looking, but he wouldn't appeal to her *in that way* in a million years, even if they weren't related.

'Well, at least you've cheered up, duck. When I first saw you, you looked as if you'd lost a tanner and found a ha'penny. Come on, let's see what the canteen's got to offer and you can hear all about Daphne's posh Christmas.'

The canteen was full. Some of the Christmas decorations hadn't even been taken down yet, prolonging the sense of festivity, although it was January now. The manageress saw no reason to dampen spirits in one fell swoop as she put it, and her policy was to take the trimmings down gradually.

The two girls saw Daphne waving to them. She was surrounded by a small posse of men in uniform. Canadian uniform. Rose's heart jolted. One of them was the fresh-faced Canadian airman she had danced with once or twice. She tried hard to think of his name, and then it came to her. Eldon McCloud. It seemed a very unlikely name for a Canadian, she had told him, and had learned that his family was of Scottish descent, and when this war was over he might go back to his roots.

He caught sight of her coming towards him now, and his smile widened at once as he slid off his stool to greet her. There was no mistaking the warmth in his eyes, nor the subdued giggles of her room-mates. Soppy things, Rose thought, feeling somewhat breathless, which must be due to the freezing air outside, and not to the sudden glow inside her as Eldon McCloud shook her hand.

'It's real good to see you again, Rose,' he said. His voice was as warm as his handshake. 'I missed you over Christmas, though the canteen gals here put on a pretty good show of welcoming us. There was no chance of me getting home, of course. I'd have liked to use my leave to go to Scotland to help out on my uncle's farm, but it wasn't worth the long journey just for a coupla days. But you look amazingly well, honey. The country obviously suits you.'

She was tongue-tied. For no good reason at all, she was momentarily tongue-tied. She had danced with him once or twice, and made small talk with him of the kind that usually passed for conversation. But in those few short sentences, she felt she knew more about him than before. If she was a country girl at heart, it seemed that he was definitely a country boy too, if the idea of helping out on a farm in Scotland in winter was so attractive! And she liked the way he called her honey. Besides which, that certain look in his eyes said he definitely liked what he saw.

'Put your tongue back in, girl, you're looking star-struck,' she heard Elsie whisper in her ear.

Daphne shushed her. 'Come and have a drink

147

with us, Rose, and tell us all about life in the wilds of Somerset. I've been telling these sweet boys that they should come and spend a couple of days at my family's home, and my room-mates must come as well, of course.' Her voice grew more enthusiastic. 'In fact, we could make it a weekend house party, providing we can all wangle leave at the same time. I know my parents would love to host it all. They're all for showing hospitality to our allied boys far from home.'

God, she lived in a different world from the rest of them, thought Rose. And catching the glimmer of amusement in Eldon's eyes, she knew he was thinking the same thing. But her heart suddenly thumped with excitement. Daphne's extravagant idea may never happen ... but if it did, how wonderful it would be to be in the company of all these lovely people for a few days, far away from the work environment and constant talk of war ... and also to see how the other half lived.

'What do you think, Rose?' Elsie said slyly, just as if she could see the workings of her mind.

'I think it sounds like a wonderful idea,' she said, her voice a bit more husky than she would have wished.

'So just as soon as we can all get the same weekend off, I'll get things moving,' Daphne said cheerfully.

Rose didn't quite know how it happened, but she and Eldon McCloud seemed to be in each other's company for the rest of the evening. He was so polite, so genuine, so everything a girl could want in a young man, and she had the absurd feeling that she might have known him for ever. Later, somebody started a sing-song of patriotic songs, and they all joined in lustily, singing their hearts out, and it was the cosiest, most enjoyable evening away from her family that Rose had spent for a long time. When it was time to leave and get back to the Nurses' Home, it felt almost like an anticlimax.

'I'd like to see you again sometime, Rose,' he said, under cover of the general goodbyes. 'Would you consider going to the cinema with me one evening?'

'Yes,' she said, before she had time to think. 'That would be nice.'

She squirmed at her naive response. But it was the way he made her feel. Young and gauche, and on the brink of going into the unknown. It was scary and exciting at the same time, and she forced herself to remember that he was only asking her out to the cinema. It wasn't a marriage proposal!

'See if you're free next Saturday evening, and with any luck I'll see you here before then so you can let me know,' he went on easily.

'With any luck?' she queried.

He gave a small shrug. 'Tonight was a great way to forget there's a war on for a little while, but we're not over here on vacation, Rose. We've got assignments and ops coming up, and even whether or not we meet again is always going to be in the lap of the gods from now on. That's why we should all make the most of it.'

He sounded serious now, so unlike the frivolous way he'd been all evening that she couldn't help but feel a shiver of fear inside. On nights like these it was so easy to forget why they were all here, in such different circumstances from normal, away from the homes and families they knew, but in the end, who knew what tomorrow might bring for any of them?

Eldon gave a sudden smile at her downcast face. 'Just listen to me, making you sad when I've just asked you for a date. Don't worry about me, Rose. My dad always said I had a charmed life, and now that I've met you, I shall think of you as my lucky charm.'

She laughed a little shakily. 'That's quite a responsibility to put on anybody. I just hope I can live up to it.'

'Don't you worry about that either, honey!' He blew her a kiss as his buddies made a move for the door, calling to him to get a move on.

Still in a bit of a daze, she went with Elsie and Daphne to collect their outdoor things, ready to walk back to the Nurses' Home.

'Well, I'd say you've made quite a hit with that one,' Daphne said. 'What was he saying to you that we couldn't hear?'

'Nothing much.' She had no intention of telling them that Eldon had called her his lucky charm. Some things were too personal for sharing.

'Oh, come on,' Elsie almost exploded. 'He's

been whispering sweet nothings in your ear for the last half hour, so what's going on between you two, and does your doctor boyfriend need to be told?' she teased.

Rose's heart gave a lurch. Until that moment she'd forgotten all about the letter from Matt that she hadn't opened yet. Even more than that, for the last couple of hours, she hadn't thought about Matt at all, and certainly not when Eldon had asked her out, and she had accepted so readily. Guilt flooded through her, and her face must have given her away, because her two friends hustled her out of the canteen and into the cold night air. She was linked between them, and she knew they wouldn't take silence for an answer.

'If you must know, Eldon asked me to the cinema and I said yes, and now I wish I hadn't,' she said, the words tumbling out.

'Why the hell not?' Elsie said. 'He's a great-looking guy, a bit of a dish if you ask me, and he certainly took a shine to you, so where's the harm in it?'

'Well, you've just said it, haven't you?' Rose said, starting to get annoyed. 'You asked if my doctor boyfriend needs to be told, so what do you think?'

Daphne gave her arm a squeeze. 'Rose, don't be so damned suburban. You're worse than Orla. I'm darned sure Matt wouldn't object, but if you think he would, then don't tell him. Such liaisons are two a penny in my circles, whether they're innocent or not.'

'Of course it's innocent!' Rose was stung into replying, but even more annoyed to be thought of as some kind of country hick and far removed from the sophisticated lifestyle of Daphne Poole. 'I hardly know the man, and it's not a liaison, either. It's just a date.'

'That's how it starts,' Elsie said dryly, and then gave a chuckle. 'For Gawd's sake, Rose, don't take yourself so bleedin' seriously. Enjoy it while you can. Who knows when we're all going to be blown to Kingdom Come, anyway? I'm damn sure I don't intend ending up without knowing what it's all about – and you know what I mean, so don't pretend that you don't, country girl.'

Rose felt her cheeks burn now, and she simply clamped her lips shut and refused to say anything more until she got back to their room. Even there, she didn't have the privacy she needed, so although she knew it would be freezing in there, she went off to the lavatory block to read Matt's letter. She shut herself inside one of the cubicles and locked the door, telling herself that whatever it said, she was glad to hear from him. He'd always been a friend, and lately, far more than that. They had an understanding. Whether or not he would understand if she told him about Eldon McCloud, was a different matter.

My dear Rose,
    I was really sorry that I couldn't get down to Bramwell for Christmas, and I hope you

had an enjoyable time with your family. Things have been fairly hectic here, but I hope very soon that I'll be sent abroad to do some field work – that is, once something really starts to happen. It seems a far cry from the excitement we both felt at joining up to do our bit. But apart from all that, what I really want to say, Rose, is that I think we should cool things between us for now, because who knows how long this war will last? We will both be meeting other people and even though I think very fondly indeed of you, Rose, and I know my feelings are reciprocated, we have to face the fact that feelings can change.

What I'm trying to say in my clumsy way, is that I don't want you to feel beholden to me in any way, my dear girl, and to forget whatever obligations you felt towards me. I think we should both be free, at least until this war is over, and then we can both review our lives. Who knows? We may yet end our old age together – but don't let's burn our bridges by making promises we may not be able to keep. I've seen too many maimed and sad servicemen in this hospital already with the legacies of war, and heard how they agonize over being a burden to their loved ones. Let's resist any thought of that happening to either of us, Rose. Let's agree to make the best of things, whatever may occur in the future. I hope you agree and that my words don't upset you too much, because I mean them sincerely and I know it's for the best. Always remember that I'm ever your close and loving friend, Matt

Rose managed not to burst into tears as she tried to calm down her thumping heart at the shock of his words. But these feelings were quickly replaced by a growing sense of fury, because this was no spontaneous letter. Matt could usually say what he meant very quickly, but the fact that he had rambled on so much, told her that this had been thought out very carefully. No matter how much he couched the letter in such lofty words, it said the same thing in the end. He was finishing with her. He didn't want to think of her as his girl any more. For all she knew, he might already have somebody else in his sights. Some more intelligent, more sophisticated girl, more his class...

She crunched the letter in her hand, feeling her fingernails bite into her palm through the paper as the bitterness seeped through her. They had joined up together, wanting to be together, to stay together, but it had taken such a little while, after all, for Matt to decide he didn't want to feel tied in any way to a village girl with ideas above her station. That was what they called it, wasn't it? She wasn't even a proper nurse. She did the menial jobs in the hospital that proper nurses didn't have to do, while Doctor Matt Stacey would be lording it over his wards, and attracting the adoring eyes of patients and nurses alike. She knew the procedure, because she witnessed it every day. Even junior doctors were the gods of any hospital, and they could have the pick of the women flitting around them like attendant worker bees.

She smothered a sob. For those few moments she completely overlooked the fact that her feelings had been cooling as well, even though she had fought hard to deny it. She and Matt had got along so well while they were in Bramwell, but she admitted that she no longer felt the same rush of emotion whenever she thought of him. All the same, it still hurt – *it bloody-well hurt like blazes* – to know that he had been feeling the same way all this time.

She thought she had only been in the lavatory block for a few minutes, until the sound of someone hammering on the door of the cubicle made her jump.

'What are you doing in there? Other people need to use these lavs as well as you, whoever you are,' she heard an angry female voice say.

Rose stuffed the letter into her pocket, leaped up from the seat and automatically pulled the chain. She pushed past the other girl with a muttered 'sorry' and gave her hands a cursory and unnecessary sluice in the wash-basin, before rushing back to her room.

She'd hoped that Elsie and Daphne had gone, but they were still gossiping on their beds. One look at Rose's heated face and they knew something had happened.

'My Gawd, what's up?' Elsie said at once.

155

'Did your bloke have something horrible to tell you? Has somebody died?'

Rose couldn't speak for a few seconds. She didn't want to tell them what was in the letter, anticipating Elsie's indignant theory that there were plenty more fish in the sea, and Daphne's cool encouragement that she already had a dishy Canadian drooling over her. But in those few seconds when she had to swallow the lump in her throat before she could speak at all, she had to agree that, no, nobody had died.

They were still in what was derisively called the phoney war, but it wasn't going to last for ever. In the enormous catastrophe that was almost certainly facing all of them, what did it matter that a possible romance between two people had fallen through? She took a shuddering breath and then began to tell them what was in Matt's letter, knowing that whatever else happened in this war, she had two good friends here, and friends were what she needed right now.

Nine

It was official. According to all the newspapers and the wireless announcers, January 1940 heralded the start of the coldest weather for forty-five years. Walter Chase grumbled that it didn't need bloody poncey weather men to tell them that. You only had to go outside your front door to feel the blast of icy air hitting your face, and freezing your fingers and toes.

'It's not the weathermen's fault, Walter,' Alice chided him.

'It's the bloody government's fault for giving us fewer and fewer rations. In weather like this, you need extra fuel inside you as well as in the fireplace. And it's only going to get worse.'

'I'm sure they're doing their best,' Alice said wearily.

She couldn't be bothered to argue with him. It was all they seemed to do these days and she couldn't be doing with it. Her back ached with the weight of the baby, and with Bobby's constant grumbles now because even though the school was still closed, lessons had to be carried on at home as best they could. She wasn't a teacher, and she wasn't equipped to check his sums or answer his questions. She knew it should be simple work for a woman of her age and experience, but it was mostly left to Lucy when she got home from work to do what she could with the boy.

That was another thing, she thought, going off at a tangent, the way her thoughts so often did these days. Rose had sent a letter home with the usual news about her daily activities and her new friends, and with just a brief mention at the end that she and Matt Stacey had decided to keep things on a friendly basis between them from now on. Since letters were read by all the family, Lucy, in particular, had been dismayed to hear this snippet of news.

'Well, this is awkward for me, isn't it?' she had wailed.

'For you?' Alice said, too concerned with what Rose might *not* be saying than her brief statement. 'What difference does it make to you, for heaven's sake?'

'Well, now that I work for Matt's family, I'm there every day, and it could be very embarrassing when he comes home on leave. I wouldn't know what to say to him – and I won't know what to say to Mrs Stacey, either, or if I'm even supposed to know about it!'

Alice was annoyed with her lack of sensitivity. 'Lucy, that's a very mean attitude, and I thought better of you. It's obvious that Rose is upset by what's happened, even if she doesn't say as much, and I hardly think Mrs Stacey is going to think badly of you because of what's happened between Rose and Matt. I'm disappointed that you haven't given more thought to Rose's feelings.'

'Oh, it's always Rose, isn't it?' Lucy said heatedly. 'I don't get a look in when Rose has a problem, do I?'

She flounced off to her bedroom, dragging a bewildered Bobby behind her as she said she'd help him with his writing, since it was all she was good for.

Ten minutes later she was back downstairs, contrite and tearful, and wrapping her arms around her mother.

'I'm sorry, Mum. I didn't mean any of those things.'

'I think you did, my love,' Alice said gently, 'but if that's the way you feel, then there's no reason for it at all. I love all my children the same, and so does your father, and when any one of you needs our sympathy and understanding, that's the one who gets it. It doesn't mean we shut the rest of you out.'

'I know,' Lucy mumbled. 'I was being selfish, only thinking of myself and not about Rose. Do you think she's very upset then?'

'It's difficult to tell from her letter, but why don't you write to her when you've had time to think about it a bit more? I know she'd like to hear from you.'

Lucy frowned, not so sure about the idea of giving sympathy to her older sister. 'Well, I suppose I could just write a few lines, even though I won't know what to say. I could always remind her that it's my birthday soon though, couldn't I?' she added.

Alice laughed. 'You could always do that, Lucy.'

It would be Alice's own birthday at the end of the month too. Last year there had been the usual celebrations for a mother and daughter with birthdays only a day apart. Last year her best friend Tilly had sent her usual cards and letter, and had talked about coming down to Somerset for a visit. This time last year there hadn't been a war on, and Tilly had still been alive.

Alice shook herself, refusing to let her thoughts descend into gloom. But she had truly never expected to miss Tilly so much. They hadn't communicated on a regular basis for years, and they lived so far apart, with Tilly still in London and herself in the back of beyond, as Tilly called it. For all that, Tilly had somehow always been there in her life, like her shadow, and now the shadow was gone.

The throaty voice that was Tilly's floated into her head, as clear as day.

'Bleedin' 'ell, gel, with the size you are now, I'd have a job to be your shadow! When are you thinking of droppin' that bab?'

'When it's good and ready and not before,' Alice muttered, not realizing she was saying it aloud.

'What did you say just then, Mum?' Lucy said.

'Oh, nothing, love. I was just thinking aloud.'

Lucy began to laugh. 'It sounded to me as if

you were talking to somebody. We don't have ghosts around here, do we?'

'Well, none that I can see,' Alice replied shortly.

The last thing she intended to do was to confide in Lucy that she frequently heard Tilly giving her advice, and nor did she want her modern-thinking daughter pooh-poohing the idea, or thinking that her mother was going strange in her old age. Besides, Walter had no truck with such things, and if he got to hear of it, he'd be more than uncomfortable. And Bobby would be too frightened to go to bed at night, for fear the bogeyman might be hiding under the bed. Yes, some things were definitely best kept private and personal.

Rose had arranged to meet Eldon McCloud at the end of the lane near the hospital on Saturday evening. She felt as nervous as a kitten. She had grown to like him more and more on the occasions they had met in the canteen, but this would be the first time she had been out with him alone, just the two of them.

She had never thought of herself as a simpleton, but right now, she was becoming desperately afraid she wouldn't be able to think of a single thing to say. There were only a few Canadians here so far, a sort of advance party, but far more of them were due to arrive next month. They spoke the same language, but there were subtle differences in their two cultures and background, but so far she liked

161

everything she had learned about them. This one, anyway.

She pulled her coat around her more closely, shivering in the cold wind, and began to wonder if this had been such a good idea after all. The cinema was always warm, but it was a good couple of miles away, and she hadn't given a thought as to how they would get there. Buses were few and far between, and her stack-heeled shoes were far from sturdy enough in this weather. It would have been far more sensible to wear thick boots and stockings, but vanity had won the day.

A car pulled up alongside her, and like the well-brought-up girl that she was, she kept her eyes averted, trying to ignore the rapid beat of her heart as the driver got out and walked towards her. You never knew who was going to accost you in these blackout nights.

'Your carriage awaits you, Ma'am,' she heard the familiar voice say.

She turned her head sharply, and looked straight into Eldon's laughing eyes.

'You've got a car?' she stuttered.

'Borrowed for the evening, and with strict instructions not to crash into anything,' he said solemnly. 'So unless you want to stand here all night and let the interior freeze, I'd suggest you get inside, Ma'am.'

He opened the passenger side door with a flourish, and Rose giggled.

'You sound just like a chauffeur now.'

'That's what I am for the evening, Miss

Chase, at your command.'

She laughed out loud now, feeling oddly reckless. It flashed through her mind that she had only ever been in her Uncle Mick's ramshackle car with the odour of animals in it, or Peter Kelsey's old van with the lingering smell of vegetables, or one of the hospital vehicles. This was different. This was a small car, but against the others, it was comparative luxury, and she was being escorted by a handsome fair-haired Canadian who seemed to like her company. Rose felt her spirits soar.

Later, she couldn't really have told anyone what they saw at the cinema. It was a love story, and the sweethearts had to go through plenty of conflict before they reached their happy ending. But that was what movies were all about – those and cheap novels. Or even the best ones, she reminded herself, remembering *Pride and Prejudice* that she had read at school. Not all novels were trashy.

What was far more important was that Eldon had slid his arm around her in the darkness of the back seats of the cinema, and after her initial embarrassment, she found herself cuddling up against him, as if she had known him for a long time, instead of only a few weeks. That was how it was with some people, though. You didn't need to know them a lifetime to know that you liked them enormously and that you felt comfortable just being with them.

They came outside to the blackout to find that the first snow had fallen in the area during those few hours. It was already lying a couple of inches on the ground and glistening on roof-tops, lightening the sky a little.

'We should have weather like this for the duration, and then maybe the Jerries would think twice about invading our little country,' Eldon said, his arm still around Rose. She didn't object. There was warmth in being close together.

'Our little country?' she echoed. 'You really think of this as being your country too?'

'Of course. Why not? We're all in this to-gether, honey.'

'But did you mean it about settling down here after the war? Well, not here, of course, but in Scotland.'

'I might. I'm keen to find out where my folks came from, and my uncle could certainly do with some young blood to help out on his farm and to keep it in the family. He and my aunt don't have any family of their own. I could give it a try with him, and if it suited me, well, who knows? Haven't you ever thought about leaving home and spreading your wings?'

'I thought that's what I was doing right now,' Rose retorted.

'But this is different. This is because the country needs us, Rose, and we have to sort all this out before we can go back to any kind of normal home life, or starting a new one. If I relocated to Scotland it would be from choice, not patriotism.'

As they walked back to where they had left

the car, the conversation had become all too serious. In fact, he was a far more serious young man away from his buddies than he had at first appeared, thought Rose, and as though to dispute her thoughts, he suddenly let go of her and scooped up a handful of snow and packed it together in his hands.

'Hey, we're getting too maudlin, kid, and this weather is only a taste of what it might be like if I lived in the wilds of Scotland, so let's make the most of it.'

He flung the snowball at her shoulder, and within seconds she too had scooped up some snow and was following suit. There was barely enough for a real snow fight, but it was enough to get them laughing like schoolkids at one another, and it only stopped when one of Eldon's snowballs hit the side of a man in firewatcher's uniform hurrying by, who yelled at them to stop acting so irresponsibly.

'Don't you know there's a war on?' he snapped, as he went on his way.

It was such a puerile question to ask a nurse and a pilot that they fell into one another's arms, still laughing helplessly, and then Rose felt his mouth on hers, and she was kissing him back just as fervently.

'Gee, I'm really sorry about that, Rose,' he said at last. 'That wasn't meant to happen, and I apologize for getting carried away by the moment. I really do respect you enormously.'

'Well, that's all right then,' she said in a strangled voice. 'Because you didn't find me objecting, did you?'

After a brief moment when she was all too conscious of her heartbeats, she wondered if that sounded too darned fast. Had she been too eager for that kiss, too brazen, and should she have behaved more like an English lady? But to blazes with it, she wasn't a *lady*, she was a normal working girl, and she had enjoyed kissing Eldon as much as he had enjoyed kissing her. At least, she thought he had.

'I'm sorry too,' she added lamely.

He tipped up her chin with his finger.. 'You don't have to be sorry for being the most delightful girl I've met since leaving home, nor the one I'd like to call my girl, Rose. What do you say? If it's all too soon, tell me now, but I've always thought that when you see some-thing you really want, you should go for it.'

Oh Lord, thought Rose. Romantic as it sound-ed, it wasn't the way of things in the sleepy little English village where she came from. But here, miles away from home, and all those thousands of miles away for Eldon, it didn't seem the wrong way at all. Especially in the circumstances they were in. But there was something about her he didn't know.

'Did you mean it about being your girl?' she said shakily.

'I never say anything I don't mean. Of course I meant it, honey. But I can see that I've spoken out of turn, and if you want to sleep on it, that's fine by me. In fact, whatever you say, is fine by me.'

'It's not that. I thought I was somebody else's girl until recently, Eldon, but we've decided to keep things friendly between us instead. So you could be getting me on the rebound and that's not fair to anybody.'

God, that sounded so stupid. Even as she said it, Rose shut her eyes in embarrassment. The next minute she felt his arms go around her.

'Come on, let's get to the car before we freeze out here, and then you can tell me all about the guy who was stupid enough to let you go, and I'll tell you why I'm hoping he's done me a great big favour.'

Rose couldn't doubt his meaning, and suddenly the blood was thrilling through her veins as his voice deepened. He was so nice ... but so had Peter Kelsey been ... and so had Matt ... and she could be heading for foolishness again. Then, right out of the blue she found herself remembering something her mother's old friend Tilly had once told her.

You've got to take chances in this life, gel. Once they've gone, they've gone for ever. Your mum knew that, leaving everything she knew for the love of your dad, and she's the lucky one, having all of you.

Eldon caught hold of her hand as they raced towards the car and almost fell inside out of the cold. She was breathless, and it wasn't only the biting wind that was making her feel that way.

Ever since she had been away Rose had been diligent in writing home, and Alice raised her eyebrows when she read the latest letter from her daughter.

'Rose seems to be moving in strange circles,' she remarked to Walter as they sat huddled over the fire that evening while he fiddled with the wireless, cursing all the while at the crackles and whines coming from it.

'What sort of strange circles?' he said, hardly listening. 'I thought she said she was working with a nice group of girls.'

'So she is, but this Daphne seems much posher than the others. It sounds as if she lives in a mansion, because Rose says she's arranging for some of her friends to go to her home for a weekend house party. Did you ever hear of such a thing?'

'*Bloody hell*!' Walter yelled in frustration as the wireless finally gave out just as he was trying to hear the latest news of the Union Castle liner that had been sunk by a mine off the southeast coast a week ago. 'I knew I should have got a new accumulator for this bloody thing. Now I'll have to go out to get one.'

'Didn't you hear what I was saying?' Alice asked him.

'Something about Rose,' he said, already halfway to the scullery to put on his outdoor coat and boots.

'I said she's going to a weekend house party at this Daphne's mansion. I hope she's not getting above herself.'

'Don't be daft, woman. Our Rose has got a sensible head on her shoulders. She's bound to mix with all sorts in wartime, and if it's with a better class of person than riff-raff, that's all to the good, isn't it?'

'I daresay,' Alice said with a frown. 'Be careful out there, Walter. It's freezing again tonight. The paper says that even the Thames is frozen over, and that'll be a tempter for some people.'

'More fools them,' he said, not too interested in what London folk got up to. 'I'll get back as soon as I can, though you won't object if I call in at the Pig and Whistle for a jar, will you? Or do you want to tie me to your apron strings until this babby's born?'

'Just don't be gone too long, that's all,' she said, determined not to get uppity or to make him think she was turning into a clinging vine.

In fact, she was quite content to doze on the sofa in front of the fire. Lucy was out somewhere and Bobby was in bed, and it wasn't often she had the house to herself – or even wanted it. But sometimes lately it was nice just to settle down in the warmth and let her thoughts drift away. The midwife said it usually happened in the last stages of pregnancy, when a mother needed to conserve all her strength for the labour that was to come. Alice didn't know about that. They were fancy words for something that was a natural occurrence, and she had already done it four times before. She knew the ropes.

Her relaxed thoughts were drifting back to a time when she and Tilly were girls, the way she did so often nowadays. They were both young and slim and eager then, full of life, and each anticipating a future with the prince of her dreams. And then came the charabanc trip to Somerset, and along came Walter Chase, bold-eyed and handsome, and unlike any of the fast-talking London boys they knew. He didn't need to be fast-talking to win Alice over, though. He and his brother Mick were real charmers, and she and Tilly had been quite ready for a bit of a flirt.

Walter had had a crush on her from the start, and when he promised to write to her, Alice had asked him teasingly if he even knew how. But when she got home and went back to the drudgery of the shirt factory, his letters had surprised and delighted her by their eloquence, and the way he described the glories of the country so well, tempting her to want to go back...

Distance could be deceiving though. There had been two brothers, both dark-haired, both charming, both trying to outdo the other in their teasing with the London girls they had their eyes on. Herself and Tilly. Not that Tilly had been too bothered. To Tilly it was just a brief holiday fling and nothing more. They had both giggled at the letters from Walter Chase, but in bed at night when Alice read them again, she had sighed over them too, thinking that here was her soulmate after all. It was just unfortunate that in her mind, she couldn't quite remember which of them was which. It didn't matter, since she had never expected to meet them again.

Then she had been invited to stay with the Chase family on her own for a short visit, and Tilly had urged her to go. It was a huge adventure for a young girl, travelling all that way on the train to Somerset, and when she arrived at the small village of Bramwell, it was to discover that the brother she thought had been sending her all those letters was not the one who so obviously intended to court her.

It was Walter, not Mick. But as she got to know them more, it was obvious that it was Mick who was the more articulate of the pair, the one with all the words, and she suspected very early on that even if they had been Walter's sentiments, Mick had been the one to put the letters together. Alice was too confused to think just how it really affected her, but by the time Walter proposed and she had accepted, it was too late. Too late to decide if it was really Walter that she loved, or Mick, the wordsmith, the poet.

A small gust of wind blew down the chimney, catching the wood chumps and sending a shower of sparks back up the chimney. It awoke Alice with a start, and she felt a small smile start at the corners of her mouth, as the memory of the dream still lingered. Those old fantasies were long gone, even though they had lasted far longer than had made her comfortable. There had even been a time when she was quite sure Mick had been in love with her too, but no more. And she was more than content with what she had, a good home and a loving, if some-times irascible husband, and four, soon to be five, healthy children.

The loving husband returned, stamping his feet to get rid of the snow, and cursing at the effect it was having on his gouty toe. Oh yes, Alice thought with a wry smile, she was the lucky one.

'Put the kettle on, woman, I'm fair shram-med,' he said by way of greeting. 'Henry Kel-sey was in a right old spin tonight because young Peter's gone missing in the North Sea.'

'What do you mean, he's gone missing?' Alice said, heaving herself up from the sofa with an effort.

'Well, not him personally, but his ship. There's plenty of Jerry mines in the North Sea now, and it's feared that his ship might have been sunk. Nobody seems to know, and the bloody War Office isn't saying until they're certain. Now I've got a new accumulator for the wireless I may be able to hear something. Get me that cocoa, girl, while I sort it out, and do me a bit of toast in front of the fire as well. It's cold enough to freeze the old doo-dahs tonight.'

Alice reacted to do his bidding automatically, ignoring the freezing of the old doo-dahs. But inside she was shaking. Hearing that Peter Kel-sey's ship was missing and might even have been sunk by a mine, just like the Union Castle, brought the war right home to Bramwell. It wasn't just something that was being fought on the battlefields of Europe, despite how slowly it all seemed to get started for those not in the thick of it. The war was also right here in a small Somerset village, where a young man she had known well, could already be drowned.

She could just imagine how Henry Kelsey was feeling. Peter was his only son, and there was no woman to share his anxiety. She had always disliked the man, and she was more than thankful when Rose had finished with Peter, but she wasn't heartless enough not to feel a wave of sympathy and compassion for him now.

'Where's that cocoa, woman?' roared Walter. 'I'm fair parched, and the wind has got right down my throat and dried it up.'

'It doesn't sound it,' Alice said tartly. 'The cocoa's coming as soon as the kettle boils, and that's one thing I can't hurry, no matter how much you bellow.'

Oh yes, she had definitely made the right choice, Alice thought, mocking herself. She had been a lively young girl, and had never been destined for a quiet life, and it would certainly never have been the same without the ups and downs of a rip-roaring man like Walter.

Ten

Tom had settled back to his job near Bristol with comparative ease. He loved the craftsmanship involved in turning a piece of wood into something beautiful, though it wasn't a very manly thing to admit. His boss understood, though, and approved of the way his young apprentice was shaping up. He had seen the potential in Tom Chase right from the start, and knew how he was wasted at the sawmill where his father worked. You had to be careful how you handled such a situation, of course. It wouldn't do for the father to think he was being belittled by implying that the son could do so much better. Fortunately, Walter Chase had been more canny than he might have expected, and was all for his son bettering himself.

'We'll make a good craftsman out of you, Tom. You have a natural eye for the wood,' James Conway said approvingly, as he watched him plane the piece on which he was working, studying it with expert eyes to make sure it was as smooth and straight as required.

'I've been meaning to ask you about that, Mr Conway,' Tom said hesitantly. 'With Mum's new baby so near, I'd like to make something for it. The old crib Mum had for Bobby is falling apart. Do you think I could do it? There's not much time now.'

'If you're prepared to do it in your own time, I'll give you the help you require,' he was told. 'It would be a fine gesture for the family, and something I'm sure your mother would treasure.'

It would also take the boy's mind off the horrific events that had occurred before Christmas, when the girl they had all been so fond of had been killed in the tragic road accident. James knew Tom had had what they called a crush on Mary, and her death had shocked him and hit him hard. Coming back here where it had all happened, must have been an ordeal for him, and James had even wondered if he would decide to stay in Bramwell and continue working at the sawmill with his father. That he hadn't, was a testament to the boy's courage and ambition, and James approved of both. It was to his regret that Graham, his own dearly loved son, didn't have the means or the skill to fulfil a father's hopes for him, but in Tom Chase he had to admit he saw an echo of himself, and he was fervently grateful to whatever powers that be, for sending him such a lad.

There were two birthdays to be celebrated at the end of January. Alice and Lucy had their birthdays a day apart, but this year, for the first time, the family wouldn't be all together. Rose couldn't get leave from the hospital to come all the way back to Somerset, and Tom had so recently gone back to Bristol that he decided to remain where he was and would be home a week or so later. He was afraid his excuses might sound feeble, but in reality he was busy working on the surprise for his mother and the new baby.

Their cousin Jack wouldn't be home from his army unit either, and he had dropped more than a few hints at Christmas that his next leave might well be his embarkation leave, a statement that hadn't gone down too well with his mother. To which Walter had remarked to Alice that if Helen had dropped a few more babs, she wouldn't have had to centre all her thoughts on her one offspring.

Alice hadn't bothered to explain the ins and outs of why Helen hadn't been able to have more children. By now, she was more concerned with the one in her belly, and in any case, now that she was almost ready to pop, in her own words, she didn't want any fuss for her birthday.

As usual, Lucy was ready to complain. She would be eighteen, and considered herself a young lady now, and wouldn't have minded a bit of a party. However, she acknowledged that she shouldn't excite her mother too much, especially when the so-sensible Mrs Stacey advised it.

'I'm sure your mother will sail through the birth of her child, Lucy,' her employer told her. 'But for all your sakes, she should try to remain as calm as possible in these last few tedious weeks.'

'Is it very painful, Mrs Stacey?' Lucy asked, knowing it wasn't something she could ask her own mother. And since Mrs Stacey was the doctor's wife, as well as having had baby Mollie, she should know about these things.

'It depends on a lot of things, my dear, including the size of the mother and the new baby. It's not something you need worry yourself about until the time comes, but your mum has been through it four times already so she'll know what to expect and how best to help herself.'

'I'm not sure I ever want to go through it,' Lucy said, stroking Mollie's head. She had learned something of the mechanics of it all by now. You could hardly do otherwise with all the medical books lying about in a doctor's household. And she was still wondering how on earth something weighing pounds could go through the procedure of birth without causing pain to the mother. And head first too...

Mrs Stacey laughed. 'You'll forget all about that when you're married and have a baby of your own. The pain is soon forgotten, I promise you, and millions of women have done it, so it can't be that bad, can it?'

'Millions of women may not have had much choice,' Lucy muttered.

'Well, you just wait and see your mother's face when she holds the new one in her arms. Don't you remember how it was when Bobby was born?'

'Not really. I was little more than a child myself then.'

'And you're such a grown-up now, aren't you?' Violet Stacey said with an affectionate smile. She had been fond of Rose, but Lucy was such an ingenue, so sweet in an entirely unconscious way, that she was drawn to her even more.

'Well, I'll be eighteen in a week's time,' Lucy said, brightening up.

'Don't worry, I haven't forgotten. Mollie and I are planning a special afternoon tea for your birthday.'

'Oh, I didn't mean anything like that,' she said, confused.

'I'm sure you didn't,' Violet said. That was one of the things she liked about Lucy. She said what she thought, never with malice, but without pausing to consider the effect it had on anyone else. It could be irritating, but more often Violet found it endearing.

Jack Chase was impatient to be sent to France. He hadn't joined the army to do endless training exercises. He wanted to be in the thick of it. He remembered how his young cousin Tom had always wanted to be a hero. That was when they were both more interested in flying than army slogging. Tom had been even keener on flying than himself, but that interest seemed to have waned recently, as it had for Jack. Getting involved in dog fights sounded fine and dandy for the Brylcreem boys, but Jack had his feet firmly on the ground now, and wanted nothing more than to get a pot shot at the Jerries. With any luck his embarkation orders would come through soon, and then he could really show what he was made of.

His mother wouldn't like it, of course. He wished to God she'd still had those evacuees with her, then she wouldn't concentrate so much on what was happening to him. His dad too, had always wanted him to be a vet like himself, but he'd rebelled against that. Working on the farm had been OK, but a farm boy was just that, and he was enjoying his new status in uniform. He had his share of good looks, and the girls in the NAAFI weren't impartial to him. Far from it.

Jack also had his own little band of cronies now, and they had a reputation for being out on the prowl in their off-duty times, and he was living up to his name. They called him a proper Jack-the-Lad, and he didn't mind it one bit. He knew it was something else his straight-laced mother wouldn't approve of, but what she didn't know, wouldn't hurt her. So far, Jack was enjoying his war, and he was going to enjoy it even more when he was sent off to Froggie-land.

Alice agreed to a small birthday party at Helen's house for herself and Lucy, providing Mick did the honours and drove her there and back. The baby was only a couple of weeks away now, and the frozen snow had made it so slippery underfoot that Walter insisted that she didn't go to the village any more than she had to. Lucy could bring back any groceries they needed, and even though Alice complained that she wasn't an invalid and didn't need to be wrapped in cotton wool, she was secretly thankful they were being so dogmatic.

She wished Rose could have come home, but she knew it was asking too much. With luck, she might get leave once the baby was born, and that would be far more important. As for Tom, he seemed to have become absorbed in his new life without much thought for his family, she thought, with mild resentment.

She chided herself, telling herself she should not act like a mother hen, and it was good and proper that children should branch out and assert their independence, and live whatever had been destined for them. She had done so, hadn't she? A little voice inside her head – her own, not Tilly's – said that nobody had destined lives to be changed because of a war, thank you very much.

But before the birthdays arrived there was far more sombre news that affected the whole village. It was announced that the destroyer HMS Grenville had been sunk in the North Sea, by a mine or torpedo. Other ships in the vicinity were able to rescue many of the crew of the stricken ship, but many others were reported missing or presumed dead. Among them was Peter Kelsey.

The village was plunged into mourning. Kelsey's shop was a focal point in the centre of Bramwell, and the same family had owned it for many years. Whatever anyone's personal feelings towards the brash Henry Kelsey, sympathy poured out towards him in his loss. The shop was closed for a day, but because the village depended on it for supplies and the meagre rations of butter, bacon and sugar that people were allocated now, he opened it again with half-shuttered windows, and he wore a black armband that would adorn his coat from then on.

'I feel I should say something to him,' Alice said worriedly. 'Peter and Rose were close for a long time, and it would be common courtesy to give Henry my condolences.'

'You'll only upset yourself if you go offering him sympathy, Mother,' Walter said. 'In your condition it's best to keep away.'

'Don't be ridiculous, Walter,' she snapped. 'When did I ever shut myself away from the world just because I'm expecting? It's bad enough that this awful weather keeps me indoors half the time without you trying to prevent me from being a good neighbour.'

'I'm not preventing you from doing anything. Much chance I'd have of trying! When did you ever do as I said? You went gallivanting off to London on your own last year, as I remember, and stayed for a week.'

Alice was speechless for a moment, and then she felt her heart pounding with rage at him.

'Are you completely heartless, Walter? You know very well why I went to London when my best friend was dying, and when I got there it was too late. Somebody had to deal with her funeral and do what they could for her, and I never thought you'd begrudge me that after all Tilly meant to me!'

She finished with her throat choking, and a sharp pain in her side.

'God Almighty, Alice love, I never meant to imply anything else. I know you did everything possible for Tilly, and I know you didn't go off gallivanting, nor ever would. My words just ran away with themselves.'

'I know where Lucy gets it from then, don't I?' she said, simply because she couldn't think of anything else to say.

For a moment neither of them spoke and then Alice felt a sob in her throat. The next minute Walter had wrapped his arms around her, and was speaking harshly in her ear.

'I know I'm a bloody rough diamond, Alice, and that's a bloody overstatement. I'm more like a bloody rough lump of coal, and the clumsiest sod on earth at times, but you know I think the world of you, don't you?'

'I know,' she sobbed against him. 'And stop swearing. I don't want this baby to come out cussing.'

Her shoulders began shaking, and so did his, and then he was roaring with laughter at what she had said.

'Do you really think he's listening?' he said

finally, pressing his hand lightly to her belly.

'I'm sure he understands every word we say,' she said solemnly, and then they were laughing hysterically again, because it seemed so unlikely. And as Alice sobered, she realized too, how awful it was to be laughing like this when they had just been discussing such terrible news. She pushed Walter aside, swallowing hard, and then spoke more firmly.

'Whatever you say, Walter, I feel I should speak to Henry Kelsey about Peter. I can't just ignore it. And I must write and tell Rose too. She'll be upset, no matter what's gone on between them.'

'All right then. But you're not going on your own. We'll go together this evening when Lucy's home to look after Bobby.'

Alice knew she would get her way. It was just a pity that it sometimes took so long. Before then she decided to write to Rose to tell her the news. She knew it would be a difficult letter to write, because long before they had started courting, Rose and Peter had known each other all their lives. It was hard to lose a friend you had known for so long. It was like losing a little bit of your past.

Her pen hovered over the writing paper, and she knew she was thinking of herself and Tilly as much as her daughter. She and Tilly had known one another all their lives too, and Tilly had been like the other half of herself. They had run wild as children in the streets of London, seeing no danger, left alone to their own devices much of the time, closer than sisters, growing up together, sharing their secrets, their hopes and dreams. With the ultimate confidence of youth they had expected to marry at the same time, bring up their babies together, live next door to one another with their families intermingling. It had never happened that way, of course, and Alice was the one left alone.

She shook herself with a start as the thought entered her mind. How could she ever think she was alone with a large and happy family? The essence of it all though, was that she had never found anyone else to confide in like Tilly. There could never, ever, be another Tilly in her life.

Buck up, gel, for Gawd's sake. Ain't you supposed to have happy thoughts so that your bab comes out smiling?

I do have happy thoughts, Tilly. Especially when I think of you, Alice whispered back.

But as she stared down at the few words she had written to Rose so far, this couldn't be a happy letter she was writing. All the same, Rose needed to know what had happened, and Alice was the right one to tell her. Lucy had long ago abandoned the idea of writing at length to her sister, and had just penned a short note reminding her of her birthday on the 27th of the month. Typical Lucy.

Alice concentrated again, and by the time she had screwed up half a dozen pieces of writing paper, she was finally satisfied that she wasn't going to destroy Rose's confidence in her own future, or worry her over what was happening

184

to the other young men she knew. She had always been fond of her cousin Jack, who was Lord knew where now, and who would certainly be in the thick of the action as soon as he could. Matt Stacey might be out of the picture, but there was a young Canadian airman Rose had mentioned. His name had slipped into the conversation while Rose was home at Christmas. She had mentioned him casually, almost too casually, and it was hardly noticed by the others, but with her mother's intuition, Alice had noticed it.

Alice and Walter walked through the village soon after Lucy came home from work. It wasn't properly dark yet, but the moon was already full, throwing shafts of light through the clouds on to the snow-covered ground, spangling trees and bushes and rooftops and turning them into a kind of fairyland. It was so beautiful, needing a poet's words or an artist to do it justice, thought Alice, as they picked their way carefully. The only things lacking were the welcoming lights from cottage windows, instead of the blackout curtains that prevented enemy aircraft pinpointing their little village as a target. Just as if any of them would, she thought scornfully, with Bramwell being so remote from any city, and so far from anything resembling docks or important military installations...

Walter held her arm firmly through his. It wasn't that far to the centre of the village and

Kelsey's shop. It was naturally all in darkness, and even now, with all the resolve in the world, Alice's heart balked at offering sympathy to a bereaved father. As if sensing her feelings, it was Walter who took the initiative.

'Come on, old girl, let's get this over with. Remember how we'd feel if it was one of ours, and let's thank God it's not,' he said, remarkably perceptive for once.

He knocked on Kelsey's side door, and for a moment Alice thought nobody was going to answer it. She had the stupid urge to turn and run ... if she'd been able to run. And then the door opened slowly, and Henry stood there, a poor, stooped figure of a man, so unlike his usual self that it made Alice's heart turn over.

He hadn't thought, or hadn't bothered, to turn off the light behind him, and Walter almost pushed Alice inside, telling Henry crisply that if he didn't want the air-raid warden after him, they'd better shut the door.

'I suppose you want to talk,' Henry said dully. 'Not that it does any good, nor makes any sense. But it's what people do, isn't it? And I've had a bellyfull of talk these past couple of days.'

Alice sat down in the small sitting room without being asked. She had never been here before, but it was the room of a man who had lived without a woman for a long time, but still kept it reasonably tidy and shipshape. There was a desk at one side of the room, covered with the usual papers and paraphernalia of a businessman, which was probably going to be his salvation, Alice thought. There was a fire burning in the grate, and on the mantelpiece there were photos of his wife, and of Peter as a child. It was somehow sad and pathetic.

'Now then, Henry, what can we do to help?' Walter said. 'We know you must be bloody cut up to hear what's happened, and I suppose there's no doubt?'

'There's no doubt he's gone. I had official word today. There's nothing anybody can do to help, but thanks for the offer.'

It was said so mechanically that Alice was sure he'd said the same words many times already. She cleared her throat.

'I'm so sorry, Henry,' she said softly. 'It's so hard to lose someone you love, and I won't insult you by saying it will get any easier, because it won't, not for a long time, anyway. You just gradually get used to the pain and start to remember the best of times. One morning you'll wake up and realize Peter's not the first thing on your mind, when I know that right now he occupies every second of your day.'

'Well, that's a bloody comfort to the man, I must say!' Walter said sharply.

'Shut up, Walter,' Henry said. 'Your wife is a good woman, and she talks a lot of sense. I've had enough do-gooders coming around here telling me it was God's will to take Peter into His keeping. I don't want to hear any of that crap, begging your pardon, Mrs Chase, when anybody with a bit of sense in their brains

187

knows it was Hitler and not God who drowned him.'

For once, Walter didn't know how to answer this, and then he took out a small bottle half full of brandy from inside his coat pocket. Ignoring Alice's look, and knowing he'd get a tongue-lashing later, he held it out to Henry.

'Then I hope you'll take a drink with me in memory of young Peter.'

For a moment Alice thought the man was going to refuse, and then he put the bottle to his lips and took a draught, before handing it back to Walter who did the same.

'To Peter,' Walter said.

'To Peter,' his father said huskily.

'And all the other brave young men who died with him,' Alice murmured, unable to resist saying it.

Henry's mouth twisted into a grimace.

'Oh ah, I know he weren't the only one, and I'm told there were the best part of a hundred all told. You'll forgive me if there's only one that I'm thinking of right now.' He seemed to stir himself with an effort. 'But where are my manners? Would you like some tea, Mrs Chase?'

Alice shook her head. 'No thank you. We just wanted to tell you we're thinking of you, and I am writing to tell Rose what's happened. I know she'll be very sorry to hear it.'

'I daresay,' Henry said vaguely. It was as if he had already gone off into his own little world again now that the enforced niceties were over.

'Then we'll be leaving, Henry,' Walter said. 'Don't bother to see us out and risk showing a light again. You can keep the brandy, by the way. Your need is greater than mine.'

They left with some relief since there didn't seem to be anything more they could say or do. It had been a necessary visit in Alice's opinion, and once they had started on the road home again they walked in silence for a few moments.

'That was a nice thing you did, drinking a small draught in Peter's memory with him,' Alice said at last.

'Really? I was waiting to hear your disapproval.'

'I'm not a prude, Walter. There's a time and place for everything, and that was the right time.' She hugged his arm close to her, feeling his strength and knowing that a hard man could be both tender and strong when needed. She counted herself a fortunate woman to have such a man.

Rose always looked forward to getting letters from home. Her mother was a good letter-writer and filled her in with all the things that were going on in Bramwell, the latest gossip, if there was anything worth telling, as well as the everyday life of the family. Sometimes Bobby was persuaded to add a few words in his scrawling handwriting, but the letters always ended in the same way, with love from Mum and Dad, Lucy and Bobby.

She opened the latest one at the end of her shift, kicking off her shoes in her room and lying flat on her bed, glad to be alone for a short while before the other girls joined her. And then she read the first few words of her mother's letter, and she sat bolt upright with a little cry.

Elsie and Daphne came into the room a few minutes later, still laughing at one of the risque jokes one of the patients had told them, and ready to share it with Rose. One look at her face sent that idea straight out of their heads.

'What's happened, mate?' Elsie said at once.

Rose could hardly speak. She hadn't expected the news to affect her quite like this. She was a nursing assistant and had seen plenty of squeamish things since working at the hospital, including a few deaths, but none of them had been personal. None of them was a boy she had known all her life, and who she had once thought herself madly in love with. None of them was Peter.

'Do you want to tell us, Rose?' Daphne said quietly. 'If it's too personal and you'd rather we went out and came in again, just say so.'

'No, of course I don't want you to do that. It's such a shock, that's all. I know it's something we all might have to face, but when it happens, you just can't take it in, can you?

'What is it, gel?' Elsie was alarmed now, seeing her white face. 'It's not your ma, is it? Nothing's happened to the new baby, has it?'

Rose shook her head. She had to tell them, even though putting it into words would make it seem even more real. But she couldn't put it off for ever. She spoke haltingly.

'It's an ex-boyfriend, Peter. I don't know if I ever told you about him. We went out together for a long time before I knew Matt. My mother says his ship was mined or torpedoed in the North Sea, and he's missing, presumed dead.'

She finished on a strangled sob, and while Daphne gripped her hand in sympathy, Elsie said the only thing she could think of at that moment.

'Blimey Rose, how many more ex-boyfriends have you got hidden away?''

Eleven

Daphne was a born organizer. She had already checked with her parents about the proposed weekend house party with her new chums, and now she decided it was just what was needed to cheer up Rose. Once she and Elsie had calmed their friend down a little, and Elsie had assured Rose she hadn't meant any harm by her clumsy remark, Daphne went off to telephone her mother.

Obliging as ever to her precious girl, the Poole mater had assured Daphne that any week-end at all would be suitable, and just to let her know when they would be coming, and how many there would be.

'It's all settled,' Daphne announced, returning to the room where the other two were still mulling over Rose's news. 'Providing the boys can get the time off, we're all going up to Kent for the weekend after next, and no arguments. It's just what we all need, and it'll be fun. Mother says the lake is frozen hard enough for skating too.'

'*Your* lake, I presume?' Elsie said with a grin.

'Of course,' Daphne said coolly. 'So what do you say, Rose? When are you seeing your Canadian again?'

Rose started, her thoughts still too full of Peter and the awful thing that had happened to think of anything else. 'I don't know. I daresay he'll be at the canteen tonight or tomorrow night. I just don't know.'

'Well, you'd better find out, hadn't you?' Elsie said, jumping off her bed, her eyes alight with excitement. 'We'll all go down there tonight, and get things settled.'

'I can't, I've got an extra duty,' Daphne said, 'But you two can find out and let me know which date is best so that Mother can get in extra supplies.'

'There *is* a war on, you know,' Rose said suddenly irritated at the way these people seemed to find it so easy to shrug off the privations that were beginning to make themselves felt elsewhere.

It seemed almost obscene to be talking about a carefree weekend, and even more about

192

getting in extra provisions, when everyone had to register with a grocer and a butcher now, to get the miserable supplies of food allocated to them every week. And this was only the beginning. Besides, if Rose had a free weekend, wouldn't it be right and proper for her to go home, despite the long and dreary train journey, not only to see her mother, but to pay her condolences to Peter's father, however much she shrank from the thought. But how could she not do so, when she had once believed herself in love with him?

'I know there's a war on, darling girl,' Daphne went on. 'But there are always ways and means, and our cook is an absolute wizard at producing splendid meals out of practically nothing. We won't starve, I promise you.'

Elsie laughed. 'You won't shame her, gel. Our Daphne lives in a different world from the rest of us, and I for one, can't wait to get a little taste of it before Jerry blasts us all to Kingdom Come.'

'I wish you'd stop saying that! We won't be expected to dress for dinner, will we, Daphne?' Rose was only half serious and more than a little sarcastic, but she was starting to take a reluctant interest, despite herself.

Daphne laughed. 'Oh, I think the parents will dispense with that idea for a group of my chums. We'll just be a jolly party, set on enjoying ourselves. Say you'll come, Rose. It would not be the same without you.'

Rose finally felt bound to agree, saying she

would do her best not to spoil things. Her heart may not be in it, but she couldn't spoil it for the rest of them. And Elsie was right. They had to make the best of things before Jerry blasted them all to Kingdom Come. She couldn't get the damn phrase out of her head now.

'You don't look yourself tonight, honey,' Eldon greeted her when he came into the canteen with his buddies, a sprinkling of snow on their heads and jackets, and saying it was getting more like Ontario weather every day.

As always the mood of the canteen changed when the Canadians arrived. They seemed to bring a breath of fresh air with them, or maybe it was the accents that were so attractive and transatlantic compared with the motley variation of regional British accents that was everywhere now. One of the old stagers had commented that Canadians were supposed to be dour, but none of the girls in the canteen had noticed any such thing.

'I don't exactly feel myself,' Rose murmured, wondering just how she was going to tell him the news without exposing her own raw feelings, and bringing the mood of the evening down.

The canteen was always crowded and noisy, but somehow he had manoeuvred her into a corner while they waited for some seats to become vacant.

'Has something happened?'

His voice was so caring and concerned that

194

Rose felt her throat constrict. She looked down at her clenched hands. Eldon followed her glance, and put a protective hand over hers. She drew a deep breath.

'Someone I knew very well has died. His ship went down in the North Sea, and it's really hit me that ordinary people like us are going to be killed in this war.'

'Was he special, Rose?' When she didn't answer, he went on. 'For pity's sake, honey, I didn't think you'd have lived like a nun before I met you, so you don't have to be embarrassed about telling me.'

His words seemed to release something inside her. 'He was special to me once and I thought I loved him for a long time. He was my first love, and I don't think you ever forget that, do you?'

It flashed through her head that she was probably doing this all wrong, making more of her relationship with Peter Kelsey than it actually was, and putting off this nice young Canadian who was obviously interested in her. But that was the least of her problems now. If he couldn't cope with this overemotional girl, and wanted to end what had hardly begun, then so be it.

'Of course you don't forget it. I still remember mine very clearly.'

His face came into focus. 'You do?'

'Sure I do. She had glorious blonde curly hair, and she was as pretty as any film star. Her eyes were as blue as the sky and I remember following her around like a love-sick puppy. I used to

195

take her a toffee every day.'

'A toffee!' Rose repeated, parrot-like.

'Oh, did I forget to mention that I was six and she was five at the time?'

His mouth curved into a teasing smile, and as she realized what he was saying, Rose was smiling back and the tension was broken.

'You see?' he went on calmly. 'You always remember your first love, but life changes all of us, and it doesn't mean that your first love is necessarily going to be your last, does it?'

He had the knack of putting everything into perspective so simply, and Rose felt a mite better than she had done since receiving her mother's letter.

'I know you're right, and I have to get over what's happened, so thank you for making me see it. In fact, that's why we're here tonight. Daphne said I need cheering up. She's arranging that house party she mentioned, and being Daphne she wants to do it quicker than yesterday now, but I doubt that you boys can get leave the weekend after next, can you?'

'You're in luck, because we're off duty that weekend. It must be fate, Rose.'

This time her heart did a double flip, because there was no doubting the meaning in his eyes. It wasn't just fate that had brought them together ... it was more likely the machinations of two governments. But whatever it was, they were here, and they were enjoying each other's company. In these hazardous days, they could not ask for anything more.

Elsie joined them with the other two Canadians in tow, wanting to know what these two were doing, huddled together in a corner.

'Nothing you need to know about,' Rose said lightly. 'I've just confirmed with Eldon that the weekend after next is all right for Daphne's house party, if you others are happy about it.'

Buzz and Dean thought it was the best idea they'd heard yet, and were keen to see more of the way these British folk lived. Daphne had been right, Rose thought later. Chatting about it in the canteen over soft drinks and beer, had definitely lightened her mood by the time she and Elsie went back to the nurses' home that evening. Even though she had to smile at the thought that the Poole household promised to be anything but typical of how 'these British folk' lived!

'You two were getting very friendly when we came over earlier, weren't you, Rose? I'd say Eldon's got a real soft spot for you,' Elsie said archly.

'Maybe he has, but wartime's no time for rushing into anything. It's far better to keep your feelings under control.'

'Blimey, what are you, a hundred years old? Make the most of it, Rose. Eldon seems a nice chap, and you never know what's around the corner. What happened to your other bloke should have told you that much,' she added, more seriously than usual.

'I know. Just don't start reminding me again that Jerry's about to blast us all to Kingdom

Come, that's all, because I don't want to hear it,' Rose said tartly. 'Now I've got to write back to my mother, and I'm also going to write a letter to Peter's father. It's the least I can do.'

'I'll leave you to it, then,' Elsie said. 'I'm going to the common room to listen to the wireless for a bit, and then I'm going to think of what clothes I'm taking for this posh weekend at Daphne's, and you should do the same. It'll be a hoot, Rose, seeing how the other half lives!'

Left to herself, Rose realized it was the first time she had been completely alone since she'd had her mother's letter. And left to herself, the reality and the horror of it all finally washed over her. Peter was dead. The first victim of the war known personally to her. Whatever her recent feelings towards him, he had been part of her life, and as her limbs seemed to turn to water, she threw herself down on her bed and wept.

The patrons of the Pig and Whistle in Bramwell paid their own kind of tribute to Henry Kelsey's loss. His cronies encouraged him not to stay in and wallow, but to share a drink of ale with them so that they could all give young Peter a kind of absent wake.

Walter and Mick Chase were among the small crowd who had gathered together in the pub that evening. Once the difficult business of the evening was over and the men started to awkwardly relax again, Henry spoke to Walter.

'I had a note from your Rose, Walter, remembering Peter. It was thoughtful of her to write, and she's a credit to you and your missus for what she's doing.'

'I'm glad she wrote to you,' Walter said, knowing that it wiped out the lingering unpleasantness between them since Rose had broken up with Peter. None of it mattered now, anyway. It was ancient history.

'You'll be ready to welcome your new babby soon, I daresay,' Henry went on with an effort to be sociable.

'It's a few more weeks yet, but we'll both be glad when it's all over.'

Henry nodded and wandered on vaguely around the smoke-filled room, listening to various tributes that were being paid to his son, and hardly registering any of them. Peter hadn't been hugely popular as a boy in the village, but all that seemed to be forgotten or overlooked now that he was dead. It was ironic that it should be so, but that was the way of things.

'Look at him, poor devil. He hardly knows what's hit him,' Walter said to his brother as they watched Henry traversing the pub. 'It's a bad thing when the son goes before the father.'

'Amen to that,' Mick said, and Walter knew he must be thinking of Jack at that moment, and the dangers for all servicemen.

'Your Jack's all right. He's the indestructible kind, always coming up roses, the same as I think our Tom would be if he was old enough to join up,' he said, privately thanking God that

199

Tom was still only fifteen.

'I hope you're right,' Mick said, draining his glass. 'Let's get out of here, Walter. I've had enough gloom for one night. Do you want to come back to my place for a yarn?'

'I'd better not, boy. Alice doesn't like me to be out for too long and I don't blame her for that. She can't sit comfortably for too long and I have to rub her feet every night. It's one of the penalties of being an expectant father!' he added, trying to be jocular.

Mick nodded, though it was many years since he'd been in that position himself, and he knew he would never be in it again. As the homely and intimate image came to his mind of Walter rubbing Alice's feet, he felt a sudden sense of loss for all that he didn't have, and which his brother did.

Alice had had a letter from Rose too. She wasn't sure what to make of it at first, but it was Lucy who said bluntly that Rose was doing exactly the right thing, because what good did it do anybody to waste time in grieving for something that couldn't be changed?

'That's a heartless thing to say, Lucy,' her father told her.

'I don't mean to be heartless. I'm as sorry as anybody over what's happened, and it must be awful for Mr Kelsey. But Rose can't do anything about Peter, and there's no sense in moping about. We all have to get on with life, don't we? Mum showed me that, after Tilly died.'

200

Alice drew in her breath. Even now, hearing Tilly's name out of the blue, could make her heart stop for a moment. To her surprise, Walter nodded.

'You've a good head on your shoulders, girl, for all that you're so young. So I think you should write back and give Rose our blessing for this weekend visit to her friend's parents, Alice. It'll cheer her up and take her mind off things.'

'If you think so, Walter,' Alice said.

He looked at her sharply. 'Is there any reason you should be against it? It's good of this Daphne's folks to invite a group of her friends to their home. Young nurses don't have the easiest of jobs, as we know.'

Providing it was only a group of young nurses, Alice thought. In her heart she was fairly sure it wouldn't be. People like Daphne Poole, living in the kind of mansion Rose had only hinted about, were far more outgoing and bohemian than insular village folk. Not that Alice thought anything bad went on, but the opportunities were there. Alice might be an insular villager too now, but she'd been born and brought up in London, and she knew a bit of what went on in the seedier parts of the city. Rich or poor, if the opportunities were there, some were only too ready to take them.

She stopped her rambling thoughts. Rose wasn't a flighty miss, and Alice could trust her girl ... she just hoped she could trust this dashing young Canadian whose name cropped up in

Rose's letters now and then. All the same, she'd bet a tinker's cuss that Eldon McCloud and his mates were going to be included in this house party in Kent. For a second, she felt an unexpected envy sweep through her mind. How wonderful it would be to be in the company of such people. To be young and free and easy and living the high life. How lucky for Rose...

The baby inside her gave a great lurch, reminding her that she had responsibilities and that they weren't going to go away. The time for Alice Chase to go chasing a dream of being young and free and living the high life were long gone.

'Where have you gone, Mother?' she heard Walter say gently. 'You're nodding, and you should put your feet up and have a rest.'

She gave him a quick smile. 'It's the heat of the fire making me sleepy.'

'Well, nobody's stopping you, girl. Once the babby's here you'll have plenty of disturbed nights, so make the most of it while you can.'

'I'll write back to Rose first,' she said, rousing herself. 'I want to let her know she has our blessing for the visit with her friends. Then I'll put my feet up.'

By the time the weekend arrived, Rose and Elsie were in a high state of excitement. Eldon and his buddies had arranged to borrow a car that was large enough for the six of them to arrive in style at Daphne's home. The weather was still bitterly cold, but the biting wind had dispersed much of the snow by now. They left early on Friday evening and planned to return late on Sunday evening which would give them nearly two full days. Rose was determined not to put a damper on things by mentioning Peter Kelsey again, especially since her mother's hasty reply to her letter had told her to enjoy the weekend with her friends.

Eldon was the driver, and although there were no street lights to guide them, and the car had its lights mostly blanked off, the roads were clear enough with Daphne's instructions, until they reached the open country. She directed him amid much laughter, and after an hour and a half's driving through darkened lanes, they turned into a long, tree-lined driveway leading up to an imposing mansion.

'Blimey, Daphne, you weren't kidding, were you?' Elsie said in awe. 'Your folks ain't royalty, are they?'

'Don't be silly, of course not, although Daddy did have a commission in India for a while. We lived there when I was a child.'

'Have you got any more surprises you haven't told us about?' Rose asked.

Daphne laughed easily. 'None that I'm aware of, darling.'

In the seat next to Eldon, Rose squirmed a little. She could never get used to the free and easy way Daphne referred to people as darling. It was a word that should be reserved for somebody special, not bandied about between friends and acquaintances. In Daphne's world it was simply an affectionate term, but to Rose, using it so freely made it meaningless.

'Don't let it worry you,' Eldon whispered, putting his hand briefly over hers. 'It's just her way.'

'Are you a thought-reader now?' she asked.

'Sometimes. When I need to be.'

Daphne broke in again, as the car neared the heavy oak front door of what looked like a very large house, even in the dark.

'By the way,' she said casually. 'Just so you'll know. You refer to my dad as Sir Dennis, and my mother as Lady Vera.'

'*Bleedin' 'ell*, Daphne!' Elsie squeaked.

But by then it was too late to say anything more. The car had come to a halt, and the Canadians were opening the doors and hauling their large bulks out of the vehicle. Daphne ran lightly up the flight of steps and pulled on a door pull. After a moment the door was opened by an elderly man whom Daphne called Jeeves.

'It's not his real name,' she said with a giggle as they all went inside. 'I called him that when I was a child and it stuck. We all call him that now, even his wife. Heaven knows what their real name is.'

'None of this is real, is it?' Rose murmured to Eldon. 'I feel as though I'm living in some kind of a play. Somebody will pinch me in a minute and I'll wake up back in Bramwell.'

The next moment two elegant people came out of the drawing room, the woman holding out her arms to Daphne, the man extending a gracious welcome to the group. This then, was Sir Dennis and Lady Vera Poole. After a moment Lady Vera turned to Daphne's friends.

'Welcome, all of you. Come into the drawing room and take a glass of sherry to warm you after your drive, and then Mrs Jeeves will show you your rooms. Dinner will be in about an hour. It will be very relaxed this evening.'

It was all so civilized, so genteel. Was there a war going on elsewhere in the world? Was England in danger of being invaded by the Germans, or was it all a dream? For the life of her, Rose couldn't get the bizarre nature of it all out of her head. Lady Vera was a very gracious hostess who made herself and Elsie feel as much at home as either of them could in such grand surroundings. It was only when she heard Sir Dennis talking seriously to the Canadian airmen that it was clear he was no landed gentry without a clue of what was going on in the world. The questions he asked were pertinent and informed, and it occurred to her that Eldon and Buzz and Dean weren't half as awed by it all as the girls.

Rose admired them for that. Perhaps living in a country that had no aristocracy, and whose king and queen were far removed from their everyday lifestyle, had made them more relaxed at meeting people in all walks of life. While for someone like her, Rose Chase, saw-mill worker's daughter, living in a Somerset village, the thought of rubbing shoulders with even minor nobility was something unimaginable. And yet here she was...

Across the room she caught sight of Eldon in earnest discussion with Sir Dennis, and she felt a flood of something inexplicable in her veins. As if aware of her glance, he looked her way for a moment, flashing her a small smile, and his eyes flickered with an answering glow before he returned to his conversation. But it was enough. In that moment it was enough.

She drained her sherry too quickly, and felt her head spin. She realized to her surprise that Elsie also seemed fairly at ease with Lady Vera now as they talked about places in London's East End that sounded quite incomprehensible to Rose.

'Rose's mother comes from London,' Daphne put in. 'She went to Somerset to marry Rose's father and never went back.'

'How very romantic,' Lady Vera said.

'It wasn't quite like that,' Rose said with a smile. 'But I always did think it was romantic for two such unlikely people to meet and fall in love.'

'It's the same in wartime, my dear,' Lady Vera went on conversationally. 'People are thrown together who would never have met otherwise, and great friendships can be formed. Although it would be unwise to forget that when it's all over, most people go back to their roots, unlike your parents who chose to make a new life for themselves.'

Was that a tiny message to her daughter and her friends, Rose wondered? Daphne certainly seemed to have her head on the right way round. She wouldn't be caught out by any wartime romance unless it was of her own choosing. Elsie was always ready for a bit of a flirt with no thoughts of any serious entanglements. While Rose ... what did Rose want, she asked herself?

'Shall we get settled in our rooms, boys and girls?' Daphne said gaily as the empty sherry glasses were being replaced on a tray.

As if by magic, which was presumably the way things happened here, a smiling Mrs Jeeves appeared to escort them all up the curving staircase to the various rooms on the first floor landing.

At their request, Elsie and Rose were to share a room, while Daphne had her old room. The Canadians each had a separate room. As Elsie had surmised there was no lack of accommodation here.

'What do you think Rose?' Elsie said, bouncing up and down on the bed she had chosen for herself. 'A bit different to the nurses' home, ain't it?'

'I'll say. It is beautiful, though. I can't wait to see the grounds in daylight, especially the lake Daphne mentioned. Our lake's frozen at home now. Well, the lake in the middle of the village, I mean.'

Just saying it, seemed to emphasize the difference between them all. Hadn't Alice said the River Thames was frozen over as well? The sherry must have gone to her head. For a moment Rose found herself wondering how it would be if everything in the world was frozen. Frozen in time and space. No yesterday, no today, no tomorrow. Just here and now. There would have been no war, and no sense of impending doom. There would also have been no Eldon McCloud on her horizon to stir her senses.

'You've gone all peculiar, Rose,' Elsie said as she seemed to jerk upright. 'They're only people, for Gawd's sake. My old gran used to say you should imagine 'em with no clothes on and that'll bring 'em down to size.'

'I don't think that's very polite!' Rose said with a laugh. 'Anyway, I wasn't worried about Daphne's parents. I think they're really nice.'

Nor was she imagining anybody else in this house with no clothes on, either, even though Elsie's flippant words had put a different kind of image into her head. It was enough to fill her cheeks with colour, and it was an image she knew she would be better off without.

Daphne burst in on them as they were still hanging up the few things they had brought with them. She had a mischievous look on her face.

'You're a dark horse, aren't you, Daphne?' Rose said at once, hoping her flushed face would calm down soon. 'You didn't tell us you lived in a stately home!'

'Oh well, it's only a minor stately home,' she replied. 'There are far grander ones than this. My parents are very much into doing what they can for the community, though, and depending on what the War Office might want later on, they're talking about offering this place as a convalescent home for wounded servicemen if need be, and just living in one wing for the duration.'

'Blimey, I wouldn't want dozens of oiks sprawling over this place and ruining the carpets,' Elsie exclaimed. 'Although it might be all right if I was one of the nurses tending to all those boys! It would beat working in our hospital, wouldn't it?'

'You wouldn't get the chance,' Daphne said, throwing a pillow at her. 'Look, when you're ready, I'll show you over the house. The boys are keen to have a look as well before we go down for dinner.'

They did as she suggested, and after what Daphne had said about the house, Rose found herself looking at it with different eyes, imagining how wonderful it would be for wounded servicemen, recovering from their injuries, to be able to convalesce in a place like this. That was what folk with money could do – those who were public-spirited enough to make such a generous offer – and she admired the Pooles even more.

Twelve

Lucy came home shivering on a slippery Friday afternoon at the beginning of February with the news that Doctor Matt had arrived back at the Stacey's house for a few days' embarkation leave.

'I don't know why our Rose didn't hang on to him,' she said irreverently to her mother as she rubbed her hands in front of the fire to get the feeling back into them. 'Everybody knows he's the best catch in the village. It's a shame he only sees me as a kid, but at least there wasn't any awkwardness because of Rose. In fact, I'd say he hardly noticed me at all,' she finished on a moan.

'There's more to life than looking at young men, Lucy,' Alice said.

'Well, I don't know how else you get to marry them and have children if you don't look at them in the first place.'

She would dearly have loved to make a pert remark that not all babies were born by immaculate conception, but she didn't dare. Not only because of the religious significance, but because of the imminent birth of the new baby in the family. Making some kind of cute remark about babies would only emphasize the fact that her mum and dad had *done* it, and she didn't think it would go down too kindly with them to hear her being so cheeky. Besides, even though she could hardly ignore her mum's size now, how she had got that way was none of her business – nor something she really cared to think about!

'Did you say embarkation leave?' Walter said sharply.

Lucy jumped. 'Well, I think that was it. It was a long word, anyway.'

'His family will be anxious for him if that's the case,' Alice said. 'There's no knowing where any of them will be sent from now on.'

'It'll be France,' Walter said knowledgeably. 'That's always the first stop for infantry fodder.'

'He's a doctor, Dad, not infantry.'

'It makes no difference what fancy title he's got. Foot soldier or doctor, if he's needed in the Front Line, that's where he'll be sent. Same as young Jack, who's chafing at the bit to go, according to our Mick. There'll be no stopping him once he gets his orders.'

Alice shivered. All this talk of war, who was going where and when, and what was going to happen when they got there, was all that men seemed to talk about these days. It was bad enough with the sombre words of the politicians on the wireless, and the endless newspaper reports. She was glad she wasn't a fly on the wall at the Pig and Whistle, having to listen to it every evening when all the men of the village got together. Not that she could be a fly on any wall nowadays, she thought, as the baby inside her gave a hefty kick. It would take a crane to lift her anywhere.

'I'm making some tea,' she said shortly. 'And Lucy, remember you're helping Bobby tonight. Thank goodness the school's opening for half days next week so he can get out from under my feet.'

She heard herself grumbling, and bit her lip. She was more weary than she let on to her family, but sometimes it just washed over her. She had never been one for sitting down and wasting time, but she did so more and more often these days, snatching five minutes here and there to put her feet up and close her eyes. It wasn't natural. It wasn't her. It wasn't the woman she wanted to be.

The midwife kept telling her cheerfully that all would be well once the bab was born. As if she didn't know that! As if she hadn't already had four of them, and knew exactly how much of a toll nine months of carrying took out of a woman. But she was older now, and even these five years since she had had Bobby had seen a change in her body and her moods. She wasn't young and sprightly any more, and she was just as likely to send the midwife off with short shrift as look at her.

Just a couple more weeks, she thought, and then it will all be behind us. The new baby will be here, and I'll be back to my health and strength, and I'll wonder why I made such a fuss. God willing.

She tried to believe it, but as she heard Bobby start to wail that he didn't want to do any more school work and he didn't like Lucy any more, she slammed the kettle down on the stove and got out cups and saucers for the tea. She ignored Lucy's complaining as she snapped at her to help Bobby with his letters.

Everybody had to do their bit in whatever way they could, here in the home and everywhere else, according to the government's directions. Doing what they could, depending on their means and where they lived. Growing vegetables, keeping chickens for their eggs, making do and mending ... which was exactly what they had always done in the country, Alice thought scornfully. It took common sense to do what you could for your family. It didn't take pompous words from ministers to tell you that.

'Are you all right, Alice?' she heard Walter say in the kitchen behind her. 'You're getting ratty again, old girl. Slow down a bit for God's sake, or you'll meet yourself coming back.'

She was about to snap back at him when she met the concern in his eyes. He was worried for her, and it wasn't fair to worry him like this. They all had worries these days. Tom was settled again now, providing the war didn't go on long enough for him to be called up. Rose – well, Rose was an adult and had made her own decisions and Alice couldn't blame her for that.

Alice only admitted to herself that she missed

Rose more than she had expected to, but you couldn't lean on children for ever. It was the wrong way of things. Lucy was still at the flighty stage and not the confidante that Rose had been, and Bobby was becoming more and more fretful because of the enforced school holiday that had begun to pall, and they were all getting on each other's nerves.

She leaned against Walter for a moment. 'Sometimes I wonder if this baby will ever be born,' she said.

He gave a short laugh. 'That's one you can be sure of, woman. It's not going to stay in there for ever! And there's no hurrying it, as you well know. Come and sit down and I'll make the tea.'

She smiled weakly. 'No more than two teaspoonfuls in the pot then. We don't want it as black as soot.'

'No, but we'll have it strong enough to taste while we still can. If the bloody government decides to ration it in a couple of months' time, we'll all be drinking it as thin as crickets' piss.'

'*Walter!*'

But it was no good. As his eyes widened in mock surprise that he'd said anything amiss, her shoulders began to shake, and then they were laughing helplessly and holding one another up. They were still there, tears rolling down Alice's face, when Lucy came into the kitchen to find a pencil, and shook her head at the sight of them.

'You two are more like a couple of infants

sometimes,' she said, stalking away from them. Which only made them laugh even harder.

Alice lay in bed that night, aware of the great mound of her belly halfway down the bed, and of Walter snoring gently beside her. She was ashamed of her earlier outburst, the way she always was. She was also calmer now. She rested her hand gently on her middle, imagining she could feel the baby breathing. She imagined she was stroking his hair and feeling the velvet curve of his cheek. Or her cheek. On nights like this, when she managed to get herself into a comfortable position, and all the world was quiet and at rest outside, she could let herself drift into a state of calm that eventually ended in dreamland.

In her dreams she was no longer heavy and awkward, nor just days away from the greatest feat of endurance a woman had to undergo. She was young and bright, slim and animated, an eager young woman in her salad days with Tilly. Sometimes she wasn't even herself, and Tilly too faded smilingly into the background. Then she was Rose, enjoying far more than the restricted pleasures open to a young woman of Alice's own generation. She was somewhere in a great mansion, mixing with different people and expanding her horizons. She was Rose, discovering life. Discovering love.

The dream never continued beyond that point. Something always woke her, whether it was a snore from Walter, or a wild animal scooting in the bushes in the night, or the hoot of an owl. Something always brought her back to reality, and rightly so. She wasn't Rose and never could be, but she had to admit that in those brief, half-waking moments, Alice felt a genuine twist of envy for all that was open to her daughter now. Such thoughts were just as quickly followed by the knowledge that Rose was only living this life because the country was at war, and how could any sane mother envy such a situation? All the same, she would always wish a mental good luck to Rose, before falling into a deeper sleep.

Rose sometimes felt intuitively that her mother was thinking about her. Alice had been very young when Rose was born, and they had always been close, and now her mum was going to go through childbirth all over again. Her friend Elsie thought it was a bit creepy that two middle-aged people should start having babies again at their age.

'They're not dinosaurs, and what's creepy about it?' Rose said crossly. Whatever her own feelings, she wasn't about to have her parents criticised by the likes of Elsie Venn!

They were fetching their outdoor clothes from the shared bedroom at the Poole house, in readiness for taking a walk around the grounds, and maybe skating on the lake. *Sliding* on it, more like, as Elsie had commented.

'I didn't mean nothing,' she said hastily now, seeing Rose's glare. 'I suppose I think your

216

mum's quite brave really, wanting to go through it again when she's got grown-up kids.'

'We've got Bobby too,' Rose reminded her. 'He's only just five, so it's not really like starting again.'

'Well, I don't ever want to have kids. Smelly little bleeders, they are, either puking at one end or plopping at the other.'

Rose began to laugh. Elsie could be coarse and infuriating, but you couldn't stay mad at her for long. And this wasn't the time, anyway. They were here to enjoy themselves, and that was what they intended to do.

'Come on, let's go, or Daphne will wonder what we're doing up here.'

'It ain't Daphne you're worried about, is it?' Elsie said slyly. 'You don't want to spend any more time away from lover-boy than you have to.'

'Idiot!' Rose said.

She was right, though. The more time Rose spent in Eldon's company, the more she liked it, and she didn't need to be clairvoyant to know he felt the same. It was exciting and scary at the same time, partly because Rose had been here before. First with poor Peter, and then Matt. Each time, she had thought she was in love with them, and how was she to know whether or not this feeling she had for Eldon would just go the same way? How did anybody know how it really felt to be in love? Or even if it would last beyond the first rush of excitement?

The two girls ran lightly down the richly

217

carpeted staircase to where the others were already congregated. The boys looked up with cheers and slow handclaps and teasing remarks about how long it took for two girls to finish gossiping before they were ready. And Rose looked directly into Eldon McCloud's laughing brown eyes as he reached for her hand as she got to the last stair. She felt his fingers curl around hers, and felt her heart pound with a reckless sense of going towards something that couldn't be stopped.

'Come on, all of you,' Daphne said impatiently. 'We don't want to waste a minute of the daylight and we've already dawdled half the morning away. Mother's preparing a light lunch for us when we get back from the lake.'

'How far is this lake?' Elsie said.

'She's complaining already,' Rose said. 'If you lived in the country like I do, you'd be used to tramping about the fields and woods.'

'She should try the Canadian forests,' Buzz put in. 'I was a lumberjack before I joined this outfit and walked for miles every day just to get to work.'

Elsie yelled. 'Are you all ganging up on me? I can walk, you know. I've got bleedin' legs – sorry, your ladyship,' she said quickly to Daphne, seeing her frown.

'I'm used to it, but don't let my parents hear you swearing, or they'll wonder what kind of company I'm keeping,' she was told.

The small incident was brushed aside as they went outside, to be met by the crisp morning

218

air. The temperature was decidedly Arctic compared to a normal English February morning, so it made sense to link arms and stride out briskly in order to keep warm. The grounds of the property were magnificent, and Rose couldn't help remembering what Daphne had said about her parents opening it up as a possible convalescent home if necessary. As it surely would be. With a sliver of insight, she knew that this place, relatively near to the south coast where wounded servicemen would be returning home by air or sea, would be a haven to them all. Rose found herself hoping fervently that it wouldn't be necessary, while feeling certain in her bones that it would.

'What are you thinking so deeply about?' Eldon asked her, once they had skirted a small copse and made their first tentative steps onto the frozen lake. The sun gleamed dully onto the surface now, but Daphne assured them the ice was so thick there was no danger of any of them breaking through.

'I was thinking about something Daphne said, that her parents were considering allowing this house to be used as a possible convalescent home. It takes two very special people to offer such a thing, doesn't it?'

'I'd say there are a lot of special people around here,' Eldon said. 'I'm holding on to one of them right now, with no intention of letting her go.'

Rose caught her breath. His words were two-edged. All the Canadians seemed to be sporty types, and he was used to skating in Canada, but she had only ever ventured onto the village pond. He was physically holding on to her now, but she knew very well he meant more than that. And she wanted him to hold on to her. She wanted it more than she had ever wanted anything in her life before.

'Hold me tight then,' she said huskily, and somehow they were gliding across the lake in perfect unison, and words were superfluous.

It was not so easy for Elsie. She was being held up between Buzz and Dean and screaming with excitement and mock fear as her feet kept sliding from under her, despite Daphne's bellowing instructions.

'I'll be black and blue before I'm finished,' she screeched out, as she finally gave up the attempt and landed flat on her backside. The boys hauled her to her feet again, and after a lot of arguments and discussion they made their muscular arms into a cradle, and glided across the ice with her between them.

'Look at her,' Daphne said, laughing. 'Isn't she a scream? You've got the idea though, Rose!'

So she did, but it wasn't so difficult when you were relaxed and had confidence in your partner. She felt Eldon squeeze her arm, and she felt a glow that had nothing to do with the healthy exhilaration that filled them all.

But they had finally had enough exercise, and they tramped back towards the house, chattering noisily. It was so easy to forget why they were all here, how they had all met, and what circumstances had brought them together. So easy to forget about the war. It was only when the drone of a plane from a nearby airfield caught their attention that Rose remembered Peter, and drew in her breath. How could they all be enjoying themselves so much, when ships were being sunk and men were dying? And how could they not, a small voice inside her said? What good did it do to them to wallow in misery? It didn't bring them back.

'Laying ghosts?' Eldon said quietly while the others were still trying to decide what kind of plane it was, and joking that they hoped it was one of theirs.

'Something like that,' she said, thankful that he understood without the need for explanation.

Peter Kelsey had been part of her childhood and her growing-up, and now he was gone and she would never see him again. It was something that had to be faced, and in wartime, such things were going to occur more and more. By the time the weekend was over, Rose felt as if she had come a very long way in a few days. It had been the very best thing to do, to get away from the hospital and be among friends, and in the company of Daphne's very genial parents. It had been the very best thing to realize that she could fall in love again, if she wanted to.

As soon as she had a few spare moments in between her hospital shifts, Rose wrote home to tell her family all about her weekend. It had been special in many ways, and she knew Alice and Lucy would love hearing about the big house and the elegant furniture, and Bobby would like to hear about the lake and how they had gone skating on it. She didn't mention any of the Canadians in particular, just that there had been several of the airmen with them, and it had just been a group of friends who had been invited to Daphne's house party.

'I wish I could meet some Canadian airmen,' Lucy complained. 'We haven't got anybody interesting down here. Uncle Mick said there were some Land Girls billetted to Dawson's Farm recently, and I think I saw one of them in the village today. She looked about my age. I think maybe I should join something,' she added vaguely.

'You're doing well enough where you are, young lady,' her father said sharply. 'And you'll be needed at home when your mother's time comes, so don't go getting any fancy ideas about joining up.'

'It's not like doing war work to be a glorified nursemaid, is it?'

'It's essential for the doctor's wife to have help, and your sister wasn't too proud to do it,' Alice put in. 'Besides, I thought you liked looking after Mollie.'

'I do. But when I hear about our Rose having such a good time at her friend Daphne's house it makes me envious. I know I only worked for the Frankleys as a skivvy in their big house, but I know how the gentry enjoy themselves.'

'Yes, well, you just remember that envy is one of the seven deadly sins, my girl, and be satisfied with your lot,' Walter told her. 'I'm sure Rose doesn't think she's enjoying herself when she's emptying bedpans and doing all sorts of unpleasant tasks for the hospital patients.'

Lucy allowed herself a smile. 'She's welcome to that,' she admitted.

'So now that you've cheered up, go and make your mother a cup of tea,' Walter told her.

'I don't want any tea,' Alice said at once. 'I've had heartburn all evening and tea will only make it worse. A drop of dyspepsia mixture will do me more good. I'd have a lie down if I thought it would help, but it's hard for me to get comfortable any more.'

Once her mother started on about her various aches and pains, Lucy knew it was time for her to leave them to it. Not that she was unsympathetic, but hearing about all the problems involving the imminent birth of the baby was making her slightly squeamish. She wished Rose was here. Rose would be far more helpful when things started to happen. Rose was a born nurse, while she was anything but. Coping with the Stacey baby was nursing enough for her, and she prayed guiltily that when Alice's labour began, she would be well and truly away from the house.

If she did but know it, Alice thought exactly the same. Lucy was a good girl, but she would be hopeless in an emergency. Anyway, babies didn't arrive very quickly, and there would be ample time, once things began, to send for the midwife. Helen had already said she would be glad to have Bobby to stay at their house while Alice was laying-in, and like the dutiful sister-in-law that she was, Helen arrived every afternoon now to check on her.

'She makes me feel like a prize sow,' Alice complained to Walter one evening when Helen's chatter had exhausted her. 'She means well, but I'd really like to be left alone sometimes instead of having to answer her endless questions. She keeps looking at me in a peculiar way too.'

'What's that supposed to mean?' Walter said, starting to laugh. 'Can't people look at you now?'

'Not the way she does, as if she's expecting me to pop at any minute. I swear that if we had a telephone in the house, she'd be sitting next to it, ready to pounce on it and send for the midwife at the first twinge.'

'She's only looking out for you, woman. Would you rather she never came to see you at all? She thinks of herself as the sister you never had.'

That honour belonged to Tilly, not Helen. The thought was in Alice's head before she could stop it.

'Oh well, I know she means well,' she said swiftly. 'I'll tell you something though, Walter. This one had better be the last.'

He chuckled. 'Well, short of cutting off the old pecker, I don't know what I can do about that, old girl.'

Her smart retort at his coarseness was cut short as Bobby tottered downstairs, woken by the chattering below, his eyes still heavy with sleep.

'What's a pecker?' he asked.

February was surely going to be the coldest one on record for many years. The fields were concrete-hard with frost, too solid for the sharpest fork to dig through, and on the farms the cattle huddled inside barns for warmth. Milking them took all the strength and stamina of the Land Girls who were learning to do tasks the men had now left behind. In Bramwell the village pond remained steadfastly frozen, and Walter Chase's chickens scratched for scraps in vain on the hard ground of their coop. If the whole country seemed to be held in the grip of an icy winter, at least it seemed to give a little respite to the progress of the war. It seemed to be more talk than action, except on the Russian Front and the invasion of Finland. That was a bugger, according to the men who gathered for their nightly jar at the Pig and Whistle. You didn't want to get tangled up with the Ruskies if you could avoid it.

Alice Chase was less concerned with Ruskies than with keeping her own family warm. That included the coming baby, and the clothes she was busily knitting for it. Poor little bab, she found herself thinking, due to be born into a wintry white world where barely a hint of sunlight got through the grey clouds these days.

Bobby and Lucy didn't seem to feel the cold so much. Bobby was playing with his toy soldiers before going to bed, and Lucy was putting the final stitches into a new skirt she was making for herself. Lucy was certainly adept with her needle. There were also half a dozen baby nightgowns upstairs, that Lucy had stitched painstakingly. The sewing workbox that Walter had made for her birthday last year, polished to such perfection, had never been wasted, thought Alice approvingly.

She was about to say as much when she felt a pain that was instantly recognizable. Almost at the same moment she was aware of a warm dampness where she sat, and she quickly counted to ten before she spoke calmly to Lucy.

'I think it would be a good idea to put Bobby's outdoor clothes on and take him to Auntie Helen's with the little bag of things I've put ready for him, Lucy. If Uncle Mick's there, ask him to fetch your father from the pub. If not, you'll have to go there yourself and get someone to call your father out. Then go to the midwife's and tell her I'd like her to come, please, but that there's no great hurry.'

She said it all as pleasantly as she could, making sure the children realized there was no great urgency, but that they needed to do as she said.

Lucy leaped up at once. Her heart was hammering in her chest as she urged Bobby to put his toys away, saying he was going to stay with

Auntie Helen for the night as he'd been promised. She desperately wished she could stay there too, but she knew there was no chance of that. She might be needed here.

'Come on, Bobby, get a move on. It'll be our little adventure to go out in the dark, won't it?' she said, her lips shaking, despite herself.

She didn't really think so at all. She didn't want to go, yet she didn't want to stay. She was filled with panic, just as she knew she'd be. It was her mother who was the calm one. Her mother, who was about to begin the great adventure, if that's how you cared to think of it. One look at Alice's steady eyes, and she was ashamed of her momentary jitters as she told Bobby to kiss his mum, and they'd be on their way. Then she hugged Alice, mumbled a whispered good luck, and took the boy out of the door and into the cold, dark night.

Thirteen

Walter and Mick were arguing the toss with a couple of cronies over what Henry Kelsey might want done about his son. You couldn't bring him home for a burial if he was fish-bait somewhere at the bottom of the North Sea, but on the other hand you couldn't let a boy's death go unnoticed, especially one who had lived in the village all his life. The vicar might well have something to say about a brief service in the boy's memory, but since neither Henry nor Peter had been churchgoers, he might also take a dim view of such a suggestion.

Neither brother looked up from their ale at the sound of another slight commotion at the door. It was only when a local farmhand called out to attract the Chase brothers' attention that they took any notice.

'Your girl's here for you, Walter. Looks like your missus is ready to drop her bab, and you're to go for the midwife sharpish.'

Walter left his pint half-drunk and made for the door, with Mick close behind.

'There's no need for you to come,' Walter said shortly before he turned to see Lucy shivering outside. 'What's happening, girl?'

'I've taken our Bobby to Auntie Helen's, and we're to fetch the midwife,' she repeated the words of the farmhand. 'Mum said it's not urgent, but it's time.'

'Then we'd best get on,' Walter said. 'We'll report as soon as there's any news, Mick.'

'Ah well, then, good luck,' Mick said impotently.

Walter nodded. 'Alice will be all right. She's as strong as any farm animal.' He spoke clumsily, saying the only thing that he thought would make sense to a vet.

'You're a bastard, aren't you, Walter?' he thought he heard his brother say, but by then he was striding away from the pub with Lucy at his heels. Minutes later they were hammering on the door of Mrs Gould, the local midwife. She answered it in her own time, peering out into the darkness at whoever was interrupting her evening.

'Is that you, Walter Chase? Your wife's time has come then, has it? You and your girl get on home, and I'll fetch my bag and follow you directly I've finished my supper. I doubt there's any need to rush.'

'Old trout,' Walter muttered as she closed the door on them.

Lucy giggled nervously at his words. 'Mum will be all right though, won't she, Dad? At her age, I mean.'

'Good God, of course she'll be all right. A woman her age has got a good few child-bearing years in her yet, and this isn't the kind of conversation I care to be having with you, young lady.'

'I'm not a kid, Dad,' Lucy said, nettled, even though she knew she had started this. 'All the same, Mum's not as young as when she had Rose and me and Tom, is she? Nor even when she had Bobby.'

In answer, he caught hold of her arm and hurried her along the frozen lanes as quickly as it was safe to do so.

'You're a sensible girl, Lucy, and once the old trout gets to the house and gives her instructions, you just do as she asks and I'm sure the new bab will be here by morning.'

'I won't have to do anything, will I?' Lucy said in a fright. When Bobby was born, the rest of them had all been sent off to Helen and Mick's until it was all over. It was scary enough that she was expected to stay in the house this time, let alone be involved in the smallest way.

Walter grunted. 'You can boil a kettle or two, and fetch towels, or whatever else Mrs Gould wants, can't you? I doubt it'll be anything more than that. Don't worry. Your mother always said birthing was like shelling peas and there's no reason to think this one will be any different.'

Lucy fervently hoped he was right. All she wanted was to close her eyes and ears to everything that was going to be happening in the house during the next hours. She felt horribly guilty to feel this way, but she just knew she wasn't equipped for this. She wished desperately that Rose was here. Rose was so capable, while she was like a bag full of jelly.

When they returned to the house they found Alice leaning over the sink in the scullery, a bowl of washing-up half done. Her forehead was beaded with sweat, and her knuckles were white from clinging on to the stone surface.

'Is it getting bad, my dear?' Walter said at once.

Alice gave up the attempt at a reassuring smile, and gave a grimace instead. 'I'd say it's a toss-up as to whether this one comes out with a rush, or whether it's going to take forever,' she said through gritted teeth.

'Well, you can be sure of one thing, old girl.

It won't take forever. There's only one way for it to go,' he replied, attempting to be jolly.

'That's easy for you to say,' Alice snapped with a burst of spirit. 'The man always has the easy job, while the woman has to put up with the consequences and get on with what he started.'

Lucy thought her dad was going to throw a fit at this, but instead she saw him put his arms around her mother. He put his hand over her swollen belly and rubbed it gently, before whispering in her ear.

'It takes two, my dear, and I'm going through it with you.'

Alice leaned back against him for a moment, and Lucy felt acute embarrassment at seeing them like this. They could shout and rant at one another, but this moment was so tender, so intimate, that she felt like an intruder in her own house. She shouldn't be here, witnessing this, and she wished she could be anywhere else rather than stuck in the middle of it all.

'Mum, leave that washing-up. I can do it,' she said jerkily. 'Shouldn't you be sitting down, or lying down, or something?'

'I'm better walking about for a while, love,' Alice said with an effort. 'This has been going on for hours already, but I'd probably be better walking about in the bedroom, then I can get on to the bed when the midwife comes. She won't be long, will she, Walter?'

She bit her lips tightly together as she finished speaking, and hoped her sudden sense of

231

anxiety hadn't sounded in her voice. It was five years since Bobby was born, and she couldn't remember the labour pains being this severe. She had always been thankful that she had never suffered too badly with all her children, but this one, this last one, was different. She was a stoical woman and hadn't bothered them with the fact that she had already been having intermittent labour pains for hours already. By now she was enveloped in the pain and there was no respite. There was no counting the minutes in between, yet there was no sense that the birth was imminent either. Something was wrong, and she knew it. She prayed that the midwife would come soon. She couldn't do this alone.

'Shall I make you some tea, Mum?' she heard Lucy's shaky voice say.

She nodded. 'That would be nice, love. Help me upstairs, Walter.'

She didn't want tea, but it would give Lucy something to do. She felt a momentary sympathy for Lucy, who shouldn't be here at all. But she couldn't even spare more than a moment's thought for her daughter with the turmoil going on inside her. She felt as if she was moving towards the stairs like a very old woman. What was wrong with her, she thought, in a real panic now? She tried to push her thoughts ahead as she and Tilly used to do when they were girls.

This time tomorrow we'll go to the park and listen to the band. This time next week perhaps we'll go to the pictures. There's a good one on at the Odeon with that dreamboat you like. This time next year we'll find the man of our dreams and get married and have babies and live happily ever after...

A sudden pain, sharper than the rest, brought Alice back to reality, and she clung to the banister rail for a moment until she felt able to put one foot in front of the other again. Walter's arms were supporting her all the way, but climbing these stairs seemed like climbing a mountain, and that young girl with her eager, high hopes had disappeared for ever. Her eyes blurred with a kind of sorrow for that girl, but as Walter murmured words of encouragement she tried to think positively.

This time tomorrow it would all be over and she would be holding a new baby in her arms. This time tomorrow ... if she was still here to see it.

She gasped as the new thought thundered through her brain. Or perhaps it wasn't new. Perhaps it had been there all along. Perhaps all the times she had thought about Tilly recently had been an omen. As she reached the landing she turned blindly to Walter and clung to him while tears flooded her eyes.

'Hey, come on now, old girl. This isn't like you,' he said roughly. 'God knows I'd have the bab for you if I could, and apart from it being a bloody miracle, we could put on a bloody freak show and we'd make our fortune, wouldn't we?'

'I'm sorry,' she gasped again, too tense to see the funny side. 'You know I want this baby so much, don't you, Walter?'

'Well, of course I do. We both want it. For God's sake, Alice, don't start apologizing for getting in the family way!' Uneasy now, he steered her towards their bedroom, not understanding the macabre direction of her thoughts.

'I don't want to leave you,' she mumbled, but so softly that he couldn't hear the words, and he made her sit down on their bed while he shouted down to Lucy to bring up that tea as soon as it was ready.

He didn't want bloody tea either, but it would give Alice something else to think about to help take the wild look from her eyes, he was thinking. He had never seen her look quite like this before, and agonizing thoughts he had never thought before began swirling around in his head.

'What can I do?' he said hoarsely.

'Just stay with me,' Alice said between gasps.

'I'll do that until the old trout arrives. Once she's here, I'll be ordered out as usual. She'll insist that this is woman's work, and no place for a man here then.'

'Well, there damn well should be,' Alice said sharply. 'Perhaps then they'll know what a woman's going through.'

Walter gave her the ghost of a smile, even though her grip on his hand was draining the blood from his fingers and making him sweat. But while she still had the guts to give back as

234

good as she got, he knew they'd get through this. A few minutes later, to his utter relief, he heard a commotion downstairs and Lucy was calling out that Mrs Gould had arrived.

The woman came bustling up the stairs, the aroma of her supper still lingering on her breath and clothes.

'Now then, how are we doing, missus?' she asked Alice directly.

'I think the bab wants to stay where it is,' Alice gasped.

Mrs Gould gave a hearty laugh. 'Well, there's no danger of that, is there? Let's take a look at you, my dear. One way or another we'll have him out of his cosy nest before morning.'

'He's not a bird,' Alice said crossly.

Mrs Gould laughed again, as if everything Alice said was funny. She jerked her head towards Walter, who was thankful to extricate himself from his wife's grasp and escape downstairs.

'I swear if that woman's going to cackle like a hyena all night long, I'll be had up for blue murder by morning,' he told Lucy savagely.

Lucy smothered a sob. 'Mum is going to be all right, isn't she, Dad?'

He took proper notice of her frightened young face then, and saw the tears she tried not to shed. He hugged her briefly, and then busied himself with the tea she still hadn't managed to prepare.

'Your mother's a strong woman, Lucy, and none of this is new to her, even if she's a bit older now than the last time. You needn't fret yourself, girl, and the pity of it is that you're having to be here at all.'

'I could still go to Auntie Helen's,' Lucy said hopefully.

Walter shook his head. 'Neither of us is going to desert your mother. Now then, do you want to take this tea upstairs or do you think you'll drop it?'

Before the girl could answer, Mrs Gould came clattering down the stairs again. Her face wasn't quite so cheerful now.

'There's nothing to worry about, but it might be a good idea if one of you fetches the doctor,' she said, her voice belying the calmness of the words.

'What's wrong?' Walter said at once. 'Tell me, woman.'

'I can't be certain how far it's gone, but it seems as if the bab's turned around and is coming out breech first. Only it seems to be stuck, and she'll need expert help. So which one of you's going for Doctor Stacey?'

'I'll go,' Lucy said through chattering lips. 'Dad will want to stay here.'

Walter was already running up the stairs, ignoring Mrs Gould's tut-tutting at such unseemly behaviour when a woman was in labour. He didn't give a tinker's cuss for that right now. Alice needed him, and he needed to be with her.

Lucy had thrown on her hat and coat, and was struggling to fasten her boots even before her dad reached the top of the stairs. Her heart was in her mouth as she sped back along the frozen lanes towards the village and the Staceys' house. She heard the catcalls of several youths staggering home from the Pig and Whistle as they threatened to block her way, and she managed to resist screaming at them as she dodged past them.

'Snooty bitch!' she heard them call after her.

She didn't care. She had a stitch in her side now and her heart was tight in her chest. All she wanted was to get to the Staceys' house and have Doctor Stacey's reassuring voice telling her not to worry and that her mum and the baby were going to be all right. She didn't want to imagine what was happening back at their own house now. The night was very dark, and it was only the whiteness of the frosty, snow-covered ground that let her see where she was going. She slithered and slipped, and fervently thanked God when at last the bulk of the Staceys' house loomed up in front of her. She hammered on the door, and fumed as she waited for an answer. Because of the blackout regulations there was no sign of any light inside, and no indication that anyone had heard her, and her panic rose.

At last someone came to the door, opening it wider when he recognised her, and she almost fell inside the house as she stammered out her message to Matt.

'Can you ask your brother to come quickly?' she gasped, holding her side where the anguish of the stitch had intensified. 'The baby's coming and Mrs Gould's with Mum, but she says the doctor's needed. It's well known that she never sends for the doctor if she can help it, so he should hurry!'

She finished on a sob, and felt Matt gripping her arms that had suddenly gone limp. Until the moment she said it, she hadn't let herself think of the implications. But everybody in the village knew that old fusspot Gouldie thought herself as good as any doctor when it came to birthing, and never sent for him unless she thought she couldn't handle it herself. So it must be bad...

'Sit down while I get a few things together, Lucy,' she heard Matt say.

She looked at him stupidly. '*No*. I said we need Doctor Stacey!'

'Well, I'm afraid you can't have him. He's already out on another call, and unlikely to be back for hours, so you'll have to make do with me instead,' Matt said, as calmly as if he was soothing a child. He was already moving towards the surgery and starting to put things into a medical bag and she trailed behind him, her thoughts in a whirl.

'We don't want you!' she finally howled. 'Mum needs a proper doctor, and you're too young. It's not right.'

His patience snapped now. 'Keep quiet, girl, or you'll wake up the entire household. Do you think any of the wounded soldiers in my hospital care about how old I am when I'm patching up their broken bodies? I *am* a qualified doctor, for God's sake. How long has your mother been in labour?'

'I don't know. Hours, I think. She's the sort who would never say anything until it was necessary, so there's no real way of knowing.' She spoke jerkily, unwilling to admit to the fear she felt.

'Then we'd better get moving,' Matt said. He snapped the bag shut with a sound of finality, making her flinch. 'My brother's got the car, but in any case it's probably safer to walk on these roads. Off we go then, and stop looking so worried. Women have babies every day.'

He knew all about the theory, of course, but he didn't bother to add that he'd never actually delivered one before.

Walter ignored the midwife's less than discreet mutterings that it wasn't done for a man to be in a woman's bedroom when she was about to give birth. It didn't need a genius to see that Alice was getting increasingly distressed, and he needed to be with her, no matter what the old trout thought.

'Where's that bloody doctor?' he grated when Alice continued to moan and thresh, despite her efforts not to do so. The thick towel she held between her teeth stopped much of the sound getting through, but it dried her mouth so much she was constantly needing sips of water.

'Language, Walter,' she said feebly, removing the towel and running her tongue over her dry lips.

He wiped the sweat off her forehead, smoothing back her damp hair. Her eyes were dark with pain now, and the baby seemed no nearer to being born. He ached to take some of the suffering from her, while cursing himself for putting her in this position in the first place.

'It will be all right, Walter,' she whispered, gathering up enough strength to reassure him. 'My guardian angel will see to that.'

'What the bloody hell are you talking about?' he muttered, wondering if her mind was affected as well. He was a straight-talking man who had no truck with the likes of angels or the supernatural.

'Tilly,' Alice said in a clearer voice. 'She'll look after me.'

'She's a bloody doctor now then, is she?'

He swore to himself, wondering if he was going loopy as well, if he could be talking about Tilly as if she was still here. He almost glanced behind him to see if she was hovering near with her blasted strong scent and her flashy clothes. He resisted the temptation, just in case ... because if she had been there, all ghostly and white, and suspended several feet above the floor, he'd probably pass out from shock, and much good that would do his wife.

'I'm glad of any help I can get right now,' Alice said, her voice fading a little as the pain continued to consume her. She gripped his hand tightly again, making him wince, but at least her grip was real, he found himself thinking. It wasn't some bloody ghostly hand clinging on to his.

It seemed a goddamned eternity before they heard noises downstairs, and then he saw Lucy hovering at the bedroom door, while somebody else carrying a medical bag came towards his wife's bed.

'What's this?' he roared. 'We need a doctor, not a whippersnapper, still wet behind the ears.'

Matt took in the situation quickly. 'I'm used to insults, Mr Chase, and there's none that will keep me away from my duty. My brother's out attending the sick, so I'm taking his place tonight, and by the looks of things, you should be glad of it.'

'Now then, Mrs Chase, will you allow me to examine you?' he said gently to Alice, as he approached the bed.

'No, she damn well won't let you examine her.' Walter barred his way and continued bellowing. 'It's not decent for a boy of your age to do such things.'

Alice spoke wearily. 'Walter, I'm still in control of my own body, and of course Doctor Matt needs to examine me. It's what a doctor has to do, and if you want this baby to arrive safely in the world, you'll go downstairs with Lucy and let him and Mrs Gould get on with their work. I'm just thankful he's here, and will know what to do.'

She was exhausted after saying as much, but she still had enough strength to flash her eyes at Walter to let him know she meant what she said.

'Please come downstairs with me, Dad,' Lucy's scared little voice said from the doorway. 'We made some tea hours ago and it will need warming up.'

She wasn't interested in any such thing, but tea seemed the one constant thing in this entire horrific night so far. Walter finally nodded, and pushed past Matt to go downstairs with his daughter. He didn't deny that he was offering up a little prayer now, to anybody who was listening.

They were still huddled together on the sofa, with Lucy finally having fallen asleep, by the time they heard the cocks crowing in the farmyards round about. The dawn light had replaced the darkness with a glorious pink and golden glow. At the same time there was a thin wailing sound from the room upstairs, and Walter jerked into full awareness, to go rushing up the stairs to his bedroom. The midwife met him at the door, preventing him from going inside the bedroom.

'Give us a few minutes to tidy things up, man, and then you can go in.'

His voice was harsh. 'Don't brush me off with that, woman. Is the bab born and is my wife all right?'

'They're both well, though they both had a hard time of it,' Mrs Gould said carefully, still keeping him on the landing. 'I'll let the doctor tell you the details in a little while. Now go back downstairs and tell your daughter the good news that she's got a new brother.'

'It's a boy,' Walter said numbly, as if he'd never heard the word before.

Mrs Gould allowed herself a tired smile. 'And as big a bruiser as I'd want to deliver myself,' she said. 'You should be giving thanks to God that your wife's a capable woman and the young doc's got what it takes. And that's all I'm saying for now. Me and the doc have still got a bit of work to do, so go downstairs and get yourself a dram of brandy to wet the baby's head, and I'll call you when you can see your wife.'

She closed the door on him, but as he heard the continuing life-affirming sounds of the baby's wailing, he found himself doing as she said, stumbling back down the stairs like an automaton. Lucy had woken now, and she stood up, swaying slightly, still rubbing the sleep from her eyes, and almost afraid to ask.

'You've got a new brother,' Walter managed to choke out.

And then he did something he never thought he would ever do. As Lucy's eyes flooded with relief, he found himself lurching towards her, wrapping his arms around his daughter and sobbing his heart out on her shoulder. In those blistering moments of release he felt as though their roles were somehow reversed. She was now the parent and he the child.

'For a God-awful time I thought I was losing her,' he gabbled incoherently. 'I couldn't believe in anything any more. But your mother did. She always had faith. Even if the worst had happened, which thank God, it didn't, she always had the comfort of knowing she'd be with Tilly. I envy her that blind faith, Lucy, and I'll never forget this night.'

But he would, and deep down he knew he would. It was even a relief to know that time would come. You couldn't live with such high ideals for ever, and the time would come when he and Alice would be ranting and raving at one another again, and life would return to normality. But right now, at this blessed moment, he sent up a fervent prayer to God and Tilly and any other being in the far beyond, for giving his wife and son back to him.

Lucy finally extricated herself, acutely embarrassed at hearing her father weeping, and being sure that he'd want to forget it as quickly as possible.

'More tea?' she asked, for want of something to say.

He shook his head. 'I've never welcomed a child of mine into the world with tea yet,' he said, sounding more like his old self. 'It's brandy for me, and you can have a little drop with water if you've the stomach for it, girl. We'll offer that young doc a dram as well when he's finished upstairs.'

Lucy smiled. 'You don't think he's such a whippersnapper now then, Dad?'

'More like a bloody hero,' Walter said simply.

When they were finally called upstairs, Matt and Mrs Gould had done a good job of clearing up the bloodbath that had so nearly cost two lives that night. But this wasn't the time for such details. That would come later when Walter Chase had to be advised that because of the damage that had been done to her insides, his wife should have no more children. She would heal, but her age would be against her bringing any more children into the world, especially one the size of this new boy.

Right now, once Walter had kissed his frail-looking and exhausted wife, and been assured that she was feeling well enough, he and Lucy gazed in awe at the child resting quietly in the crib alongside her. Lucy couldn't keep her delight in check, but Walter felt such a mixture of emotions it was hard to control them. He was thankful it was a boy, though he wouldn't really have cared either way, except that some devil inside him had hoped that his wife wouldn't insist on a girl being called Tilly. He couldn't be doing with any incarnation of her old friend.

They hadn't even thought of any names yet, although Bobby had been told he could choose it, as long as it was something sensible and not Bonzo after his friend's dog. But this boy, this fine, healthy-looking boy, was a mixture of Tom and Bobby, and Walter's heart swelled with pride at the sight of his little head with its fuzz of dark hair, and his perfect features.

And oh yes, there was a God, he thought reverently. How else could there be such a miracle as this?

Fourteen

Some while later Mrs Gould went on her way, well satisfied with her night's work, and ready to tell the village at large that young Doctor Matt was as fine a doctor as his brother ever was, and she'd hear nothing to the contrary. Lucy was sent with her, so that she could report the glad news to her aunt and uncle, and Bobby of course, that the new baby had arrived. Helen would also be asked to telephone the nurses home later in the day to let Rose know the news, and also Tom in Bristol.

'I doubt that Tom will be too bothered about it,' she commented to Mrs Gould as they trudged towards the village in the early morning light. 'Boys aren't all that interested in babies, are they?'

'Not until they're grown into men and become fathers themselves,' Mrs Gould agreed. 'I daresay you and Rose will be looking forward to having babs of your own one of these fine days, when you find yourselves a husband, o' course. First things first!' she added with a laugh and a cough as the cold frosty air took her breath away.

'Perhaps, though being in the house with

Mum tonight, I'm not so sure I'm all that eager,' Lucy said.

Mrs Gould was dismissive. 'Oh, you should not let a little mishap like your Ma had this time worry you, ducks. The child was a monster compared with young Bobby, but I've no doubt he'll be all the stronger for it, and not have as many ailments as Bobby did at first.'

'I wasn't thinking of the child,' Lucy muttered. 'I was thinking of what Mum had to go through.'

The midwife patted her arm. 'And I'll guarantee that she'll have forgotten the pain before you know it. We women are made of stronger stuff than men in those circumstances, girl. I don't imagine a man would survive very long if he had to go through giving birth.'

She cackled again, making Lucy wish she'd never mentioned it at all, and was thankful that they were soon within sight of Mrs Gould's house.

'Well, thank you, anyway,' she said awkwardly. 'I know Mum will want to thank you properly when she's up and about again.'

'And you tell her I'll be there to see her tomorrow to see how she's getting on with putting the little tyke to the teats and everything,' the woman said comfortably. 'Now I'm going to get my head down for an hour or so before I get my old man up for work.'

Lucy left her before she felt a strange compulsion to ask too many questions about what had happened to cause such ructions during the night. She had a natural curiosity about it, but mostly, she didn't want to know. Mrs Gould might be all too eager to tell her more gory details that she felt able to deal with.

She hurried on to the vet's house, knowing there would be only pleasure and relief there that the baby had been born, and great excitement from Bobby, now that he wasn't the youngest any more. They were all still in bed when she arrived, but her Uncle Mick had acute hearing, and he and Helen came to the door in their dressing gowns after she had rung the doorbell a few times, both anxious.

'Is it over?' Helen said at once.

Those three words were all it took for all the pent-up tension to leave Lucy's body, and to her horror she burst into tears. Helen pulled her inside the house, while Mick stood by helplessly, not knowing what to expect from this reaction, and fearful of what she was going to tell them.

'For God's sake, Lucy, tell us your mother's all right,' he said roughly.

Without warning, all the feelings he had ever had for his brother's wife came rushing to the fore at that moment. All the envy for his brother, and the way their lives might have been so very different if he'd spoken up years ago. If he'd admitted that he'd fallen in love with Alice the moment he saw her ... and all the lingering regret for the fulfilment of a married life he might have had with her, and the children they might have had ... He caught sight of his wife's eyes over the top of Lucy's head, and he smothered the feelings angrily, as he had always done.

'Come and sit down in the warm and catch your breath, Lucy love.' He tried to sound as normal as possible, considering that brief eruption of emotions. 'Your auntie hasn't been able to sleep properly all night, so tell us if it's a boy or a girl.'

He led them both into the sitting room, where the remnants of last night's fire still warmed the room, and sat them down on the sofa. Lucy gave a shuddering breath and finally managed to babble out the words.

'It's a boy, and he's lovely, but Mum had a bad time, and I don't think she'll be having any more,' she gasped out in a rush. 'I had to go for the doctor to help the midwife, and you'll never guess who came. It was Doctor Matt. He was the one who delivered the baby. What do you think our Rose will say to that?'

She had to say everything at once, or she felt she'd never get it out at all. And until that moment, she hadn't admitted to herself how terrified she had been for her mother, and suddenly she was weeping quietly in Helen's arms.

'That's right, love, let it all out,' Helen said soothingly. 'It's been a bad night for you as well, but as long as everything's all right, that's all that matters. Let's have some porridge to start the day, then you can tell us all about the new baby.'

She kept talking in order to calm Lucy's

nerves. The girl was obviously feeling the after-effects of a sleepless night and the worry over Alice, and it would do her good to get some food inside her and then have a sleep. There would be enough excitement when Bobby woke, and she prayed that he'd be dead to the world for a couple of hours yet.

Her futile hopes were soon dashed when a sleepy-eyed five-year-old trailed into the kitchen where the three of them were sitting down with steaming bowls of porridge in front of them.

'I'm hungry,' Bobby complained. 'Can I have some of that too?'

'Of course you can,' Helen said. 'And Lucy's got something to tell you.'

He climbed onto his sister's lap. He was damp and muzzy with sleep, but she fleetingly thanked the Lord that he hadn't wet his pyjamas. Even though that would have been the least of her worries ... but seeing his curious face now, she felt her heart begin to lift.

'Guess what we've got at our house?' she said mysteriously.

'Is it my new bike?' he shouted. 'Dad said he was going to mend my old one and turn it into a new one!'

Lucy laughed, hugging his moist little body close.

'It's something better than that. It's a new baby brother for you, and later on today you can come home with me to see him. I expect Auntie Helen will want to come with us too.'

She smiled at her aunt, drawing her into the intimate world of women and children, and unintentionally shutting Mick out.

'Can Uncle Mick come too?' Bobby shouted excitedly.

'And Uncle Mick too,' Mick replied evenly. 'I'll take you in the van.'

'What's he like?' Bobby went on, his thoughts dodging from one thing to another. 'Will he play ball with me?'

'Not yet,' Lucy said. 'When he's bigger he will, but right now he'll sleep a lot of the time, like you did when you were a baby.'

Helen could see the disappointment begin to dawn on Bobby's face that the baby wasn't a ready-made companion, and remembered what Alice had told her.

'Weren't you supposed to be thinking about giving him a name, Bobby? Finish your breakfast and let's think about that while I take you upstairs and get you dressed.'

Lucy watched them go. 'She's so good with him, isn't she, Uncle Mick? She should have had lots of babies, shouldn't she?'

'Yes, she should,' he said without expression.

He cleared his throat, and Lucy felt awkward for a moment, wondering if she had said something she shouldn't. Such topics were personal between man and wife, and she had no idea what regrets they might have had. She tried to think of something else to say, and then remembered.

'Dad wants you or Auntie Helen to phone

Rose and Tom,' she said.

'Of course we will,' Mick said, relieved that the moment had passed. 'I'm sure Rose will get home as soon as she can get some time off. She'll want to see your mum as soon as possible.'

'I wonder how she'll feel when she finds out Doctor Matt was the one to deliver the baby!' she said again.

Nearing midday a telephone call came for Rose Chase at the nurses' home. She answered it eagerly, hoping it was the news she had been waiting for. Her auntie's voice was clear and excited over the line, reporting that she had seen the baby and that he was a beautiful big boy, and that her mother was feeling as well as could be expected, considering the hard time she had had. Lucy was looking after the house while she was confined, and Helen added that Alice wanted to assure her that all was well. But it was the final bit of information that left Rose stunned and shocked.

Daphne and Elsie came off their shift and caught up with her while she was still standing by the telephone, her face paler than usual.

'What's happened, kid?' Elsie said, knowing the news she had been waiting for and hoping nothing had gone wrong. Though, from the look on Rose's face, something must have done.

'Come and sit down, Rose,' Daphne said, steering her to a window-seat.

Rose shook her head. 'No, I'm all right. It was just a shock that's all, and something I never would have expected.'

'Your mum ain't had twins, has she?' Elsie said, trying to lighten the moment.

Rose managed a smile. 'No, it's just the one. A very large boy, by all accounts. My auntie said Mum had a pretty bad time, but they're both all right.'

'Well that's good news,' Daphne went on. 'We'll have a drink in the canteen tonight to wet the baby's head.'

Rose shook her head. 'I'd rather see if I can get some leave. I want to see Mum for myself. It's something else that shook me.'

'What is it then?' Elsie was getting impatient now. She didn't like riddles, and preferred folk to say what they meant without going round in circles. Besides, her feet hurt, and she needed to kick off her shoes and flex her toes.

Rose spoke rapidly. 'The midwife had to send for the doctor to help deliver the baby, but he was out with another patient, and the only one available was Matt.'

'*Your* Matt?' Elsie squeaked.

'Cripes, Rose, that's a turn-up, isn't it?' Daphne said uneasily, not sure how to take this news.

'Well, he *is* a doctor,' Rose said defensively. 'Only it does seem peculiar that he should be the one – you know – seeing to it all.'

'I should bleedin' well think it is,' Elsie said, blunt as ever. 'I wouldn't want my bloke peer-

253

ing up me mum's whatsit.'

Daphne pinched her arm. 'Shut up, Elsie. I daresay when you're in labour and need help, you wouldn't care if a regiment of soldiers marched through.'

Rose had heard enough of all this. 'I'm going to see Sister now to see if I can get some time off. When I explain what's happened, I'm sure she'll let me go.'

'Just remember to come back, darling,' Daphne said keenly. 'There are people here who love you too, and I don't mean just Elsie and me,' she added meaningly. 'Weren't you meant to be seeing Eldon tonight?'

'You can tell him what's happened. He's the last thing on my mind now,' Rose said.

An hour later she had packed her bags and was on her way to the station with Sister's blessing and a week's leave. She had made a phone call to Mick and asked him to meet her at Temple Meads station. It would take forever to get home, but home was the only place she wanted to be. The family ties had always been strong, and never more so when she ached to be with her mother right now – and to relieve her poor sister of the undoubted panic she would have been in during the night. Poor Lucy, she thought sympathetically.

Hours later she stepped out of the train at Bristol and stretched her limbs. She looked around eagerly for Mick's van and couldn't see it immediately. Then a car she didn't recognize pulled up beside her, and the driver got out, causing her heart to give a massive jump.

'It seems I'm destined to carry on being your family's good Samaritan, Rose,' Matt Stacey said with an apologetic smile.

'Where's Uncle Mick?' Rose stammered, unable to think of anything else for the moment.

'Called out to a farm where a cow's stuck in a ditch,' he said briefly. 'So if you want to get home and see the new arrival at your house, I'm your man. I've only hired this car for a couple of hours, so get in, before you freeze to death.'

She obeyed, because there seemed nothing else to do. She was acutely embarrassed at seeing him like this, partly because they had gone their separate ways as far as being romantically involved was concerned – and also because she was so aware of what he had done for her mother last night. But then her nursing instincts took over.

'Is Mum really all right, Matt? I know what happened, and it must have been a serious situation.'

'It could have been. The baby was breeched and the cord was around his neck. I had to improvise pretty much and go by instincts. It was an ordeal for all of us, not least your mum, of course, but she and the baby both survived. My brother went to visit them, as they are his patients, this morning, and they're both thriving.'

'Thank goodness for that.' She hesitated. 'It was a wonderful thing you did for Mum last night, Matt. I know my dad must be very grateful you were there.'

He grinned. 'Well, he didn't think so at first. Apparently, anyone my age isn't old enough to be a doctor. I think he's changed his mind now, though.'

'I'm sure he has.'

She didn't know what else to say. They had always been so easy together. But now there was a barrier between them. It wasn't just the birth. It was the fact that they had both moved on. She didn't know if he had been seeing other girls, but she had Eldon now, and she had begun to realize that he meant a great deal to her.

'It's all right, Rose,' he said at last as they drove through the outskirts of Bristol and onto the country roads. In the town the thin layer of snow had been mostly turned to slush by the traffic. Here, it was still virginal white and extraordinarily beautiful with the sun glinting on the distant Mendip Hills and the glistening hedgerows.

'What is?' she mumbled.

He put his hand over hers for a brief moment.

'You and me. Or rather, *not* you and me. I'd like to think we were good friends, and that we'd always feel that way about each other. And good friends can talk to each other about anything, can't they? So how's your love life lately?' he said cheekily, and taking her by surprise.

She laughed. 'How do you know I've got one?' she asked, but feeling freer than she had expected to feel with him. That, coupled with the relief that her mum was going to be all right, was like a breath of fresh air.

'Oh, come on. A lovely girl like you is bound to have someone on the horizon. And you know what they say about a nurse's uniform attracting the boys, don't you?'

With sudden insight, she countered. 'All right, I'll tell you mine if you tell me yours. Is there a certain nurse you've got your eye on?'

'I asked first. Who is he, Rose?'

It was amazing, she thought later. The awkwardness had been almost palpable at first, at least on her part. But they were suddenly confiding in one another, the way good friends did. And she heard all about the dark-haired hospital nurse called Judith, and she had told him about a certain Canadian airman called Eldon Mc-Cloud.

'You want to be careful of these fast-talking colonials,' Matt teased her. 'Before you know it, they'll be whisking you over the Atlantic, never to be seen by your family again.'

'Actually, Eldon's not fast-talking at all, and he's not going to be whisking me anywhere. As a matter of fact, he's thinking of settling in Scotland when the war's over. That's where his family's roots are, and he has an elderly uncle there who would like him to take over the reins of his farm.'

'So do you see yourself as a Scottish-Canadian farmer's wife?'

'Good Lord, we haven't got as far as that yet! Anyway, he hasn't asked me.'

'But if he did?'

Rose felt her heart jump again, but this time with a different emotion.

'I don't know. I might.' She laughed. 'And that's all you're going to get out of me, Matt Stacey. So how long are you home for, anyway?'

'Two more days. I shouldn't be telling you this, but just between you and me, this is embarkation leave, Rose. Judith and I are off to foreign parts soon.'

Her heart really jolted then. He said it so casually, but they both knew what it meant. He could be sent anywhere in the world now. But at least his dark-haired nurse was apparently going with him. It was what he didn't say about her that let Rose know she was somebody special. It didn't make her jealous, only glad for him. But it was a strange feeling too, since Rose had thought she would be the one to be going abroad with him when the orders came.

It was good to be on the old friendly footing with him though, with no other ties involved. It was something that had never happened with Peter Kelsey, and Rose couldn't help regretting that they had parted so sourly, and now he was dead. Not that it was any fault of hers, but it was a sobering thought.

They finally arrived at Bramwell and the final mile to Rose's home that always seemed the longest. Her heartbeats quickened as she saw the smoke curling out of the cottage chimney. And then Lucy was opening the door and rushing down the path to greet her, her feet slipping and sliding on the hoary ground, but still laughing with excitement and relief that her sister was home. Walter and Bobby soon followed, showing relief that they were all together again. Nearly all, anyway. Matt was ready to leave them to it, but after they had all hugged one another, they insisted that he should come inside to take another look at the baby, since he was so personally involved.

'You'll never be free of us now,' Rose said, with a smile that was friendship and gratitude all rolled into one.

'Just for a minute then,' he agreed. 'I must admit I've got a special feeling for young Master Chase.'

'Let me go first,' Rose said, putting a hand on his arm. She was quite sure her mother would prefer to see her alone, rather than with Matt, or anyone else, and it seemed to be tacitly agreed, despite Bobby's excited shouting that he was still calling the baby Bonzo.

Rose threw off her hat and coat and sped up the stairs, her heart thumping with anticipation at seeing this new baby brother. Alice would be confined to bed for the next two weeks, though Rose guessed she might well be defying doctor's orders in that respect. Alice had never been a lay-a-bed. But she had a little shock when she went into her parents' bedroom.

Alice looked more frail than Rose had ever seen her. She was resting against the pillows, apparently dozing, and for a moment Rose felt afraid for her. Had Matt told her everything about what had happened that night? And then Alice stirred, opening her eyes and giving her daughter a welcoming smile as she held out her arms, and everything in Rose's world turned the right way up again. She moved swiftly to the bed and put her arms around her mother.

'I was so thankful to hear the news, but are you really all right, Mum?'

'Of course I am, and I can't thank young Matt enough. It was a blessing he was home on leave, since we heard later that Doctor Stacey's car broke down on his way back from a case and he didn't get home until morning. Things might not have gone so well if Matt hadn't been here to help the midwife.'

She tried not to shudder as she spoke, having only just learned about how fortunate she had been. But there was no sense in crying over spilt milk, and Alice Chase had never been one to do so.

'Aren't you going to say hello to your new brother?' she went on with a smile, when Rose seemed in no hurry to disentangle herself.

Rose cleared her throat and looked at the sleeping baby in the crib alongside the bed. She drew in her breath at the sight of him in the winceyette nightgown Lucy had made, so perfect, so adorable, and so *big*!

'He's absolutely beautiful, Mum,' she breathed. 'But what a size he is. Were any of us that big?'

Alice laughed, wincing slightly as she did so.

'If you had been, I doubt I'd have had any more of you!' she said dryly. 'But this little charmer is definitely going to be the last. That's the doctor's orders, and I'm more than happy to go along with it.'

'Can I pick him up?' Rose said.

'Of course you can. And Rose, I'm so happy to see you, my love.'

Her breath caught then, because for a time, an awful, unreal time, she had wondered if she was ever going to see any of them again. But true to form, and unknown to anybody but herself, Tilly's practical voice had entered her senses, telling her not to be so daft, and that she had a lot of living to do yet.

Rose had already picked up the new baby and was gazing in awe at his perfect features. He might be big in terms of a new-born, but he was still the tiniest scrap of humanity she had seen since Bobby was born five years ago.

'He's beautiful, Mum,' she said, with a catch in her voice. 'Has he got a name yet? I hope Bobby's thought of something other than Bonzo by now!'

Alice looked at her warily. 'We're still trying to think about it. He did have one idea, but we're not too sure about it.'

Something in her voice told Rose what it was without asking.

'Not *Matt*?'

'Well, not exactly. Matthew, perhaps. Doctor Matt's something of a hero in Bobby's eyes now, being a soldier and a doctor as well. I must say he's a rather a hero in my eyes too,' she added in some embarrassment.

The initial pain and shock of that night had faded a little now, but she knew in her heart that if Matt Stacey hadn't been around, things might have ended very differently. But she couldn't overlook the fact that Rose might be upset at naming the new child after an ex-boyfriend.

Before Rose could think of a reply, Walter came storming upstairs, hardly pausing for breath before bursting out with what he'd just heard on the wireless.

'There's news that a large number of British prisoners of war have been rescued in Norway. They were all taken off ships sunk by the *Graf Spee* and have been kept aboard a German tanker in a Norwegian fjord. The tanker was spotted by HMS *Cossack* and a boarding party attacked it and found the prisoners. There'll be hell to pay for somebody on this. Why didn't the Norwegians do something about it? Apparently when the tanker called at Bergen it was searched, but nothing was found. Pretty bloody unbelievable, wouldn't you say? How hard could they have searched, or couldn't they be bothered to get involved? I thought Norway was supposed to be neutral. I wonder how old Kelsey will be feeling about it. He'd have preferred his kid to end up as a prisoner of war rather than snuffing it.'

He ranted on, barely taking a breath, while the two women glowered at him as the baby in Rose's arms awoke and began wailing loudly.

Rose cuddled him into her, while Alice huffed at Walter for being so insensitive, especially his last remarks about Peter Kelsey. She hardly dared look at Rose. What with being obliged to tell her about a possible name for the baby, Walter had to remind her about Peter.

'You are an oaf, Walter,' Alice snapped. 'You've upset the baby and Rose as well. I thought I was getting a few weeks' peace from all this war talk.'

'It's all right, Mum,' Rose said, in a muffled voice while she had the snuffling baby close to her face.

'No, it's not. Your father never had an ounce of tact, and he never changes.'

'You should be used to it then, shouldn't you, woman?' Walter growled. 'The war don't stop just because you've had a baby. And stop getting in such a mither. You'll curdle your milk.'

He turned and stumped out of the bedroom, while Rose bit her lip at hearing her father say such a thing in front of her. Alice held out her arms for the child, fumbling inside her nightgown to put him to the breast.

She spoke far more tolerantly than Rose would have done. 'Take no notice of your father, Rose. I know the gout's playing him up again, and it'll all blow over by tomorrow. He's just getting agitated over what's happening in the war.'

'Well, he still shouldn't talk to you like that when you're lying-in,' Rose said passionately. 'Nor in front of other people.'

Alice gave a small smile, more relieved that the baby was sucking contentedly on her nipple now than fretting about a few harsh words from a man she'd loved for more than twenty years. Rose would learn that in time.

'He'll be sorry about that too, I daresay. But I'll tell you one, thing, Rose. This young 'un might have a fine pair of lungs, but whatever Christian name we decide to give him, it won't be the same as his father's. One Walter in the family's quite enough!'

Fifteen

In early March there was a special church service in the village of Bramwell in memory of Peter Kelsey, which brought down the mood of the whole village for a while. The fancy title of a phoney war might have been bandied about in many quarters, but to a bereaved parent it was never that. The war couldn't be taken as anything less than serious as more and more troops were being sent abroad, and many of those were returning as casualties.

As he had expected, Matt Stacey had been sent abroad soon after his leave when he'd unexpectedly had to assist the village midwife, but the largest contingent of British troops finally set sail for Europe on April 12th.

Jack Chase had been one of the earliest to go, and was now 'somewhere in France', which was all his letters home allowed anyone to know. Many of the remarks he wrote were heavily censored, anyway, with thick black markings over words or phrases that could be construed as being useful to the enemy, should they be intercepted.

'I hardly think our Jack could be considered a spy,' Helen told her sister-in-law in exasperation, after showing her Jack's latest scrappy letter. 'Who do they think is going to get hold of one boy's scrappy letter home and decide he's trying to give information to the Jerries, for goodness' sake?'

Her indignation that her precious Jack could be thought of as being unpatriotic for a single moment made Alice smile. She bounced the heavy baby on her lap, making him gurgle with pleasure after his feed and the necessary belching. Alice was far more concerned with her own family's welfare than hearing Helen constantly complain over Jack, knowing that in her heart she was very proud of him – and for all her anxiety over him, she was sneakily pleased too, that he was the only one of the Chase children to be in the thick of the fighting.

Tom was still too young to join up, of course, and Rose seemed perfectly settled where she was. Whether or not Lucy would get itchy feet if the war went on much longer, was anybody's guess, and Alice didn't want to let her thoughts go that far ahead.

Right now, she had plenty of other things to think about. The baby's christening had been arranged for Sunday April the 21st, and Alice was planning on having a little celebration spread for her family once the church service was over. The two godmothers were going to be Rose and Lucy, since she wouldn't have one without the other, and the godfather would be Mick, who had been uncharacteristically moved when she and Walter asked him. No, right now, Alice was more concerned with how she was going to juggle the meagre rations so that it looked more like a feast than a famine. But she might have known that Helen wouldn't let her do everything alone.

'You must let me help, my dear,' she said at once. 'You've got plenty to do with the family, without worrying all the time over preparing food. And didn't you say Rose had asked about bringing a friend with her? Is it one of the nurses she works with? Not the posh one, I hope.'

Alice laughed, knowing Helen would rise to the occasion whether it was Daphne or the more down-to-earth Elsie, whom they had all heard about by now. But so far, Alice had avoided mentioning just who Rose wanted to bring home for the brief forty-eight-hour leave they had both managed to get. It was silly to put it off for ever, though, and no reason why she should do so. In any case, there was something else she still needed Helen to do for her. She took a deep breath.

'It's not one of the nurses. I may have mentioned the Canadian airman Rose has been seeing lately.'

'You mean it's a young man?' Helen exclaimed. 'But how thrilling, Alice. A Canadian too. Do they eat the same things we do?' she added without thinking.

'Well, he's not from Timbuctoo, so I daresay he does. He's been in England long enough now to get used to our food, such as it is nowadays.'

'Is it serious then?' Helen went on excitedly. 'I realized there was nothing more going on between her and young Doctor Matt, of course, and poor Peter Kelsey was never the right one for her, was he?'

'If you let me get a word in edgeways, Helen, I'll tell you,' Alice put in. 'I'll put this little one down for a sleep and then we can talk in peace.'

Helen watched her enviously as she went upstairs. Seeing how complete this family was now, only made her loneliness seem more acute. She shouldn't be lonely, of course. She had her voluntary work at the church, and she had Mick to care for, but it wasn't the same as having a large loving family, and she missed Jack even more.

She even missed those irritating little evacuee kids more than she had ever expected to, and there didn't seem to be any more of them being sent to the country. Besides, she wasn't sure she could cope with training any more of them to her own high standards, whether that was churlish or not.

She put the gloomy thoughts aside and put on a bright face when Alice returned to the sitting room and picked up her endless pile of mending and darning as she sat down beside her. Alice's hands were never idle.

'Tell me then,' she said quickly. 'Is it serious between Rose and this Canadian fellow?'

Alice licked the strand of grey wool before threading it on to the darning needle, as she prepared to attack the holes in Walter's socks.

'I think it might be,' she said. 'He sounds very nice, but you know how Rose is. She's cautious about saying too much about anything until she's sure.'

'She must think enough of him if she wants him to meet you all. Let's hope it doesn't put him off,' she added, not meaning to be sarcastic, but somehow it came out that way.

Alice paused in her darning. 'What's that supposed to mean?'

Helen felt her face flush. 'Well, nothing, really, except that he may not come from such a large family, and they can sometimes be a bit overwhelming, can't they?' she said, floundering.

'I don't think my lot are overwhelming,' Alice said with a laugh. 'But I don't know too much about Eldon yet, and for all we know, he may come from a larger family than ours. I don't suppose they have much else to do in the Canadian wilds.'

Helen laughed with her, relieved that she

hadn't put her foot in it again as she was wont to do.

'I'm pleased for Rose, anyway,' she said sincerely. 'I sometimes wonder if our Jack will ever think of marrying and settling down. It would be nice to think of grandchildren some day,' she added wistfully.

'You know you're always welcome to have a share in any of mine,' Alice said, more briskly, before she began to feel unnecessarily guilty for having the children that Helen didn't. 'So if you really do want to help, Helen, let's think of what we can provide for the christening feast, shall we?'

'Yes, but where is Rose's young man expecting to stay while he's here? There won't be room enough here, with Tom home as well, will there?'

'That was something else I was going to ask you about,' Alice said.

Rose snuggled up to Eldon in the picture house, and marvelled at her luck. That they had both managed to get a forty-eight-hour leave for the weekend of her baby brother's christening was wonderful, but added to that was the fact that Eldon was so keen to meet her family. He had even said teasingly on one occasion, that he wanted to do the right thing and make an honest woman of her.

Not that he had done anything that he should not have done yet, and it was just an expression. A bit of mild petting was all that existed between them, but his passionate kisses told her very well how he felt about her. Just as she knew very well that she felt exactly the same way. She was in that delicious stage of falling in love, and knowing that nothing could be done about it yet, because there was a war on, and nobody in their right minds would think of getting too serious until it was all over. Some did, of course, but then they risked so much anxiety and heartache if things went against them – and everyone knew that they so often did.

It made her shiver sometimes, thinking how strange it was that she and Eldon had even met. If it hadn't been for this dreadful war, they would still have been living worlds apart, with an ocean between them. It was the kind of stuff you saw on the silver screen, or read between the covers of a romantic novel.

She drew in her breath, wondering if it was so very wrong to be grateful for the circumstances that had brought them together. If it hadn't been for the war, she might even have ended up with Peter Kelsey, and lived a humdrum life as the wife of a village grocer. Or she might have married Matt Stacey and become a doctor's wife ... but however dreary the one sounded, and how exotic the other, neither of them would have given her the fulfilment she knew instinctively that a life with Eldon would give her – someday. And it was for the simple and most important reason that she really believed she had found true love at last. But she was still in

no hurry to make it permanent yet. She sometimes faced the fact that she was in love with
being in love, and that was where it ended.

'Not cold, are you, honey?' Eldon murmured,
hearing her soft sigh. He tightened his arm
around her in the dimly lit back row of the
cinema which was the most romantic part of the
place, and where all the lovers chose to sit.

'Not cold, just happy,' she whispered back, as
the flickering screen told them something was
about to begin. But before the film started they
had the inevitable news bulletin, which was
always announced by a well-educated, positive
voice to make everyone feel good about the
way the war was progressing, and which the
cynics knew was as much of a propaganda
exercise as anything put about by the Germans.

If people believed everything they saw or
heard, they'd think it was all going to be over
tomorrow, when there wouldn't have been any
need for the thousands of British troops now
being sent to France and elsewhere. Rose Chase
had seen enough casualties returning from
France needing urgent medical attention, and
heard the often lurid stories of the desperate
hand-to-hand fighting and the injuries inflicted
on both sides. She had the added personal
anxiety when Eldon flew his plane on the nightly raids over Germany, and even though he
rarely told her any real details, she had heard it
from other airmen, and her vivid imagination
supplied the rest.

It was then that she and Daphne and Elsie had

made a kind of vow that none of them would be persuaded into any kind of permanent relationship until the war was over and they could see a clear future ahead of them.

The newsreel ended to a few cheers, and the comedy film they had come to see took its place, allowing the audience to relax and laugh at the antics of the actors and to forget about the existence of the war for a couple of hours.

When they came out of the picture house later, they adjusted their eyes to the blackout from the brightness of the interior when the lights went up, including the hasty reversal to decorum for the couples in the back rows. The bitter cold of the first few months of the year had given way to a milder spring, but the evenings were still chilly enough for Rose to be glad of her coat.

'Let's find a pub and get something warming inside us,' Eldon said. 'There's something I want to talk to you about, and I need a bit of Dutch courage to do it.'

Her heart thumped. Surely he couldn't mean what she immediately thought he meant. They hadn't known one another very long, and even though the romantic novels implied that it took no more than a heartbeat to fall in love, everybody knew it was foolish to mistake a wartime romance for an everlasting love. Wasn't it the very thing she and her friends had so often discussed?

She knew she was virtually trying to deny the very thing that in her heart any girl would want.

Because of course she loved Eldon, and she wanted it to be a forever kind of love. But if tonight was the night he was going to ask her that very important question, she wasn't at all sure how she was going to answer it. She had always wondered if she was fickle, and this was just one more thing to make her wonder. She so wanted to believe this was *really* love. She was sure that it was - and yet something still seemed to hold her back, as if the moment that the thing she most desired was in her grasp, she was going to deny it. She felt panicky, wondering what in heaven's name was *wrong* with her – it was as if attaining the goal she most wanted was going to make it worthless after all.

'Don't rush me, Eldon,' she heard herself mutter.

She didn't think he heard her, because they were suddenly in a crush of people all trying to get out of the picture house at the same time. He caught hold of her hand, and they hurried along the dark streets to where a pub sign creaked in the wind, and Rose knew there would be warmth and cheer inside – and people too. And her spirits immediately lifted, because he could hardly be intending to ask her to marry him in the middle of a crowded pub!

They went inside, careful not to let any chink of light filter out of the door. It was as crowded as Rose had expected, and she felt a moment of relief. This certainly wasn't the time or place for any emotional revelations! They found some seats, and she claimed them as Eldon fought his way to the bar. He was tall and elegant enough to command attention wherever he went, Rose thought, and she couldn't deny that it felt good to be seen with him. Daphne had remarked that they made quite a striking couple when they walked into a room. Rose had laughed in embarrassment at that, but she was flattered to think that it might be true.

By the time he came back with two glasses of cider, she felt more relaxed. Someone had struck up a tune on the old piano in the corner, and people were singing. At times like this it was easy to forget that across the English channel and on many other war fronts, people were fighting one another. Easier still to forget that tomorrow night, Eldon would probably be one of the pilots flying over enemy territory, with the ever-present risk of being shot down and killed.

No wonder some girls gave in to whatever their sweethearts asked of them, knowing that there might be no tomorrow...

She took a long draught of the cider, feeling it course down her throat and warm her insides. Could she ever be one of those girls? There was a name for them – good-time girls – especially those who played fast and loose with any good-looking chap who came their way.

'A penny for them Rose,' Eldon said, when she seemed to be gazing fixedly into space.

She gave a nervous laugh. 'You wouldn't want to know.'

'I wouldn't have asked if I didn't want to

know, but if you don't want to tell me, that's OK. Besides, I told you I had something I wanted to talk over with you.'

'In here?' Rose asked faintly. 'Is this the best place?'

'Sure. Why not? I don't want to leave it until we get to Bramwell for your brother's christening. I'd like to have your approval before I broach the subject with your folks.'

Oh God. She didn't want to have to make any decision here and now, with the raucous singing going on all around her, and the smell of stale beer spoiling what should surely be a romantic moment. She was more than a little surprised that Eldon should think it such a good idea too. Unless he was as nervous as she was...

'Hadn't you better say it then?' she asked.

It wasn't the best way to urge a young man to ask a girl to marry him, but if he didn't hurry up and come out with it, she was so tensed up with nerves she thought she was probably going to faint.

'It's about my uncle's farm in Scotland. I told you about it.'

Rose was completely taken aback by this statement. It was a very unlikely way to go about proposing!

'Yes, you did,' she murmured.

'I've told him and my aunt all about you, and since you've so generously included me in your family celebrations for the christening, I'd like to invite you to spend a few days in Scotland to meet my folks, whenever we can get some leave together, maybe in the summer. What do you say? Do you think your father will let you come? It would be all above board, I promise.'

It was one of those weird moments when all the noise in the room seemed to stop at the same time. The song had ended, and it was a brief instant of suspended time before the applause rang out for the pianist.

And just as it started up again, so did Rose's heartbeats.

'I think it's a marvellous idea,' she said, her voice breathless. 'It would be exciting to see Scotland after all you've told me about it. If your aunt and uncle approve, I'm sure that when my mum and dad have met you, they will too.'

'That's great, sweetheart. I've always believed in doing things right, and this seems the perfect way to go about it, to be together in our own environments. Providing we can get a long enough leave, we'll have all the time in the world to get to know each other properly, and even if we haven't, we'll pretend that we have.'

The words seemed far too prophetic for comfort, but that was something Rose didn't even want to think about. She felt ridiculously relieved that this night hadn't meant a proposal after all, even if there was a hint of disappointment about it too. She wouldn't have been human if she hadn't felt that.

But she knew she was being totally dog in the manger about it now, and the thought of sharing two carefree holidays in this lovely man's company was excitement enough. And just as she had said, she was sure her parents couldn't help but approve of him.

He raised his glass to her, and she smiled back into his eyes. As if she had a sudden burst of her mother's insight when it came to her old friend, she could almost imagine she heard Tilly's voice in her head, whispering at her to make sure of this one, because he was definitely Mr Right.

'By the way,' Eldon went on more casually, just as if his own heart wasn't jumping because this wonderful girl was becoming so very special to him, 'what's the final name for the new baby, or is Bobby still set on naming him Bonzo?'

Rose grinned, because Eldon was not only a lovely man, but so ready to be involved in her family's doings. Oh yes, Tilly, she thought, without even being aware that she did so. This one is definitely my Mr Right.

'It's going to be Frederick, after my dad's father,' she told him. 'He'll probably be known as Freddie, but he'll be christened Frederick. Mum said that between them all, they've been slyly putting the idea into Bobby's head that his grandfather was a hero in the last war. So when he suddenly came out with the name for the baby they all told him he was very clever to think of it. They're devious people, my family,' she finished with a laugh.

It was a minor miracle how Eldon managed to

get enough petrol to drive all the way down to Bramwell, and Rose thought it wisest not to ask. Canadians seemed able to get anything ... He even said he hoped to be able to drive them to Scotland later in the year as well, but if not, they would have to go by train. The thought of such a long journey in a stuffy and crowded train wasn't too appealing, but that was for later, not for today.

Right now, as they set off from the hospital on a bright April morning for the long drive westwards, Rose couldn't help thinking how different everything looked from the last time she had been to Bramwell, visiting her mother just after Freddie was born. Then, she had been so apprehensive. It had still been bitterly cold, and then there was the shock of seeing Matt waiting for her at the railway station.

Now, she was here in the car with Eldon, eager to be with her family again, and sitting beside the man she loved. Each time the words entered her head, she became more sure of that fact, and wondered how she could have been foolish enough to doubt it.

'Tell me a bit more about these folks of yours I'm going to be staying with, honey,' he said companionably.

'My uncle Mick's a vet, but I'm sure I've told you that, and his surgery is alongside their house. Auntie Helen's lovely, and their son Jack's away in the army, and overseas now. I think Helen would have liked more children, but it never happened, and that's why she's always been so good with all of us. They did have a couple of evacuees from London a while ago, until they went back home again.'

'Was that a wise move, do you think? Old Hitler hasn't even started with the country yet. There's plenty more trouble to come.'

'I'm sure you're right,' Rose said with a shudder, wishing he hadn't suddenly got so serious. 'But if their family wanted them back, there was nothing anybody could do about it.'

All the same, she wished Helen still had the evacuee children to care for. She seemed to have got a whole new lease of life while they were there, despite the little annoyances. At least it must have made her feel as if she had a real family, like Rose's own. Uncle Mick must have sensed it too.

'I can't wait to see Freddie,' she said now, switching her thoughts. 'He was a huge baby, much bigger than the rest of us, Mum said, and he must have grown even bigger in these last couple of months.'

'He's a lucky kid, to have so many adoring brothers and sisters,' Eldon said with a smile. 'I was an only one, like your cousin Jack. You had ready-made playmates, didn't you?'

'Well yes, when Lucy and I weren't squabbling! And poor Tom got a lot of teasing from the two of us. When Bobby was born, we made a pet of him, because he was so tiny and often poorly with bad chests. At least Freddie should be spared all that, I hope.'

'It sounds as if you had great growing-up

times, honey. No wonder your Auntie Helen felt that life had dealt her a bit of a raw deal.'

She looked at him. 'I didn't say that, did I?'

'You didn't need to. You all sound so close it was obvious.'

'So what will your parents think if you decide to settle down in Scotland?' Rose asked, deciding there had been enough dissection of her family for now.

'I'm rather hoping they may decide to do the same thing. My dad's always saying how much he's drawn to the old country, so who knows? Once this war is over, there'll be quite a few changes of direction, I reckon.'

Rose snuggled down more comfortably in her seat, not wanting to reveal how much his words had warmed her. If the whole Canadian McCloud clan moved back to their roots in Scotland, well, who knew what might happen? Scotland might be in the north of the British Isles, but at least it wasn't an ocean away.

It was late in the afternoon when the village finally came into view, just as sleepy and olde worlde as Eldon probably expected it to look. She hoped it wouldn't seem like *too* much of a backwoods for him, but she needn't have worried.

'This is great,' he said enthusiastically. 'It's just how I imagined it would be. We have a painting of a small English village on our sitting-room wall back home, and it could easily have been this one.'

'Must be fate then,' Rose said with a grin,

feeling her heart flip. 'Drive straight through the centre and past the church, and then go down the lane to our house. Once we've seen the family, and I've introduced you to them all, we'll go to Auntie Helen's later. Is that all right?'

'Whatever you say is all right with me, Rose,' Eldon told her.

His words gave her a glow as always. He was so nice, so correct in his manners, and yet so exciting too. Rose felt a thrill run through her, knowing in her heart that this was going to be an important day in her life. Bringing a young man home to meet her parents was quite different from walking out with a boy who had always lived in the village, or one who just happened to be the local doctor's brother. How would her parents react to him, she wondered?

She couldn't help wondering too, how Eldon would feel, to be thrust into the midst of a noisy country family like hers. The minute the car pulled up outside her house, she didn't have to wait much longer to find out. Bobby was in the front garden, hopping up and down with excitement as he saw the car stop, and shouting in his usual way that they were here at last, before he crossed his legs quickly in a familiar movement Rose recognized at once.

Sixteen

The door opened and Lucy came rushing outside, barely pausing to yell hello to Rose before she grabbed Bobby and shoved him indoors, ignoring his shouting.

'Welcome to the Chase family,' Rose said to Eldon with a grin.

And then her mother was in the doorway with the baby in her arms, and Rose forgot everything else but how well Alice was looking now, and how glad she was to be home. She hurried towards her, arms outstretched, and hugged them both for a moment, before marvelling at how large the infant Freddie had grown.

Alice smiled. 'He's a real beauty, isn't he?' she said, with justifiable pride, and then she looked beyond her daughter at the tall young man standing behind her. Such a handsome young man...

As if aware that he was momentarily being left out of the family circle, Rose turned and held out her hand to him.

'And this is Eldon,' she said simply, and with a mother's intuition, Alice knew in an instant that this was the man for Rose.

'I'm very pleased to meet you, Ma'am,' he

said, 'and honoured that you've allowed me to be part of your family celebration.'

Good manners too, Tilly's voice echoed through Alice's head.

'We're pleased to have you here,' Alice said warmly. 'Come inside and meet the rest of us, Mr McCloud.'

'I surely will – and the name's Eldon, please.'

She was thankful that Walter was in a cheerful frame of mind, glad to have Tom home for the weekend, and ready to play the magnanimous host. He shook Eldon's hand, and told him it was good to have some of their overseas compatriots lending a hand in this war, and that between them, they'd soon whip the Hun.

'Now Walter, we said we'd have no war talk this weekend,' Alice told him. 'This is Freddie's celebration, so let's forget for once that there's a war on.'

Although, seeing Tom's eager face as he took in the elegant sight of the newcomer in his smart air-force blue uniform, she knew there was as much hope of that as seeing snow in August.

'What's it like, flying planes over Germany?' he asked Eldon, as memories of his one-time ambition to be a flyer came rushing back.

'Don't bother Eldon the minute he's got inside the door,' Rose put in. 'And you heard what Mum said. No war talk!'

'You heard the ladies, Tom, so we'd better obey the rules,' Eldon said with a smile. 'But maybe I'll tell you later.'

It was easy to see he had everyone's approval, Rose thought happily. She could see that Lucy, coming downstairs a few minutes later with Bobby in clean trousers after his lapse, was charmed by the way he spoke and the way he fitted in so easily to this noisy household. As for Bobby, he couldn't take his eyes off the uniform and the badges, and especially the wings that signified that Eldon was a pilot. A squadron leader, no less, Rose had told her family proudly, but he didn't want to stand on ceremony here. He had even toyed with the idea of coming down in civvies, but Rose had assured him that they would all be devastated if he didn't wear his uniform. And because he was finding it hard to deny her anything, he had agreed.

By now, Rose was cuddling Freddie in her arms, chucking him under the chin to make him laugh, and Eldon thought he had never seen anything so lovely. What a perfect mother she was going to be, one day. The mother of his children...

He ignored the tantalising thought and turned his attention to Bobby before his expression gave him away. As usual, the child couldn't keep his voice down as he asked if Eldon had shot any Germans yet, and Alice threw up her arms in despair. However much she wanted to keep this weekend a war-free time, she knew it was going to be impossible, with one boy seeming to revive his interest in flying, and the younger one agog at the thought of shooting

284

Germans.

'Why don't we all have a cup of tea?' she said, resorting to the usual recipe for all ills. 'I'm sure Rose and Eldon must be parched after such a long journey. Lucy, you put the kettle on, and I'll set the table.'

'That reminds me, Mrs Chase,' Eldon put in. 'I hope you don't think it presumptuous of me, but I've brought a few items from our mess that I thought you could use. There are a few tins, and some tea and sugar.'

'It's not presumptuous at all, boy,' Walter boomed out. 'It's mighty thoughtful of you, as the cowboys say in your neck of the woods. Isn't that right?'

Tom gave a huge guffaw. 'It's all wrong, Dad! That's what the Yanks say, not the Canadian Mounties. *They* always get their man!'

'Oh well, you know I don't go to the flicks myself. It's just what I've heard you young 'uns say,' Walter went on amiably.

Alice laughed, her face pink with pleasure. 'Well, never mind all that. It's very thoughtful of you, Eldon, and much appreciated.'

She took the brown paper bag he handed her, seeing how he and Rose exchanged smiles. She could almost read her daughter's thoughts – and unconsciously, she echoed them.

Well done. You couldn't have done anything better if you wanted to make a good impression on Mum and Dad.

'When we've had a cup of tea I want to show Eldon round the village,' Rose said. 'I'll want

285

to take him to meet Auntie Helen and Uncle Mick too, as he'll be staying there for a couple of nights.'

She wished he could have stayed here, both of them in the same house, under the same roof. But there was no room, and they were pushed enough as it was, now that they were a family of seven. Lucky seven, she found herself thinking, seeing how contented they all were, and how well baby Freddie was thriving.

'Can I come for a walk with you?' Bobby shouted at once.

'Maybe tomorrow morning,' Rose said.

Almost jealously, she didn't want anyone to share this first day with Eldon. She wanted to see the village through his eyes, letting him see the places she knew and loved, and where she had grown up, gone to school, got her first job.

The thought of that reminded her too vividly of Peter Kelsey. It was in his father's shop where she had earned her first money, and now Peter would never stand behind the counter again, or drive the van in which he had taken her to the seaside on more than one occasion. As she gave a small shiver, she clutched Freddie too tightly, causing his mouth to pucker and let out a wail.

'He needs his afternoon sleep,' Alice said. 'Put him down for an hour in my bedroom, will you, Rose? He's already outgrown Tom's crib, and your dad's had to make a cot for him instead.'

It was all so homely and Rose hoped again

that Eldon wasn't finding it all too much so, but by now he was in conversation with Walter, and she hoped too, that he wasn't going to mention the holiday in Scotland too soon. But she knew he wouldn't. He was tactful enough to choose the right moment, and that would be once they had all got to know one another properly – most likely tomorrow afternoon, when the christening was over, and they were all mellow with a drop of Mick's home-made elder-flower wine he'd promised to bring them.

'So what do you think? Was it as you expected?' Rose said later, when she and Eldon had managed to shake off Bobby's bleating to come with them, and they were walking back through the lane towards the village now.

She was aware that he had waited until they were well away from the house before he tucked her hand in the crook of his arm.

'I think you've got a great family, but I never expected anything less, knowing their wonderful daughter,' he said.

Rose laughed, feeling almost light-headed after the long drive, plus the relief that her family all seemed to take to Eldon as if they had always known him.

'Flattery will get you anywhere,' she teased him.

'Is that a promise?'

'Well, maybe half of one,' she added.

His arm tightened on hers. 'I may hold you to that before you know it, honey. So start pointing out landmarks so that I can write home and tell my folks all about this quaint little English village.'

His first remark was almost lost in the second, and as they reached the Green Rose pointed out the doctor's house where she had looked after baby Mollie, now in Lucy's charge; the grocery shop where she had her first job; the church where all the Chase children had been christened, and where Freddie would be the star attraction tomorrow, with the church hall alongside where local events went on. The Pig and Whistle was another landmark never to be missed, and finally they came to the vet's house and surgery where Eldon would be sleeping while he was there.

'We could walk back through the woods and I could show you the sawmill where Dad works. Tom worked there too until he got his apprenticeship. He's going to be a clever carpenter, if he doesn't change his mind again and join up as soon as he's old enough. He was always changing his mind when he was younger, and for a while he was mad on being a flyer like you, Eldon.'

'I could tell, and I don't think the enthusiasm's entirely gone yet.'

'Would you encourage him?' Rose asked.

'It depends whether you're asking me from the sheer joy of flying, which I can never deny, or from the perspective of an anxious sister. When all's said and done, war's brutal, Rose, and flying's a dangerous thing.'

'Don't you think I know that? Don't you think I worry already?' she said, betraying herself more than she intended.

'About me?'

'Of course about you,' she muttered.

He caught her hand and pressed it briefly to his lips. It was such a sweet, spontaneous gesture that it took her breath away for a moment.

'It's good to know there's someone worrying about me,' he said. 'But don't you know I've got a charmed life? I must have, if fate brought me all this way to find you.'

Much as his sincere words thrilled her, it was becoming all too intense for Rose's peace of mind. There should be a proper time and place to express sentiments like these, with moon-light and roses and all the romantic stuff of the movies, not walking through an English village in daylight, with people she knew nodding to her or saying hello, or simply looking curiously at this tall man in an air-force uniform who was acting so familiarly with her.

She gave an awkward laugh. 'Be careful, Eldon. The folk around here are good at putting two and two together. If you don't stop paying me compliments like this, they'll have us married off in no time.'

'Would that be such a bad thing?'

She waved to one of their neighbours, and spoke shortly.

'You know it would. I thought we both felt the same way about that. I didn't think we were going to get too serious.'

Even so, Rose had the feeling they were already getting serious if she could even be saying such a thing to him. She felt him squeeze her arm.

'You're right, and I didn't mean to rush you, honey. Let's just enjoy our time together. I'm certainly enjoying seeing the way you people live.'

You people! Was that a derogatory comment, or simply the way someone from a different part of the world spoke? But she was sure he didn't mean it in any way other than the obvious. He was too open a person to mean anything other than the words he spoke. And why the dickens was she becoming so critical? Or was it not that at all? Was she just over-anxious that everyone in her family would like him as much as she did?

'We're here,' she said in some relief, as her aunt and uncle's house came into view. Eldon gave a low whistle.

'Some place,' he commented.

'Well, I suppose it looks grander than it really is, because half of the building is the vet's surgery where Uncle Mick works.'

'I'd be interested to take a look at that if he'll agree, especially if I'm going to be a Scottish farmer after the war.'

'With that accent?' Rose said with a grin, thankful that the intense moments seemed to have passed.

'Och aye, and with a bit of practice, lassie,

I'm sure I can fool the natives,' he joked, exaggerating the words in a way that wouldn't fool anybody.

They were still laughing when Helen opened the door to their knock.

'Come in, both of you. It's good to see you, Rose, and this must be Mr McCloud who I've heard so much about,' she said with a smile, even though she'd actually heard very little about Rose's new friend.

'It's Eldon, Ma'am, and I'm very grateful to you and your husband for allowing me to stay here for a couple of days.' he said at once.

'You're very welcome,' Helen said warmly, and her voice told Rose at once that she liked what she saw.

Mick appeared almost at once to greet them, and the first moments were taken up with introductions and Helen's insistence that they should sit down and have some tea before they did anything else. Rose could almost sense Eldon's smile at wondering if the English were besotted by having the tea ritual at every opportunity.

Later, after he had been shown the bedroom he was to use for the two nights they were in Bramwell, Mick took him into the surgery to show him around, and she and Helen were alone for a few minutes.

'So what do you think?' Rose asked.

Helen laughed. 'I think you should hang on to this one,' she said frankly.

'Why, Auntie Helen, how very modern of you!' Rose teased.

'I wasn't born in the Dark Ages, my love, and it's obvious that he's only got eyes for you, and if I'm not mistaken, you feel the same way. Don't let convention get in the way of your feelings.'

'I'm sure you don't mean I should lose all sense of propriety,' Rose said archly, and her aunt blushed.

'You know very well I mean nothing of the sort, Rose. But it's all too easy to let the chance of happiness slip by, and spend the rest of your life regretting it.'

Rose felt her heart jolt. Occasionally, over the years, she had had the fleeting sense that but for chance, it was her mother and Uncle Mick who had been destined to be together. There had been times, like now, when she heard the faintly sad note in her aunt's voice, that made her wonder if she too, had wondered.

Impulsively, she gave her aunt a hug.

'I know you're right, and Mum and Dad are good examples of not wasting the chance that they were given, aren't they? If they hadn't met and fallen in love, I wouldn't even be here!'

'So make the most of it, girl,' Helen said.

'Well, can I ask you something then? I may need your support, actually, and there's nobody who can give me better advice than you.'

With those few words, she drew her aunt into her world, and knew she had done the right thing by the way Helen responded.

'You know I'll always help you in any way I can, Rose, and if I had a daughter I would want her to be just like you.'

'Stop it now, or you'll make me blush. But this is in confidence. Eldon's going to ask Dad if he can take me to Scotland to his uncle's farm in the summer if we can both get some leave. Eldon may think of settling there after the war, and he wants me to meet some of his family. What do you think Dad will say?'

'I'd say that if that isn't a clear indication that he's serious about you, Rose, I don't know what is. And I'm sure he'll be tactful enough to ask Walter in the right way. If there's any fuss about it, just leave your father to me!'

'That's what I hoped you'd say,' Rose said happily.

'What's tickled your funny bone?' Eldon said as they walked back an hour or so later, diverting through the woods as Rose had suggested. 'You've had a soppy grin on your face ever since your uncle and I came back from the surgery.'

'Just something between Helen and me,' she said mysteriously. 'Women's talk, that's all.'

'In that case, I don't want to know! So when do you think I should broach the subject of Scotland with your dad?'

'Were you listening?' she said at once.

'No, I'm just psychic,' he replied. 'Does she approve? I can tell you set a lot of store by her opinion.'

'Since you're asking, yes, she approves of you, and she approves of your asking Dad to

293

take me to Scotland. I thought it was only women who fished for compliments.'

He laughed, and Rose marvelled anew at how easy they were with one another. It flashed through her mind that there was none of the sometimes difficult moments she had had with Peter Kelsey, always trying to fend off his octopus hands. And none of the vague feeling with Matt Stacey, much as she had loved him, that with his background he was more intelligent than she was. With Eldon, she felt his equal in every way.

'I wish days could always be like this,' she said without thinking. 'Dad won't be talking about the war all the time, Mum's busy and happy with Freddie, and we're all going to be together for the christening tomorrow. And you're here.'

She stopped talking abruptly, because she hadn't meant to say that at all. There was a soft carpet of leaves underfoot, their footsteps making no sound. Above them, the trees swayed gently in the breeze, the late afternoon sunshine dappling through the burgeoning network of spring leaves. It was the perfect country afternoon, and Rose's heart was suddenly beating faster as Eldon pulled her to a stop and put his arms around her. They were completely alone, in a verdant world of their own. His kiss on her lips was cool and restrained at first, but as she responded with a soaring passion, she knew at once that this was the man she wanted to spend the rest of her life with.

He folded her into him, his hands stroking her hair, his body so moulded to hers that she could feel his matching heartbeats. And everything else.

His voice was hoarse. 'Do you know what you do to me, honey? Do you know how hard it is to hold back when you're everything in the world to me?'

'I do know, Eldon,' she said weakly. 'I'm not a saint.'

The sudden rustle in the trees as a small flock of birds went skywards, had made her swallow back the smart remark she may have made. Because this wasn't the time. This definitely wasn't the time. But the small movement overhead had made them both glance upwards, enough to make them both pause.

'Nor a sinner, I think,' Eldon said, more subdued. 'And I want you to know, Rose sweetheart, that however much I want you, and God knows that I do, you'll be perfectly safe with me in Scotland.'

And if I don't want to be safe? The thought was in her head before she could stop it, because more than anything else in the world she knew how much she wanted to be a part of this man, and for him to be a part of her. Did he think that a woman wasn't capable of as much desire as a man?

The sound of light giggling told them they were no longer alone, and they reluctantly broke apart as another young couple came into view. But even as they passed them and went on their way towards Rose's home, she knew in her heart that this was the love of her life, and that she could be whatever he asked of her. She would be able to deny him nothing ... and it was both an awesome and frightening thought.

Late that evening, Eldon left Rose and the family and drove the hire car back to Helen's house. It was a straight road, and he assured them he couldn't get lost, even in the dark. In any case, pilots had night vision, he joked. It was arranged that he would drive Helen and Mick to the church for the christening the following morning, and then they would all go back to Alice's house for the spread afterwards. The usual Sunday dinner would be abandoned in favour of the tasty snacks and puddings that Alice and Helen had prepared between them. There was also a cake to welcome Freddie into the family properly, scraped together with the small amounts of ingredients they could acquire between them. Luckily, Walter's hens had provided enough eggs to make it a worthy effort, and with Eldon's generous offerings, there would be enough little luxuries to go around in future days.

She hadn't missed her girl's heightened colouring when the two of them had returned from Helen's yesterday. She knew the signs of love when she saw them, and she prayed that Eldon was an honourable young man. They looked so happy together, so perfectly matched, and she sent up another silent prayer that this war wasn't going to wrench them apart in any way. When she and Rose were getting breakfast for everyone that morning, she ventured to put the question she had been longing to ask.

'Are you happy, Rose?'

'Very happy, Mum. I don't think I realized it myself until now. It's just as though it's suddenly hit me, like a thunderbolt, if that makes any sense,' she added self-consciously.

'I don't think love has to make any sense, my dear. It can be overwhelming when it happens. Just be careful, that's all. You know what I mean.'

Rose felt her face grow hot. 'Of course I will.'

She turned away, thankful that Freddie was waiting to be fed, and that her mother would be occupied with him for the next twenty minutes or so.

'I'll finish getting breakfast ready, Mum. You go and see to the little whopper,' she said quickly.

It was always odd to think of parents having the kind of feelings young people did. You never wanted to think of them making love or being carried away by passion, but it was a fact of life that if they hadn't been, none of the Chase offspring would be here at all.

'Why are you standing there staring at the wall, Rose?' she heard her father say. 'I thought you were getting the breakfast ready. Some of us are starving in there and I'm that parched waiting for my cup of tea it feels as if my throat's been cut. Get a move on, there's a good girl.'

Rose laughed as her father came into focus, his hair not yet combed, his chin not shaved, and not yet spruced up for the church service. Back to earth then, and definitely no time to be thinking of her parents in a passionate mood!

'You could tell Lucy to come and help,' she said tartly. 'I'm not the only skivvy around here, remember.'

Walter chuckled. 'It's good to have you home, girl,' he said.

A couple of hours later the Chase family walked into the village to go to church as they had always done. Alice and Walter walked ahead with Freddie in his pram; Rose and Lucy held Bobby's hand, swinging him between them when he protested that it was too far to walk ... and Tom brought up the rear, dreaming of the time when he'd wear some kind of a uniform like that dashing Eldon McCloud. He wasn't even bothered any more about which kind it was, just as long as he looked as good as Eldon and caught the eyes of the girls.

The hire car was already outside the church when they arrived, and her aunt and uncle were standing outside with Eldon, and passing the time of day with neighbours as they went inside. Rose felt her heart lift. It was strange how he had used those particular words yesterday about holding back ... she knew he meant them in a different context, but she had been holding back all this time too. Holding back from

298

admitting that she was madly, gloriously in love, and that he was the one for her. The one and only.

Helen Chase was thinking the same thing as she watched her elder niece perform the ritual of chief godmother to the infant Freddie. The occasional glances between Rose and Eldon confirmed it in her mind. She just hoped Walter wasn't going to get stuffy about his daughter going to Scotland with her beau later in the year – and even more so, she prayed that all was going to turn out well for the two of them. Only a fool could deny that the war was becoming ever more serious. Hitler had invaded Denmark and Norway, and Britain was rallying to their defence. Helen feared for her own son, with no idea where Jack was now. And as a pilot, Eldon's life could be in increasing peril as the war in the air was becoming more vital.

When men got together it was inevitable that they discussed such matters, and listening to Mick and Eldon discuss the progress of the various campaigns in some detail last evening as she made them all a bedtime cup of cocoa, Helen guessed that such thoughts were not only in her own head on this bright April morning when all seemed as serene as ever in a small English village.

If such thoughts coloured the enjoyment of this day as young Frederick Chase was welcomed into the church, Helen determinedly ignored them. The ceremony was finally over, with Freddie behaving himself admirably, and later they were all crammed into the small living room of Alice and Walter's house, with much laughter and chatter as they shared the refreshment she and Alice had prepared.

Rose and Eldon spilled out into the garden, ostensibly to make some room indoors, but in reality to snatch a few precious moments together, which they had hardly been able to do all day so far.

'I'm going to ask your father about Scotland this afternoon,' he told her. 'I can't think there'll be a better time for getting him in a good mood.'

Rose laughed, happy to be here on this lovely spring day, happy to be with her family, and most of all, happy to be with the man she loved.

'You're getting as devious as the rest of us,' she said. 'But you're right – and now that he's met you, how could he possibly refuse?'

Seventeen

After the fall of the Scandinavian countries, Holland and Belgium seemed poised to succumb to the German onslaught next, and there were rumours everywhere that Hitler's great plan was soon to invade Britain. So much of France was occupied now, that it seemed inevitable he would try to cross the Channel. In any case, whatever the newspapers and the wireless announcers didn't tell you, the man in the street made up, and the rumours got ever wilder and more preposterous. As expected, Walter Chase was very vocal in his comments and opinions.

'God knows what would happen if the bastards tried to take over this country,' he roared, 'and don't nag me for cussing, woman. If a man can't cuss in his own home in defence of his country, when can he?'

'I wasn't going to nag you for that,' Alice said crossly, 'only for waking up Freddie before I'm ready for him. And don't spoil Rose and Eldon's last day before they go back.'

'I'm damn sure Eldon's heard his fair share of cussing, and done plenty of it himself when he was in a tight corner,' Walter retorted. 'You

301

women have a cushy time of it back home while your menfolk are away fighting your battles.'

Alice almost exploded at that. 'A cushy time of it indeed! You try juggling rations around to try to make ends meet, my lad, and since when did you go fighting any battles? The only scar you've got is the one on your face from getting into a scrape with some anti-war louts at the village hall last year.'

The sight of her incensed face calmed him down a little. His daughter and her young man were taking another walk through the woods on their last morning here before driving back, and he wished to God Rose never had to go back at all. He wished he could keep all his family safe for ever, but the way the world seemed to be rushing ever nearer to disaster was something that frustrated him more than he ever let on.

'You're right as usual, Missus,' he grunted, 'and I'll put on a more cheerful face before they leave. At least I feel comfortable about that young man's behaviour towards her despite his foreign accent.'

Alice just managed to stop herself snapping that Canadian was hardly a foreign accent, but that was Walter ... but in any case she didn't want to provoke him on that score, since she was pleased and amazed at how agreeable he had been to Eldon's well-mannered request last evening. For someone as parochial as himself, Walter seemed to have suddenly realized that foreign travel wasn't such a bad thing – not that

302

Scotland was a foreign country – and nobody went abroad just for fun these days.

Remembering how the evening had ended so amicably, she gave him a quick hug. 'Your heart's in the right place, Walter, I'll give you that,' she said.

'So your dad said yes?' Elsie almost squeaked when Rose told her friends the news while she unpacked after her forty-eight-hour leave. 'Blimey, I always did say them Canadians had the gift of the gab, and now I know it.'

'It's lovely news, Rose, and how did the christening go?' Daphne asked. 'Was the baby well-behaved?'

'He was beautiful,' Rose told her. 'Everybody was in such a good mood and Eldon picked just the right time to ask Dad about Scotland. Anyway, it's months away yet, so I'm not even going to think about it for now.'

'You're not backing out, are you?' Elsie said.

'No, of course not. I'm just keeping my fingers crossed that things will turn out the way we want them to – which isn't always easy these days, is it?'

She didn't want to sound too sober, but everyone knew the news wasn't good. The Germans definitely seemed to be winning on all fronts, and if so many countries were being overrun, there was little to stop them invading Britain. There was just the little matter of the English Channel between them and the poor Allied countries that were so quickly coming under the heavy German jackboot. It didn't bear thinking about, and yet any sane person couldn't help thinking about it.

She gave a shudder. 'Anyway, have you two got any news? I know I've only been away for a long weekend, but it seems like for ever.'

'Daphne has,' Elsie said at once. 'But I'll leave it to her to tell you. I've got to be on duty in ten minutes, so I'm off.'

She left their shared room and Rose turned to the other girl, glad to divert her thoughts to something else.

'Come on then, Daphne,' she said more cheerfully. 'Which young chap's heart have you broken now?'

Daphne laughed. 'It's nothing like that. I phoned home while you were away and had a long conversation with my mother. I told you ages ago what my parents were considering about the house. Well, now they've done it. They've offered the use of it to the powers that be as a convalescent home for the duration. They're going to keep one wing of it for themselves, of course, but the rest of it will be for the use of the military medics.'

'Good Lord. I know they talked about it, but I didn't think it was going to happen so soon. But what about all their lovely things, Daphne, and the carpets too! Can you imagine army boots tramping all over them?'

'The poor devils will hardly be wearing their army boots by the time they get back to England in an ambulance, will they? As for our

304

lovely things, well, things can be replaced, can't they?' Daphne said with a shrug. 'They're going to take all the carpets up and put in storage, anyway. There's no guarantee how many or what kind of people will be accommodated, but the rooms will be turned into some sort of semi-hospital wards, so linoleum will be more practical,' she added delicately.

Rose listened in some awe to think of that elegant house being turned into a kind of hospital for the duration of the war. And how must Daphne feel, with all her childhood memories of that beautiful place?

'I think your parents are wonderful,' she said impulsively, 'and so are you to be taking it all so calmly.'

'Well, since it looks as though I'll be away from home for the foreseeable future, it hardly makes much difference to me, does it?'

'But what about when you go home on leave?'

Daphne laughed. 'Oh, I'll still have my own room in the West Wing, and I'll also have access to all the lovely convalescent chaps, won't I?'

She sounded cheerful enough, but privately, Rose guessed she was just making the best of it. It wouldn't be Rose's wish to turn her own home into a kind of repository for the war wounded – not that her home in Bramwell was big enough to house any of them! No, people like Sir Dennis and Lady Vera Poole were definitely a special breed, she decided.

News on the war front was becoming ever more alarming. In early May a sick Mr Chamberlain resigned from the government and Winston Churchill was now prime minister. The girls listened to as many wireless bulletins as their duties and their stomachs permitted. Air raids over Germany had intensified, and contact with any of the Canadians at the nearby base was minimal now. The occasional phone call was about all that Rose could expect to let her know that Eldon was all right. Then, a few weeks later some news from home brought her up sharply. Alice wrote to say that Tom was coming back to live with them and taking up his old job at Wakeman's Sawmills. Tom's employers had been anxious over their son's health for some time, and now it had been discovered that he was suffering from TB.

'The poor boy has to go to a sanatorium in Wales for treatment,' Alice wrote. 'These things take a long time, so the whole family has decided to sell up and move there to be near him. Tom had the offer of transferring his apprenticeship to the new owners of Conway's business, but he didn't fancy it. He seems to be as contrary-minded as ever, and you probably know about the announcement on the wireless that there's to be a group called the Local Defence Volunteers open to all males between the ages of fifteen and sixty-five who aren't already called up. Well, you can just imagine what that did for your father – and Tom as well.

The pair of them went straight to the local police station and signed up. I ask you! I don't know what things are coming to when they want boys and old men. The whole world seems to have gone mad. It said in the newspaper that by the next evening over two hundred, and fifty thousand volunteers had joined this new group, so I don't know what they're supposed to be doing. Anyway, that's enough of all that. You'll want to know how Freddie's doing.'

Rose felt as though she had to catch her breath after reading this long epistle from her mother. The fact that it had been written with barely a pause told her how steamed up her mother felt over these new happenings. Tom coming home was one thing. Leaving his valued apprentice-ship was another, and the fact that Alice had said so little about Walter's reaction was some-thing else.

But through it all, Rose wondered if Alice wasn't secretly glad that Tom was leaving Bristol. Hitler hadn't set his sights on Bristol yet, but the docks there were sure to make it a prime target one of these days, like all the other cities that could be paralysed by bombing. And for all her Dad's imagined ranting at him for coming back home, he'd be glad to have his boy under his wing as well. For now, anyway.

Before she could write back to her mother, she was surprised to get another letter from her. This time the news was brief.

'We've had news of your cousin Jack, from Norway of all places,' Alice wrote. 'He's been

307

wounded and is being sent on a hospital ship back to England. Poor Helen doesn't know how bad he is, and she's very upset. If it didn't sound so awful, I'd tell her to be glad he's just been wounded and is coming home, but however much I try to comfort her, there's no talking to her at the moment. You might drop her a line, Rose. You always know what to say.'

Rose's heart was thumping by the time she finished reading this letter. No, she *didn't* know what to say. It was one thing to be dealing with strangers in a hospital ward, and Lord knew that wasn't always easy when the injuries were so terrible you knew there was going to be no recovery. It was something else trying to comfort a relative when there was no knowing what Jack's injuries might be yet.

Her thoughts raced on, wishing she was clairvoyant enough to know what was happening. It was impossible to think or to hope, that Jack might turn up here, of course. Even more so, to hope that Daphne's parents' home might be ready to receive convalescents and that he might be billeted there. Those were crazy and impossible thoughts. Besides, if he was somewhere in Norway, it was logical that he'd be taken to the nearest hospital in the north of England.

If she had to write something to Aunt Helen, then that was the only thing she could think of to tell her. That, and the fact that once he had recovered, he'd be coming home for some leave. At least that should comfort her a little.

But the news made her more and more disturbed. The war was coming home to them. It wasn't just in some distant part of the world, but getting ever closer. It had taken Peter, and now her own cousin had been wounded. And it didn't take a genius to know that Tom was getting restless all over again. How long before he slipped away from home and put up his age? He was big enough and brash enough to get away with it too. She vowed to have a few stern words with him on her next visit home. It would not only break her mother's heart if anything happened to Tom, but her father's too.

There was something else as well. Something she hadn't told anybody. Each time she heard of something bad happening to someone close to her, she wondered if her luck was running out. Matt was 'somewhere in France' as far as she knew. How long before he was the one being sent home on a hospital ship - or worse? How long before it was Eldon being shot down on one of those nightly missions when they were all aware of the drone of the aircraft on their way to Germany?

She tried to get the horror of it all out of her mind, and her room-mates found her still poring over the words she was trying to write to her aunt and uncle. It was difficult since her hands were shaking so much. A fine nurse she was turning out to be, she berated herself angrily, but she told them quickly what had happened.

'You know what you want, don't you, gel?'

Elsie said. 'You want to get out of here and get some fresh air into your lungs. Me and Daphne are going to the canteen tonight. You want to come with us and forget all your troubles.'

'I can't forget them,' Rose said flatly.

'Maybe you won't, but Elsie's right, darling,' Daphne put in. 'You won't do any good sitting here and brooding. Leave the letter until tomorrow when you're feeling calmer, and come out and enjoy yourself for a couple of hours.'

It was too much to expect. How could she enjoy herself when her world was falling apart? She had no idea where Eldon was right now, nor even if he was coming home again. Her imagination soared to places she didn't want it to go. What if he didn't? What if his was one of the empty chairs in the airmens' mess she had heard talk about, saying they were filled up as soon as they were empty, so as to keep up morale. She could feel herself disintegrating, just thinking about it.

'Here,' Elsie said firmly, thrusting her coat into her hands. 'We're not taking no for an answer, so get your bleedin' coat on and let's go.'

She did as she was told, knowing that these well-meaning friends would stand over her until she did. She had always considered herself to be a strong person – as strong as her mother – but it just proved to her how vulnerable anyone could be given the right circumstances. And how you could rise above it too, she thought, gritting her teeth.

'All right, I'm coming,' she said.

Daphne smiled in relief. 'Good girl.'

They linked arms as they walked briskly down to the canteen that evening. The place was always cheerful. There was always plenty of refreshment as well as music and laughter and dancing. It was as though all talk of the war and what was happening outside these four walls was strictly taboo. It was a good place to be, Rose acknowledged. It calmed the nerves and made all the tension unwind, at least for a little while.

She smiled as Elsie let herself be whirled into the middle of the floor by a good-looking sailor with a bandage around his head, which obviously wasn't going to stop him having a good time.

'Just look at her,' Rose said with a grin. 'Is that meant to be a waltz or is she about to eat him?'

'It sounds like a good idea, so why don't you try it for yourself?' someone said behind her.

Someone whose voice she knew and had practically given up on. Her heart soared with joy as she whirled around, straight into Eldon McCloud's arms.

'You're back,' she stammered.

He nodded. 'So I am, honey. I know I've been out of contact for days, and my squadron hasn't had an easy time of it, but I'm back at the base for the time being, God willing, and more than glad to see my girl again.'

If she hadn't been so tense over everything that had been happening, she might have realized that his casual words hid a tension of their own. As it was, Rose simply felt a sudden, unreasoning anger.

'And wasn't there any way you could have let *your girl* know what was happening?' she blazed.

She didn't quite know how it was happening, but as if her words had triggered something in himself, he was bundling her out of the canteen and out into the soft, dark night. He gripped her arms fiercely.

'Don't you think I would have done if I could? Don't you know there's a war on and strict secrecy on our movements has to be observed, even from those we love the best? If you don't know that, then you don't know me at all, Rose.'

She stared at his silhouette, outlined against the reflected light from the sea. She swallowed hard, because of course she knew it. Of course she knew that they were all heroes, every one of them, and she sensed the words he hadn't said.

'But now that it's over?' She had to ask, however fearful it made her. 'Was it a successful mission?

'Not entirely,' he said briefly. 'Buzz and his crew didn't make it.'

Oh God, this was awful. She remembered Buzz so clearly. He was one of Eldon's best buddies, and one of the three bright and breezy young Canadians who had taken her and her two friends to visit Daphne's home for that glorious weekend house party. It was hardly any time ago, and yet how quickly everything had changed for all of them.

'Darling, I'm so sorry,' she whispered.

He cleared his throat. 'Well, hearing you call me darling is something to cheer me up,' he said. 'So do you want to go back inside and dance the night away?'

'I'd much rather walk along the seafront with you. I've got things to tell you too,' she said. 'It seems like a good night for sharing our sorrows.'

As they walked, she couldn't help thinking of other days along other seafronts nearer home, where she had once walked with Peter Kelsey in the days before there were blackouts and barbed wire along English beaches to keep out invaders. Life had been so simple then, and now it all seemed so long ago, and so sad that it had come to this. Eldon felt her shiver, and tucked her hand in his arm.

'What's happened?' he said quietly.

'My cousin Jack's been wounded,' she said in a strangled voice. 'I don't know how badly, nor where he is, but Auntie Helen thinks he'll be sent to a hospital in the north of the country, which will be too far away for her to visit him easily, though I know she'll be desperate to see him. He's her only one, you see,' she finished on a sob.

'I know. I saw the photographs, and I'm sorry,' Eldon said.

He sounded so flat that she looked at him sharply. But what could she expect? He was grieving over the fact that his best buddy had been killed – probably blown to bits out of the sky, and here she was, moaning about Helen being unable to get to see Jack, who was only wounded. But Helen's pain would be as deep as his. And until she knew for sure how bad her son's injuries were, she would be frantic - and probably in that sad state of non-communication with Mick that Rose had too often been aware of before.

'I know it's not as bad as being killed,' she said before she could stop herself. 'But Helen's a very sensitive woman, and she'll be imagining all kinds of things.'

He stopped walking abruptly, gripping her arm tightly, hurting her...

'Of course she bloody will,' he said savagely. 'Just as I'm imagining all kinds of things about the way Buzz bought it. That's one of the hellish things they don't tell you about in their brief little telegrams or neatly worded formal notes. They think that by wrapping it all up tidily it will make the truth less painful. But it doesn't. It bloody well doesn't. It just makes you realize they only think of you as battle fodder. They drag us in and spit us out, and you have to get the gory details from your buddies who witnessed it. They give no thought to who we might have waiting for us back home. Buzz had a girl that he was going to marry when all this was over, but do they care about that? Do they even know? Of course they bloody don't, but somebody's got to tell her, and his parents.'

Rose was stunned by the vehemence of his reaction. He was always so polite, never swearing, and she had never seen him show such raw emotion.

'I'm so sorry,' she whispered, her voice shaking. 'If I sounded heartless I didn't mean to. You must know that. I'm so very sorry, Eldon,' she said again, because she hardly knew how to handle this situation.

Did he want her to go? Did he want to be alone? Did he regret the foolishness of ever going to the canteen that evening and facing people having a good time, when his heart was clearly breaking for the loss of his friend?

His arms folded around her, and she could feel how fast his heart was beating now. She knew it was not with any arousal, or love, but with the sheer pain of putting into words the way he was feeling.

'I'm sorry too. I shouldn't have poured all that out on you, Rose. It wasn't fair after what you just told me, and I'm really sorry about your cousin too.'

'Well, if we're not careful we're going to spend the evening saying sorry to each other,' she said shakily. 'Have you spoken like this to anyone else, Eldon?'

'No. Only you. That's a hell of an admission to make isn't it? I see my girl after a few weeks apart, and ruin her evening.'

'You haven't ruined it. I'm touched that you

felt you could confide in me like that. It helps me understand how you feel when something terrible happens. Women can let it all out by weeping, but men have to bottle it all up don't they? I see that every day in the hospital, but it doesn't mean they don't feel the same pain. And you'd better tell me to shut up or you'll think I'm acting like a head doctor or something.'

'You're acting like my lovely, understanding girl,' he said, calmer now. 'And the more I know you, the more I know that I want you to be my girl for always.'

She caught her breath. 'Eldon, don't say it, please.'

'Why not? Do you think it's because of Buzz? Well, maybe it is. Maybe it's partly because I feel as if I've stared death in the face as well as him. But mostly it's because I'm surer than anything in my life before, that I want to know I've always got you to come back to. I want you to marry me, Rose, not now, not next week, but sometime when we feel ready. All I want is the knowledge that we're going to be together for always.'

She shouldn't say yes right now, not like this. The timing was all wrong. The moments were far too emotional, with him still grieving, herself so sad after what he had told her, and her own distress over Jack. She had already heard of too many hasty wartime marriages that had ended in widowhood. But when would the timing ever be right? Tomorrow, when it might

316

be Eldon's plane blow out of the sky? How would she feel then?

'You know I want to say yes,' she began slowly.

'Then say it. If you change your mind tomorrow, I'll understand. I won't like it, but I'll understand. I just want you to say yes tonight.'

She could see instantly how important this was for him. It was something to hold on to, no matter what the future might hold. And what would that future be without him?

'Then of course my answer is yes, and I won't change my mind tomorrow, or ever,' she said quickly, before common sense took over.

It was crazy, of course it was, although Elsie and Daphne thought it was exciting and wonderful, despite the devastating news about Buzz. But they were practical too, reminding Rose that you had to take your chance on happiness these days, and although she assured them they needn't get any ideas about wedding bells just yet, her heart glowed every time she thought about being unofficially engaged to that lovely man. She still had her own family worries, and they had agreed that their news was going to be kept private until they each chose to share it. Besides, it wouldn't be fair to flaunt their happiness when Helen was so upset over Jack.

A few days later she was told there was a phone call for her, and she went to the communal phone with a great fear in her heart, terrified

317

of what she was going to hear. It would probably be Uncle Mick, and that could mean only one thing. And then she felt a huge shock when she heard her mother's voice at the other end.

'What's happened, Mum?' she said. 'Are you with Auntie Helen?'

Because now she knew it had to be something to do with Jack. It had to be.

'I am, love, and we're all at sixes and sevens here, but there's no need to sound so worried. Helen asked me to phone you to tell you the news that Jack's back in England and in a hospital somewhere in the north of Yorkshire. His injuries aren't as serious as was first thought, and they're hoping to transfer him to the Bristol area soon, and then he'll be coming home for some leave.'

'That's wonderful,' Rose said, her heart jumping again now, because not all news was bad news after all. It was something to hold on to, and to remember. 'I'm so pleased for them all, Mum.'

Amazingly, she heard Alice laugh. 'Ah, but that's not all! You won't have realized how low Helen has been feeling lately, and even more so when she heard about Jack, of course. I was quite fearful for her at one stage, but now this other thing has happened and she's her old self again.'

'Are you going to tell me, or do I have to guess?' Rose demanded.

She couldn't guess, anyway. Her mother sounded mysterious and elated at the same

318

time. Surely Lucy hadn't got herself engaged? Not before her older sister! Rose felt a moment's indignity at the thought, and then she made herself listen properly to what her mum was rabbiting on about. As always, when she was excited, Alice's voice quickened, her London accent becoming more pronounced, as if she had never been away from her roots...

'You remember those little evacuees Helen had here before? Their names were Patty and Johnny Gregg. Well, they're coming back to Bramwell!'

'*What*? How did that happen? And slow down, for goodness' sake, Mum.'

Alice laughed again, and then sobered a little. 'Well, I shouldn't laugh, of course. But it seems the old granny who was looking after them has had a stroke and can't look after them any more. The dad who was working at the docks can't cope with them either - or doesn't want to, more like – and when the social people came sniffing around, the kids said they wanted to come back to stay with their Uncle Mick and Auntie Helen, and if they weren't allowed to, they were going to bleedin' well run away. Pardon the language, Rose, and you know I don't approve of it, but that was exactly what they said. So any day now they're coming back to Mick and Helen's for the duration. What do you think of that?'

By the time she stopped for breath, Rose was laughing too. It was turning out to be a such a good day. Such a stupendous day. It seemed

319

like only yesterday that things had seemed so dire, and now everything had changed again.

'I think it's wonderful. And while we're all feeling in such a good mood, Mum, I've got some news of my own to tell you,' she said, her voice catching, and then she couldn't contain herself a moment longer.